More for Mad Dog Vengeance

"*Mad Dog Vengeance* is Mark Rubinstein's best thriller yet—a powerful tale that pulls the reader in, faster and deeper than swirling water in the roughest rapids. If you haven't met Dr. Roddy Dolan before now, don't dare to miss this pulse-pounding book—it's a real winner."

   —Linda Fairstein, bestselling author of the Alex Cooper series

"In *Mad Dog Vengeance*, Mark Rubinstein once again displays the skills and creativity that make him one of the thriller genre's best writers. The story is a tension-filled adventure that exposes the reader to an array of emotions that shock, amaze, and frighten. What will a man do to protect those he loves, regardless of the price he might pay? Yes, it's about vengeance, but it's also about love, friendship, loyalty, morality, courage, and redemption."

   —Joseph Badal, Amazon #1 bestselling author of *Dark Angel*

"*Mad Dog Vengeance* is a master work of impossible choices and life-changing decisions. A scintillating pop culture mix of *Goodfellas* and *Breaking Bad*, Mark Rubinstein's concluding chapter in his Mad Dog trilogy both talks the talk and walks the walk. Rubinstein never stops challenging his characters in a fashion akin to Harlan Coben and Lisa Gardner."

   —Jon Land, *USA Today* bestselling author of the Caitlin Strong series of thrillers

"Mark Rubinstein is one of my favorite writers. Period."
   —Simon Toyne, internationally bestselling author of The Sanctus Trilogy and Solomon Creed series, and host of the CBS crime show *Written in Blood*

"*Mad Dog Vengeance*, the final installment in Mark Rubinstein's Dr. Roddy 'Mad Dog' Dolan's trilogy, is a thriller in the truest sense of the genre. Expertly drawn characters drive a plot that will keep you up late. Plan on losing some sleep and immerse yourself into a novel written by a true pro. I loved it."
    —Scott Pratt, *Wall Street Journal* bestselling author of the
        Joe Dillard series

"Don't tell Dr. Roddy Dolan, the world's most unlikely hitman, that there's no such thing as an impossible choice. Rubinstein's *Mad Dog Vengeance* is an excellent set-up matched only by its execution."
    —Reed Farrel Coleman, *New York Times* bestselling
        author of *What You Break*

"Fans of *The Sopranos* will love this fast-paced thriller of Italian mafia versus Albanian gangsters versus an everyday guy who just wants to protect his family. Loved the explosive end!"
    —Lisa Gardner, *New York Times* bestselling author of
        Right Behind You and the D. D. Warren series

"Stuck in the middle between warring thugs, Army-vet-turned-doctor Roddy Dolan is the perfect guide to the highs and lows of New York City. A moody, atmospheric tale about how buried secrets never stay buried long. And how a Faustian deal can lead a good man to do some very bad things. Think of a *Sopranos* crossover episode with *Trapper John, MD*. Great fun and exciting."
    —Ace Atkins, *New York Times* bestselling author of *The Fallen* and *Robert B. Parker's Little White Lies*

"Mark Rubinstein is a superb storyteller. His novels tap into the deepest of human emotions."
    —Raymond Khoury, bestselling author of the Sean Reilly
        series

Praise for Mark Rubinstein's Other Novels

The Lovers' Tango

"The tension in these pages never lets you go. Rubinstein is a born storyteller."
  —Michael Connelly, bestselling author of the Harry Bosch series

Mad Dog House (Book 1 in the Mad Dog Trilogy)

"I stayed up all night to read *Mad Dog House*. I couldn't put it down. It was fantastic, riveting, suspenseful, twisting, loving, horrific."
  —Martin West, film and television actor and filmmaker

Mad Dog Justice (Book 2 in the Mad Dog Trilogy)

"*Mad Dog Justice* speeds along with more turns than a Vespa cruising through traffic. It's a smart, twisting thriller that grows into weightier issues of friendship, vengeance, and betrayal."
  —Andrew Gross, bestselling author of *Everything to Lose* and *The One Man*

Mad Dog Vengeance

Also by Mark Rubinstein

Fiction

Stone Soup

Mad Dog House (Book 1 in the Mad Dog trilogy)

Mad Dog Justice (Book 2 in the Mad Dog trilogy)

Love Gone Mad

The Foot Soldier, A Novella of War

Return to Sandara: A Novella of Love and Destruction

The Lovers' Tango

Nonfiction

The First Encounter: The Beginnings in Psychotherapy
with Dr. William A. Console and Dr. Richard C. Simons

The Complete Book of Cosmetic Surgery
with Dr. Dennis P. Cirillo

New Choices: The Latest Options in Treating Breast Cancer
with Dr. Dennis P. Cirillo

Heartplan: A Complete Program for Total Fitness of Heart & Mind
with Dr. David L. Copen

*The Growing Years: The New York Hospital-Cornell Medical Center
Guide to Your Child's Emotional Development*

Bedlam's Door: True Tales of Madness & Hope

Beyond Bedlam's Door: True Tales from the Couch and Courtroom

Oct. 9, 2017

To Kait & Lenora

Mad Dog Vengeance

A Novel

Book 3 in the Mad Dog Trilogy

MARK RUBINSTEIN

We miss you guys! I think you'll get a kick out of this — the last book in the Mad Dog trilogy.

Best & warmest wishes,

Thunder Lake Press

Thunder Lake Press
25401 Alicia Parkway, #L512
Laguna Hills, CA 92653
www.thunderlakepress.com

Publisher's Note: This is a work of fiction. It is a product of the author's imagination. Any resemblance to people, living or dead, is purely coincidental. Occasionally, real places or institutions are used novelistically for atmosphere. There is no connection between the characters or situations in this novel to any real-life events, people, places, institutions, restaurants, bars, nightclubs, diners, lounges, social clubs, golf clubs, organizations, or companies of any kind. Any resemblance to human nature is not coincidental.

Ordering Information
Quantity sales. Special discounts are available on quantity purchases by corporations, associations, and others. For details, contact the "Special Sales Department" at the address above.

Orders by US trade bookstores and wholesalers. Please contact BCH: (800) 431-1579 or visit www.bookch.com for details.

Printed in the United States of America

Cataloging-in-Publication Data

Names: Rubinstein, Mark, author.
Title: Mad dog vengeance : a novel / Mark Rubinstein.
Description: "Book 3 of the Mad Dog Trilogy" | Laguna Hills, CA: Thunder Lake Press, 2017.
Identifiers: ISBN 978-1-941016-27-5 (pbk.) | 978-1-941016-28-2 (ebook) | LCCN 2017912123
Subjects: LCSH Friendship--Fiction. | Manhattan (New York, N.Y.)--Fiction. | Detective and mystery stories.
Suspense fiction. | Psychological fiction. | FICTION / Thrillers / General
Classification: LCC PS3618.U3 M33 2017 | DDC 813.6--dc23

First Edition

21 20 19 18 17   10 9 8 7 6 5 4 3 2 1

As always, for Linda

Sometimes it is better to forgive and forget than
to take revenge and remember.
—EDMOND MERKO

I shall be telling this with a sigh
Somewhere ages and ages hence:
Two roads diverged in a wood, and I—
I took the one less traveled by,
And that has made all the difference.
—ROBERT FROST

November 2016

Chapter 1

Though he'd rather not think about it, Roddy Dolan is certain the other shoe will drop after the disaster at Snapper Pond.

There's no escaping that grim reality: it will happen. And when it does, he and Danny Burns will pay the price for having committed murder. Roddy's certain he has a lifetime of lamentable moments.

He stands in front of Geppetto's, a trattoria on East 186th Street, in the Belmont section of the Bronx. It's the borough's version of Little Italy, though other ethnic groups have moved into the neighborhood over the last few years.

When his cell phone rang last night, it had been Vinzy Masconi, his old medical school buddy, inviting him to join him at this trattoria. "Hey, man," Vinzy had said, "the last time we talked you wanted to buy a piece, remember?"

His thoughts shoot back to the day, a year ago last September. He'd called Vinzy, asking for help. So Vinzy had set up a meeting for him with a neighborhood guy named Charlie "Cheese," the owner of Carlo's Latticini, a guy who could sell him a pistol.

At the time Roddy had had strong misgivings about asking Vinzy for a favor. There had always been more than a whiff of mobbed-up stench about this friend, whom he met over a cadaver on the first day of medical school. But it was because of that connection that Roddy knew Vinzy not only could hook him up with someone who'd sell him a piece but could ask around to learn the identity of a loan shark, one John Grange, who it turns out was really named John Gargano, a made man in the Staten Island mob.

So, in the rear room of the cheese store where he made fresh mozzarella, Charlie had sold Roddy an untraceable Taurus pistol, the weapon he'd thought he needed when it seemed the Staten Island mob was coming after him, Danny, and their families.

"Still have it?" Vinzy asked.

"I got rid of it. Not worth the trouble."

"Hey, every doc should have one in the office. I'm never without mine."

"So, what's up, Vinzy?" *A generic question, just to change the subject.*

"Nothin' much. I'm tryin' to avoid my three exes. They're houndin' me for money. But listen, Roddy. I called to see if we can get together for dinner."

"I don't know, Vinzy. I've been busy lately."

"Ah, c'mon. Why not take a quick trip down to the Bronx? There's a great place on a Hundred Eighty-Sixth Street, right off Arthur Avenue. It's quiet and we can laugh about the bad old days. It's called Geppetto's. How 'bout tomorrow night, eight o'clock?"

Am I reluctant to see Vinzy because the guy's a weasel? Over the last year and a half, I've dealt with enough dirtbags to last a lifetime.

"All right, Vinzy. I'll see you there—at Geppetto's—eight o'clock tomorrow night."

So here he is, standing in front of the trattoria. Located next door to a travel agency. Geppetto's is a storefront restaurant with a red convex-shaped awning over the entrance. Diaphanous curtains hang from a brass bar, covering the lower part of the front window. Sitting prominently on the inside sill and visible to the street is a three-foot-tall wooden Pinocchio marionette, decked out in the traditional red and green colors. Geppetto's son, Pinocchio.

Cute. Sends a positive vibe.

Funny, though, no menu is posted on the window.

No problem; if nothing else, Vinzy knows good Italian food.

As he enters the place, the room's warmth is a welcome respite from the November chill. The aromas of red sauce and cheese fill Roddy's nostrils. There are about twelve nicely spaced tables, each napped with a heavy, white linen tablecloth. Dark brown bentwood chairs sit atop the black-and-white-checkered tile floor. A service bar with two stools is at the rear of the room. The place seems quiet and welcoming.

The sound of veal being pounded emanates from the kitchen, off to the right. Beige walls are covered with framed black-and-white photographs: Toscanini, DiMaggio, Marciano, LaGuardia, Fermi, Scorsese—all famous Italians.

The restaurant feels old-world, comfortable, authentic.

The room is nearly empty on a cold Monday night in November. No surprise there. The patrons are older couples, probably among the last remnants of Belmont's dwindling Italian community. They're dressed somewhat formally, an old-timer's custom in keeping with the room's ambience. No cell phones on the tables, no music coming through a sound system, the murmur of conversation—mostly in Italian—all make for a cozy feel to the place.

A visual sweep of the eatery: no sign of Vinzy. Not unusual. He's always late for their rare get-togethers.

A short, wiry waiter wearing a yellow vest, bow tie, and black pants approaches him.

"Yes, sir, my name is Franco. May I help you?"

"Sure, Franco. I'm meeting someone."

"May I ask who, sir?"

"Vincent Masconi."

"Ah, Dr. Vincent," says Franco, smiling. "He's expecting you. Please, come with me."

So, Vinzy's known here—a good sign. A good meal is definitely in the works.

Roddy follows Franco along a side aisle to the rear of the restaurant.

Franco pushes open a heavy sliding pocket door, revealing a smaller back room with only four tables. Private dining. A thick haze of cigar and cigarette smoke chokes out the aromas from the kitchen.

Roddy feels an electric bolt of alarm when he sees two men sitting at the table nearest the door. They radiate menace.

One guy is steep-jawed with a stubbled face and slicked-back dark hair, Fonzie-style, like it's still the 1950s. He wears a sports jacket and a black shirt, open at the collar. A gold chain tangled in dark chest hairs hangs around his thick neck.

The other man, dressed in jeans and a black leather car coat over a black T-shirt, has a thin, angular face with a deep scar furrowed across one eyebrow. A blue-black spiderweb tattoo adorns his neck.

Mafia.

"Roddy Dolan, my *man*," Vinzy calls, shooting to his feet from where he sits at the rear corner table with two men.

Same Vinzy as always: thin, dark curly hair shining with gel, narrow face, pockmarked nose.

Vinzy approaches quickly, his olive-black eyes gleaming. Before Roddy can say a word, Vinzy's hand slashes through the air, grabs Roddy's, and pumps it like a piston. "How're ya doin'? Good to see ya." Vinzy's other hand claps Roddy's back.

Unease slithers through Roddy. As he's always suspected, Vinzy's mobbed up. Or at least "connected" in some way.

The two men sitting at the rear corner table set off Roddy's internal alarm. Born of instinct as much as experience, it signals peril. Roddy's heart rate accelerates. A cold sensation spreads from his neck to his upper back.

The older guy smokes a cigar. He looks to be in his fifties.

He's dressed in a tailored, pin-striped gray suit with a pale blue shirt, which is set off by a charcoal-colored silk tie, most likely Hermès. A high-end ensemble, at least a thousand bucks of threads sitting on his back.

His full head of black hair, probably dyed, is carefully coiffed.

There's something ferociously aggressive lurking beneath that groomed appearance.

There's no mistaking it: he's got that John Gotti look.

As Roddy approaches the table, he feels this man's hooded eyes boring into him. The guy removes the cigar from between his teeth and rolls it with a thumb and forefinger, revealing perfectly manicured fingernails, buffed and polished.

The other man is younger—early forties—thin and rangy. He has a weak chin and thinning, dark hair with an obvious comb-over. He wears an ill-fitting sports jacket, and his eyeglasses have cheap, plastic frames. Looks like a follower, a sycophant. He crushes out his cigarette and immediately lights another. He appears nervous and fidgety.

This place is mobbed up. What am I doing here?

Vinzy gestures toward the older man. "Roddy, I'd like you to meet Carmine Cellini. He's a good friend. And this is his associate Anthony DiNardo."

Cellini's lips spread into a semismile as his eyes narrow.

"Sit down, Dr. Dolan," Cellini intones in a Bronx-inflected accent, one not very different from the patois of the Brooklyn streets where Roddy grew up. "Join us for dinner. You're my guest. This is the best Southern Italian cuisine you'll find anywhere. Everything's fresh and nothing's out of a can. Isn't that right, Tony?" he asks, turning to DiNardo.

He knows I'm a doctor. This is no one-on-one with Vinzy.

DiNardo nods, exhaling contrails of blue-white cigarette smoke.

Roddy sits next to Vinzy, across from Cellini, with DiNardo to his left.

As he sits opposite Cellini, Roddy's thoughts barrel back to that night in the rear room of McLaughlin's, when he'd sat across from Grange, the loan shark who not only had been out to drain him and Danny dry but had sealed his fate by molesting Roddy's ten-year-old daughter.

He virtually sees himself spiking the mobster's scotch and relives the trek he, Danny, and that lowlife gambler Kenny Egan had taken upstate to Snapper Pond, where he'd shot that fat bastard dead, using his old army pistol. Then, months later, thinking the mob was after him, he bought a piece from Charlie Cheese. *Charlie Cheese, whose store is right around the corner from where I'm sitting now.*

Though McLaughlin's Steakhouse—that nightmarish investment he and Danny had been roped into by Egan—was a galaxy removed from Geppetto's, sitting in this back room with these mobsters brings back everything about that restaurant.

Now, the room feels close, overheated. The thugs sitting at the other table raise the room's temperature.

"Allow me to order for the table," Cellini says with an expansive sweep of his arm. He bends his index finger, and Franco appears at the table.

Cellini orders a platter of antipasto followed by risotto, after which will come grilled veal chops for everyone. "And a plate of broccoli rabe sautéed in garlic and olive oil for the table," Cellini says. "And, Franco, keep the Brunello coming. And keep my boys over there happy." He points at the two men at the table near the door.

Yes, Cellini's a conquistador, a man who never takes no for an answer—the personification of every mob movie Roddy's ever seen. A top-of-the-food-chain guy, he exudes arrogance and danger—in spades.

This guy could explode and do a Jack Nicholson, like in *The Departed.* It could happen in a millisecond. It's as obvious as the huge star sapphire ring he wears on his left ring finger.

A glance at Vinzy.

His eyes are cast downward; he won't look at Roddy. Fucking weasel.

Why'd Vinzy invite me to dinner with these mafiosi?

Regret peppered with discomfort seeps through Roddy. *I never should have agreed to this dinner.*

"Vincent tells me you were once a boxer," Cellini says. "A Golden Gloves champion."

"A long time ago."

Vinzy's told him more about me than I'd ever want this guy to know.

"And you were an army ranger, too?"

A hum begins in Roddy's chest and travels through his neck to his head—a signal he long ago learned denotes danger.

"Very impressive, especially for a doctor . . . a surgeon at Lawrence Hospital, right?"

Roddy nods again. His tongue feels thick, coated with paste.

"Thank you for your service," DiNardo says.

A rote mantra, habitually recited bullshit Roddy hears any-time someone learns he was in the army, especially since 9/11 and Iraq and Afghanistan.

What do these guys want?

Cellini makes conversation—small talk—about Bronxville, Lawrence Hospital, the changing demographics of the Bronx.

Roddy barely hears the conversation. The words ricochet off the walls, swarming around his head like white noise barely pen-etrating his brain.

It's clear this back area serves as Cellini's domain, or at least a meeting place where business matters are discussed. *What kind of business?*

As Cellini talks on, Roddy's thoughts swirl on a separate track. There's a purpose for this gathering—this sit-down—and it involves him.

Roddy notices a small rectangular matchbox—the kind that holds wooden matches—sitting on the table. While Cellini talks, Roddy focuses on the matchbox's multicolored cover, an artful depiction of old man Geppetto—white haired, mustachioed, bespectacled—carving a piece of wood as a half-formed Pinocchio emerges from the log. Cartoonish. Obviously emblematic of the restaurant. Geppetto's. Cute.

But this back room isn't cute. It's intimidating, actually frightening.

Still zeroing in on the matchbox, he barely hears Cellini blather on about the Hispanics, Russians, and Albanians. Vinzy says something about Medicaid cutbacks—how he can no longer double bill with impunity; he's gotta be careful how he does the books. But it's all background babble.

It's a distant drone as Roddy's thoughts turn to home: what are Tracy and the kids doing tonight? Tom's watching *Monday Night Football*. Tracy's probably thumbing through *Fine Cooking* or *Food & Wine*. Sandy's doing homework or working on a biology project. The house is warm and dinner's aroma still lingers in the air.

I wish I were sitting with Tracy in the den with the fireplace glow flickering through the room.

When the food arrives, Roddy's appestat is dampened. The aroma of risotto brings on queasiness. A spurt of acid washes up from his stomach, burning the back of his throat. It's a distaste far more than just gustatory.

He takes a few bites of veal, but his stomach gurgles in protest. He picks at his food, pushes it around on the plate, and does his best to tune out the conversation.

"What's wrong, Doc?" DiNardo asks. "You don't like the food? Maybe we can order up some Irish stew for you." He lets out a low chortle.

Roddy shoots him a weak smile.

Cellini's brow furrows. He shoots DiNardo an annoyed look.

DiNardo's smile evaporates.

Roddy wants to push away from the table, stand, apologize, fabricate an excuse—he has an early morning in the OR, he doesn't feel well, anything will suffice—and then leave, but the thugs near the door will stop him. He can almost feel them breathing on his neck.

His hands feel weak, like they can barely lift his knife and fork, and ice water trickles down his spine.

Cellini, Vinzy, and DiNardo savage everything on their plates. DiNardo grunts and chews with an open mouth. Cellini, on the other hand, eats heartily, but without a caveman's brutishness.

Vinzy occasionally glances at Roddy when he thinks Roddy won't notice.

Typical Vinzy. Sleazy. Sneaky.

When the waiter serves Sambuca in clear shot glasses, Roddy sucks his down. The anise tastes bitter on his tongue and burns going down. Maybe the alcohol will seep into his bloodstream, percolate everywhere, bring on a warm, hazy feeling, and slow his brain from sprinting with a thousand thoughts about what this sit-down portends.

"So, Roddy—I can call you Roddy, right?" A smile permeates Cellini's voice.

"Sure."

"And call me Carmine. Lemme ask you something." Cellini produces another cigar, snips the end with a gold-plated clipper, lights up, and takes a few puffs. He squints and regards Roddy. "When you came into the restaurant, what'd you see next door?"

A brief thought, a recollection. "A travel agency . . ."

"Right. You notice anything about it?"

"I wasn't really looking."

"Sure," Cellini says, sucking on the cigar, exhaling smoke in a perfect ring. "It's an Albanian agency. Ten years ago it would've been an Italian agency. Get my drift?"

Roddy nods. *More about the Albanians.*

"The neighborhood's changing," DiNardo cuts in, lighting a cigarette. "Plenty of Albanians here now. There's graffiti all over the place. The black double-headed eagle, their national symbol—it's everywhere.

"We got mostly older Italians these days; the young ones don't wanna stay," DiNardo continues. "They go into the professions, like Vinzy here. They leave for the burbs. But Vinzy, he's a *paisano*. He's stayed right here in the old neighborhood."

DiNardo winks at Vinzy, who says nothing—a level of reserve rare for Vinzy, who usually rattles on like an auctioneer on speed.

Roddy glances at Vinzy. The guy's mouth twitches.

Something's coming, a statement or proposal Roddy would rather not hear. He knows it.

He's reminded of Dr. Melfi on *The Sopranos*, afraid she'd hear some revelation from Tony that could put her in jeopardy—like a crime about to be committed, or one that's already gone down.

"Whaddaya know about the Albanians?" Cellini asks, sipping the last of his Sambuca.

"Not much," Roddy hears himself reply.

"Of course, living in Bronxville, you wouldn't run into them, except maybe for one guy, but we'll get to him later."

There's a "later"—something's coming.

Cellini puffs on his cigar, taps the end, and nods to the waiter.

Another glass of Sambuca arrives at the table.

Cellini eyes Roddy and continues. "We got a whole Balkan thing going on here. I'm talkin' heroin, cocaine, Oxycodone, weapons, counterfeit sneakers, you name it. The Albanians have ties to groups in their homeland and in Kosovo, or maybe it's Serbia. I can never get those lousy countries straight."

Peering steadily at Roddy, Cellini continues. "They'll stop at nothing, especially the young ones. They're into muggings, home invasions, murder for hire. They're animals. They got no class.

"There was some Albanian guy—crazy bastard—he storms into Vinzy's clinic. He thinks his wife came down with VD—who knows what? So this crazy son of a bitch goes up to the reception-ist and demands to see his wife's medical records. At *gunpoint*. He terrorizes Vinzy's place, goes home, and shoots his wife. Then he finds her lover and kills him. After that he puts the gun to his own head and blows his brains out."

Roddy does his best to anticipate what's coming—something about Albanians—but what does it have to do with him?

"If a restaurant doesn't pay for protection, they'll wreck the place, or worse," Cellini continues. "There was an Albanian café around the corner—Balkan Palace—where the owner wouldn't pay up. They charged into the place and went from table to table slashing people's faces. The guy's outta business in no time."

"And they're movin' in on us," DiNardo interjects. "Take a small thing like pizzerias. Every new place is Albanian. Not Italian, *Albanian*. They pass their stuff off as authentic pizza, but it's crap."

"More important," Cellini cuts in, "the FBI, the DEA, and Immigration are trying to get a fix on 'em. But it's tough because these Albanians work in very closely tied clans. They don't call them 'families,' like we do. They're *clans*. They keep their mouths shut, like the old-time Sicilians with *omertà*. So the government ends up looking at *us*.

"They smuggle thousands of kilos of marijuana and prescrip-tion drugs into the States from Canada, and Mexico, too. They hide it in tractor trailers along with legit cargo, and the drugs are stashed in warehouses all over the Bronx before they're distributed."

"They really have *cojones*," DiNardo adds. "They even pulled guns on some members of the Gambino family during a sit-down. They fear no one."

Cellini says, "They're collecting protection money and gambling proceeds from social clubs here in the Bronx, even some of the small clubs *we* still run."

Cellini pauses and clasps his hands on the tabletop. Roddy notices his deformed knuckles—once broken, healed badly, bulbous swellings on thick, crooked fingers—no doubt a legacy of fistfights from earlier years. And that star sapphire ring reminds Roddy of Grange's ring, another obscene hunk of jewelry. Must be a mob thing. Yes, that ring reminds him of snapping Grange's finger off with a cable cutter while the mobster was unconscious lying in the dirt upstate; they'd had to get the bauble off before they'd rolled him into the hole at Snapper Pond. Then how he tossed the finger, ring, shell casings, and his old army .45 into the muck-ridden water hole where they'd never be found. No way could anyone ID a thing.

Cellini's eyes crawl over Roddy, as though he's waiting for him to speak.

"All this is very interesting, Carmine," Roddy says with his heart hammering. "But why are you telling me this?"

"A good question, Roddy," Cellini replies. "Before I get to that, let me ask *you* a question."

"You want to ask *me* a question?"

"Yeah, an important one. A very important one."

Chapter 2

The room is so quiet, Roddy feels every beat of his heart, each pulse of blood as it rushes through his body. And he feels overheated—fiery—as a drop of sweat trickles down his torso.

Cellini makes a subtle waving gesture. The two men at the far table get up and leave.

The pocket door slides into a closed position.

Only four men remain: Roddy, Cellini, DiNardo, and Vinzy.

Cellini picks up his cigar, mouths it, and then sets it back in the ashtray. The end glistens with his saliva. He regards Roddy with those dark eyes. "Ever hear of Edmond Merko?"

"No."

"He heads up the most powerful Albanian clan in the Bronx. He's in the import-export business—at least, that's his cover. Merko's clan is moving in on us."

"So, what's this about, Carmine? Why should I know anything about this Edmond Merko?"

"Because he's scheduled for knee-replacement surgery in less than two weeks."

A whooshing sound reverberates through Roddy's skull. The room's heat is incendiary.

"He's due for surgery at Lawrence Hospital, in Bronxville."

Silence. The sensation in Roddy's head is now a pounding.

"I don't get it. What's this got to do with me?"

"You're on staff at Lawrence Hospital, yes?"

"Yes."

"We don't want any violence with the Albanians. No bloodshed, if you know what I mean . . ."

"I do and I don't. Why are you telling me this?"

"Because we have plans for Merko."

The room seems tomblike. The heat is gone. Ice water surges through Roddy's bloodstream—a sudden chill envelops him; tightness grips his heart.

"Plans?" he whispers through paste lining his mouth.

"Yes. It'd be a shame if a man like Merko ups and dies. He's fifty-five, massively overweight, must weigh a good two hundred eighty pounds, and on top of that, he's got a heart condition and diabetes. He's a prime candidate for sudden death. Know what I mean?"

Cellini's face erupts in a Cheshire-cat smile.

"It'd be a shame if an overweight and not-very-well man like Edmond Merko developed complications in the hospital after knee-replacement surgery. You know, something that might happen to him after the operation. There's always a risk after any surgery, right?"

High-pitched whining begins in Roddy's ears.

"You get my drift?"

In a small voice Roddy asks, "Just what are you driving at, Carmine?"

"What am I driving at? Are you *dense*?" Cellini again rolls the cigar between his thumb and forefinger. "We don't wanna get into a war with the Albanians. They have way more soldiers than we do, and the other families won't help us."

Cellini leans forward. "So, *Doctor*, since you're on staff at Lawrence Hospital, it would be easy for you to help Mr. Merko make a quick exit from this world."

Something inside Roddy shifts as his guts spasm.

The room sways.

With a surge of strength, he rockets to his feet. His chair and coat tumble to the floor behind him.

Cellini glares at Roddy with eyes that've stared down many men. Eyes that radiate rage, eyes of fire, eyes with a vocabulary of their own—whose look conveys menace and intimidation, eyes that command obedience. Cellini's look has a lethal cast. His lips spread into a thin half smile. "No need to get upset, Roddy—or should I say *Dr.* Dolan?"

Roddy casts a look at Vinzy. His medical school friend looks down at the table.

"What?" asks Cellini. "You gonna say it goes against your medical ethics, Doc?" Cellini's voice goes frigid. "Your ethics are questionable, Doc. Very questionable."

Vomit bubbles in Roddy's stomach. He starts to turn away.

"Hey, *Doc*."

He turns back, doing his best not to scowl.

"Don't get on your high horse. We know what you did."

"What are you talking about?" Roddy asks through a phlegm-filled throat. His chin begins quivering.

"I'm talkin' about the fact that a while back you called Vinzy here and asked about buying a piece, didn't you?"

Roddy feels his jaw clench.

"So Vinzy sent you to Charlie Cheese, the guy at Carlo's Latticini, just around the corner from here, and you bought a piece . . . a Taurus. Set you back nine hundred, right?" A knowing nod of Cellini's head. "You gotta know that Charlie Cheese is a friend of ours. And why'd you need that piece?"

Roddy simply stares—long and hard— and says nothing.

"And while you had Vinzy's ear," Cellini continues, "you asked about a guy named John M. Grange, a loan shark. You described him as a fat guy who called himself Ghost, right? You remember calling Vinzy?"

Roddy hears himself say, "I was calling for a friend." Even as the words leave his mouth, he tastes the lie.

Cellini lets out a bark of disbelief and then glances at DiNardo. DiNardo shrugs.

"As if you didn't know," Cellini continues, a smirk spreading across his lips, reaching his voice, "this guy Grange was with the Brunetti family out of Staten Island. His real name was Gargano. Sound familiar? Yeah, Vinzy here gave you the dope on Gargano."

Roddy says nothing.

Is this really happening? Grange, the mafioso who tried to extort close to a million bucks from Danny and me, who we disposed of at Snapper Pond, the guy I killed and then whose partner I had to shoot when Kenny Egan drew a pistol . . . it's all coming back?

"Notice I said *was* . . . not *is*? Gargano *was* associated with the Brunetti family."

Roddy shakes his head. His thoughts swarm.

"You know what, Doc? Gargano—the guy you knew as Grange or Ghost—he's been missing for more than a year." Cellini nods with a knowing look on his face. "Now, why would a respectable doc like you, a fancy Westchester surgeon, even *ask* about a guy like that? Why would you ask about a mob guy outta Staten Island?

"And why would you buy a piece off Charlie Cheese? Huh? You wouldn't . . . unless you had some bad intentions. Unless you were gonna get rid of someone. So, don't give me any of that innocence bullshit. You're up to your teeth in bad shit. Isn't that right, Vinzy?"

Vinzy nods, still avoiding eye contact with Roddy.

"And one more thing, Doc: isn't it true you went belly-up with that Mickey Finn accountant, Daniel Burns, your partner in that restaurant you amateurs owned? McLaughlin's? Yeah, that's the name of the place. Lost your shirt on that one. And Gargano the loan shark goes missing and you buy a hot piece from us all at just about the same time.

"Right, Doc?"

Roddy stares into Cellini's eyes and stays silent.

"Some people thought Gargano went into WITSEC, but there's no way that happened. No fuckin' way. He had nothing for the feds. *Niente. Nada.* He was an old-timer. Didn't know a damned thing. He just vanished. So it doesn't take a scholar to figure out what happened. The way we see it, *you* made Gargano go off the radar. Know what I mean?"

With sweat stippling his upper lip, Roddy bends and grabs his coat from the floor. He stands and begins to turn away.

"Don't get your balls in an uproar," DiNardo says, barely stifling a grin. The room's lights reflect off his glasses. The guy looks like a gargoyle. "Gargano didn't mean a damned thing to us, but I'm sure the Brunettis would be . . . Let's just say they'd be very upset to learn that a top-notch Westchester surgeon named Roddy Dolan, a guy livin' in Bronxville—a guy with a wife and two kids livin' in a nice house on the edge of the Siwanoy Country Club, a guy with a good practice, a guy who's on staff at Lawrence Hospital—that this Roddy Dolan character made one John Gargano, aka Ghost, disappear off the face of the earth just because maybe John Gargano was leanin' on him and his partner, one Daniel *friggin'* Burns. Like maybe Gargano was pushin' these two losers to pay back the money he loaned 'em to go into the restaurant business, all while the juice was runnin' big-time. No, that wouldn't sit well with the Brunettis, who never let a fuckin' thing go unanswered."

Roddy's legs liquefy.

Sepulchral silence.

Is this really happening? Am I hearing this now, after everything Dan and I have been through with that restaurant and Grange and Snapper Pond?

"We're not gonna do anything for the time being," Cellini says, that quasi smile still perched on his lips. He sets the saliva-ridden cigar into an ashtray. "But if you think we're not serious, just be aware that one call to the Brunettis settles everything. And you know what I mean . . . No one in your family will be safe, especially you."

How did I get into this?

"We looked into the restaurant—McLaughlin's," Cellini says. "A seedy operation run by your partner Kenny Egan, a lowlife gambler who's down the drain, somewhere on this earth. Seems he's missing, too. For quite some time. Since the time Gargano disappeared. Who knows, maybe he's in the Jersey Meadowlands. Only you would know, right, Doc?

"But we don't care about him. Egan means nothin' to us. And we don't give a shit about Gargano, either. We care about *you* and your partner, a guy who was also the restaurant's accountant—this hotshot money guy Danny Burns, right?"

Even if they're just guessing, they know enough. It's all they need.

"We could definitely use the services of a skilled accountant . . . someone who can, shall we say, balance the books? Don't you think so, Anthony?"

"If you say so, Carmine," DiNardo answers, sucking on his cigarette and squinting.

"What do you think, Vinzy? You could use some adjustments to your books, right? All those Medicaid cutbacks and whatever's gonna happen with Obamacare."

"Absolutely, Carmine. Things're gettin' real tough in the medical business." Vinzy still avoids looking at Roddy. His brow shines with sweat.

Cellini turns to Roddy. "So, Doc, we can use you for Merko and we can use Burns for the books. We have plans for both of you." Cellini pauses, squints, picks up his cigar, sucks on it, and exhales a mouthful of gray smoke. "So, why don't you go home, Doc? Just relax, take it easy. Go about your usual business. Don't even think about us telling the Brunettis you wasted John Gargano. Don't worry about it at all. Right, Anthony?"

DiNardo nods.

"But please, Doc, think about it. We can really use your medical skills to our benefit. That's what you do, isn't it? You help people? *Medically*, right?"

Cellini fingers the cigar, purses his lips, and looks up at Roddy with arched eyebrows.

"We'll talk in a few days to make arrangements," he adds. "We'll give you all the details you'll need since we have contacts at the hospital."

Roddy realizes his mouth is agape.

"In the meantime, I'm sure you can think of lotsa ways to put a sick guy like Edmond Merko out of his misery—you know, a little somethin' in his IV, somethin' that'll kick a sick old man over the edge, make him go for the long sleep."

Heat rushes to Roddy's cheeks. Every pore in his body opens.

"You got any questions, Doc?"

Roddy shakes his head.

"Good. You just sit on it and we'll get in touch." Cellini waves his hand dismissively. "Oh, and one other thing, Doc . . . drive home carefully. Those roads in Westchester are dangerous."

Chapter 3

Roddy drives north on the Bronx River Parkway. He clutches the steering wheel so tightly, his hands ache. The oncoming headlights are blinding with diffraction spikes radiating outward. A corona of dark purple surrounds them. He squints, trying to discern traffic, and for a moment thinks he's going off the road, about to smash into the median divide. He jacks the steering wheel to the right; the car fishtails, swerves, and then veers to the right lane; and the rumble strip vibrates beneath the wheels.

He swings into the left lane and slows down. The radio's playing but he can't recall turning it on. He's spaced out, his mind running on continuous loop, yet he's driving a 3,500-pound vehicle on a busy highway.

Floating in a dreamscape.

Kenny Egan, Danny, McLaughlin's, Grange, getting rid of him, and now this: mob guys knowing about my involvement with Egan, Danny, and Grange. They'll own me forever. And Danny, too.

Turn me into a killer? I'm already a killer, but not because of a feud between a mob and a clan.

Use medicine as a weapon. It's unreal.

It circles through his mind again, then again. He can't shut off the thoughts; they career through his brain, a ceaseless carousel.

Did it happen the way he recalls? Did he *really* sit there and listen to a scheme about murdering a patient? How does he make sense of it? And what does he do?

A horn blares so loudly his body spasms. Brilliant light fills the car's interior as the guy behind him flashes his brights. Roddy's in the left lane and has slowed to thirty miles an hour. He shifts to the right lane, lets the car pass, knows he can't drive anymore, and turns on his flashers.

He's at his exit, Midland Avenue, so he pulls off the highway, rolls to the midway point of the exit ramp, jumps the curb, parks on the shoulder, and pulls the emergency brake, keeping the engine running.

He's got to get control of himself, but his thoughts swirl in a mercurial circle.

Geppetto's. That back room.

Cellini and DiNardo. The casual cruelty of their words, of their intentions.

Grange, better known as Gargano. A guy who's eating dirt upstate at Snapper Pond.

The whole sick scenario began the night when Kenny first came to him—decked out in an Armani suit—with the proposition that Roddy become a silent partner in a restaurant.

It's an investment, Roddy. Don't you invest? For your family, your future?

"I invest through my financial advisor."

So, what did I do?

I send Egan to my lifelong friend Danny Burns. And what happens? We three became partners in a Manhattan steakhouse and it's just fine . . . for a while. Danny especially loved owning McLaughlin's; and our wives enjoyed dining there as a foursome. But, from the start, I always felt uneasy about the deal.

Why didn't I realize Kenny Egan was the same lowlife I'd known as a kid and was the same guy who talked me into committing a burglary when I was a teenage punk? Kenny wasn't the polished businessman he presented himself to be but was Grange's extortion partner. The two of them played Danny and me like the naive Irish fiddles we were. In a few months, the place was hemorrhaging money, and Grange was squeezing us to the tune of half a million bucks he "loaned" Kenny, all in collusion with Kenny.

Roddy's mind replays every step in the scenario that's taken him to this moment. He relives the afternoon when his ten-year-old daughter told him a fat man with stinky breath came to the house and kissed her on the cheek as she played earlier that day in front of the house.

And how the fat man said he'd be back to take her for ice cream, while handing her his business card to give to her daddy: it was Grange's. That fat slob had actually come to his house and sweet-talked and kissed his daughter, his child.

His thoughts careen to the night at Snapper Pond, where after Roddy drugged him, he shot the comatose fat man with the .45 from his army days. And he'd wound up killing Egan when that slimeball reached to an ankle holster. He sees himself tossing his pistol into that leech-infested murky pond. He hears Danny beside him that night—at times urging him to finish off Kenny and then on the way home invoking God's mercy.

Roddy can't stop the flood of memories long enough to get himself composed so he can drive the rest of the way home.

And now this, being ordered to execute a hospital patient.

Why in hell did I ever do something so stupid as going to Vinzy to line up a piece? Why did I ever ask him to get the lowdown on a guy named Grange . . . Gargano?

But he knows the answer: after Danny got shot in what looked like an office robbery, Roddy was convinced the mob was coming after Danny, him, and their families.

Turns out I was wrong, but I couldn't know that then.

Now the mob is coming after me—to do its bidding.

All because I tapped Vinzy for a favor.

And that one lousy decision led to the ugly terrain in which he's now mired.

Now the Bronx mob has a plan.

The plan: a sick plot—go to the hospital, slip Edmond Merko something. An old standby is potassium chloride. K-Dur is the commercial preparation. The injectable form: if a sky-high dose is shot into his IV tube, Edmond Merko's heart's rhythm goes haywire, and then comes cardiac arrest. Within minutes Edmond Merko's as dead as a skunk flattened on the Taconic Parkway.

And potassium chloride is tough to detect on a tox screen, though it's doubtful a post-op cardiac arrest in a massively over-weight fifty-five-year-old diabetic with coronary artery disease would warrant an autopsy. Or a toxicology report.

It would be an easily explainable death.

Happens all the time in every hospital, anywhere.

And here he is *thinking* about it. Actually *considering* doing it. *Jesus Christ.*

Killing a patient. Using his medical training to do murder. He can't believe he's actually turning it over in his mind after this viciously warped sequence of happenings leading to tonight's sit-down at Geppetto's: the slaughter of a hospital patient—a man who's never done anything to him or his family. It's despicable. Contemptible.

What kind of lowlife am I?

He's living up to his youthful moniker. He's an animal, a beast, a Mad Dog.

He can't polish that turd.

He's seized by a tide of nausea. His stomach clenches and he gasps for breath.

He clamps his mouth shut, pushes the car door open, stumbles away from the car, gets to the guardrail, bends at the waist, and leans over it as his chest constricts. His gut spasms and a

glottal sound erupts from his throat. His insides explode in a torrent of vomit, retching, coughing, and choking. He's frozen in
place, dizzy, as cars stream by in a whooshing rush, and he's in
a near faint, and then, after emptying his innards, wobbling on
rubbery legs, he totters back to the car, grabs the door handle,
and nearly topples over but manages to keep his balance.

After the last residue of bilious fluid drips from his lips, with
foul breath vapor pluming from his mouth, he turns, sinks back
behind the wheel, and pulls the door closed.

Weak and depleted, he sits in a daze.

Here he is, late on a Monday night, sitting in his car amid
the reek of vomit. His guts are purged and he's hiccupping, then
coughing, and he's parked on an exit-ramp shoulder of the Bronx
River Parkway as traffic streaks by in the night. He's gripping the
steering wheel like it's a lifesaver ring, as though he's bobbing in
the blackness of a vast ocean while sweat dribbles from his forehead, yet he shivers as if ice flows though his arteries, and he
wishes he could shut down his mind, but he replays the chilling
chain of events leading to the sickness his life has become—one
as horrific as a soul-devouring cancer.

Chapter 4

He pulls into the garage. It's nearly eleven p.m. The stench of vomit clings to him as he enters the kitchen through the door from the garage.

"Roddy?" Tracy calls from the den.

He mumbles something, his thoughts still seized by the nightmare of Geppetto's. His legs are so unsteady, he's not sure he can make it upstairs.

"Roddy?"

"Yeah." He can barely speak. His throat feels raw.

He tosses his coat onto a chair, rips off his jacket, and moves toward the staircase.

Halfway to the top, he hears Tracy.

"Roddy, what's wrong?"

"Nothing."

"How was dinner with Vinzy?"

"Lousy."

"Why? What happened?"

"I can't talk about it."

"Roddy?"

He turns back toward her, gripping the banister to keep from falling. The staircase elongates, as though he's looking down a distorted corridor in a funhouse.

"You're so *pale*. Are you all right?"

"Yeah." He mumbles something, turns back, and heads upstairs, afraid he'll retch more fluid. His hand shoots to his mouth as he stumbles up the last few steps.

"Where are you going?"

"I gotta shower."

"Shower?"

He mutters something else, but it's garbled. At the top of the stairs, he hears some hip-hop shit bleeding through Tom's bedroom door. Why does his son listen to such primal, lowest-common-denominator garbage? God, how ugly the world has become.

Jesus, no time to think about that.

In the bathroom, he strips off his clothes, staggers, and stubs his toe on the sink stand.

He slams the bathroom door shut, opens the stall door, turns on the water, and ratchets the handle to Hot.

As he waits for the water to heat, his thoughts churn in a frenzy. He barely hears Tracy calling him. He momentarily feels dizzy, and the bathroom pinwheels.

Steam rises in the shower. Vapor coats the bathroom mirror; he lurches into the stall, trembling beneath the cascade of water. He closes his eyes, turns his face into the stream, rubs his lips, opens his mouth, gurgles in the hot water rush, and nearly chokes.

A stream of cold air gusts into the stall.

"Roddy, what's going on?"

She's in the bathroom, standing outside the glass door. She left the bathroom door open. His teeth begin chattering. His body shakes.

"*Roddy*. What's happening?"

"Nothing. I need to shower."

"Why?"

"I feel sweaty."

"Sweaty?"

"Yeah." Slathering soap on his face, chest, arms, and thighs, he goes light-headed, about to faint.

"Roddy . . . ?"

"Tracy, close the *fucking* door. I'm freezing."

"Roddy . . . ? Talk to me. What's going on?"

Water pours over his head and face. Thoughts streak through his brain; an incoherent mélange of images and Tracy's words—shrill, piercing, intolerable—echo off the tile walls.

"Roddy." Her voice is cold, severe. "Are you washing off some woman you were with?"

A surge of nausea. He leans against the wall as water pounds his back.

This can't be happening. My whole life's turning to shit.

"Roddy, tell me the truth. Are you seeing someone?"

"Fuck, no." His mouth is parched. Despite the hot water, he's shivering.

"Really? What're you hiding, Roddy?"

"Nothing. Not a goddamned thing."

"Really? I get the feeling you've been hiding something for months."

A bolt of rage flares through him, so sudden his body spasms. His heart slams against his breastbone, feeling like it'll rupture and he'll bleed out. It's fury at Cellini and Vinzy, at everything, it's pure vitriol, a firestorm, a blaze of napalm, and it's ready to spew—wrong time, wrong place, wrong person.

"Tell me the truth, Roddy. Tell it to me *now*. You've been in another world for months. You haven't been *you*, and I'm sick of it. I wasn't born yesterday." Her voice screeches off the tiles, piercing him as hot water crashes onto him; his eardrums nearly burst, and he squeezes his eyes shut, wishing he was deaf as Tracy shouts, "Something's going on, and I have to know what it is. Is it a woman? I can't live like this anymore."

A flame of fury ignites and sears him with shocklike intensity. "Jesus Christ. Will you leave me the *fuck* alone?"

"How *dare* you talk like that to me!"

"I'm not . . . I'm just . . . ," he sputters amid the water torrent. He shouts something—it's gibberish bellowed in a roaring, wet voice, echoing in his ears—and he slips on a soapy puddle and slams his head against the shower wall. A momentary flash, star-bursts in his eyes, and his thoughts scatter. "Leave me the fuck alone. Just give me some peace. *Please*, for Christ's sake, leave me alone." His voice rips at his throat.

Water, heat, steam, nausea, the bitter taste of bile—he retches as his guts heave, but there's nothing left to puke so he dry heaves, again and again and it feels like his insides will spew out. He coughs, chokes on his saliva—down the wrong pipe—his body goes spaghetti weak, and he presses his head to the tile wall.

Despite the shower deluge, he hears the bathroom door slam shut.

He's filled with fear and fury and helplessness.

Another *thump*: he's been locked out of the bedroom.

Chapter 5

Two evenings later Roddy sits at a table in Rocco's, a trattoria on 4th Avenue in Pelham, New York, waiting for Danny Burns. And waiting for yet another shoe to drop.

He's certain it's inevitable: more bad news. Danny's about to let him know there's a final reveal about Snapper Pond—some disastrous bit of news he's learned that'll bring them closer to their comeuppance—a development that'll take them down for the count.

Danny, a lifelong friend, the kemosabe he truly loves, a guy so burdened by guilt he's barely able to keep secret the murders Roddy committed that night at Snapper Pond. And Dan was party to it. And when Dan gets worked up, his asthma shifts into high gear. His lungs turn into broken bellows. If Roddy lets him know what's going on with Cellini, Dan will drown in an ocean of asthma-driven phlegm. He'll lose it completely.

No, Roddy won't mention a thing right now.

At eight o'clock on a Wednesday evening, the restaurant is filled with patrons dining on belly-busting portions of Southern Italian food. And there's the same aroma as when he walked into Geppetto's: the air is redolent of tomato sauce and gorgonzola cheese. Cloyingly strong, the aromas bring on a swell of nausea. Geppetto's—just the thought of the place will haunt him for a long time. Of that he's certain. He does his best to focus on the surroundings.

Rocco's—a high-end place—is filled with a typical Westchester crowd: mostly middle-aged, upscale, many of them commuters who a half hour ago were sitting bleary-eyed on a Metro North train after a day's work in some soulless Manhattan office. The restaurant hum creates a steady backdrop as Roddy waits, wondering why Danny called about something he absolutely needs to discuss. The tone in Dan's voice was urgent. "We gotta talk tonight," he said.

A raucous laugh erupts from a table across the room. Roddy glances up expecting to see some mobster types—the kind he'd seen all too often at McLaughlin's when he, Danny, and Kenny owned that Manhattan steak joint. Or a laugh he'd hear in that back room of Geppetto's two nights ago.

Has it been only two days? Seems like a lifetime ago.

But the source of the laughter at Rocco's is a table of business types, especially one man, a young guy with a severe overbite.

Over the last two days, "Musetta's Waltz," Roddy's cell phone ringtone, alerted him to several calls, which he could see on the readout were from Vinzy. He let them go to voice mail. His smoldering rage, mixed with fear, kept him from playing the messages. He couldn't stomach the thought of hearing that snake's voice, and as irrational as it was, he hoped by ignoring the calls, this horror might just disappear.

But by the end of the second day, he'd forced himself to listen to the first message.

Roddy, if you know what's good for you, call me back. Your problem isn't going away.

Vinzy's usually jocular tone was gone, replaced by one rooted in deadly seriousness.

He hasn't returned the call.

But it's only a matter of time before he'll have to deal with the reality that's invaded his life.

A medical murderer. Like something in a bad movie.

Unbelievable.

And if he did agree to murder Edmond Merko?

Then what?

Live with that on his conscience?

A killer in scrubs.

A surgical assassin.

I can't do it. I won't.

He may not be shackled with Danny's religion-driven qualms, but he's not a conscienceless psychopath—he's a far cry from Vinzy Masconi, who never saw a devious scheme he didn't love.

While Roddy's younger years were filled with rage and fear—driven by the harsh reality of the streets—he'd never faced anything like the evil that had slithered into his life two nights ago.

And now he's living two separate lives.

He has a foot planted in each of two different worlds.

World One: the hospital, the OR, sterile preps, argon beam coagulators, hydraulic operating tables, surgeries, teaching residents and interns—the world of medicine, of preserving health and saving lives. The world of Tracy and the kids—which he's fucking up, big-time. The comfortable, predictable life of a suburban physician, a day-to-day life of ordinary routines—helping his daughter with her school projects, a movie at the multiplex, dinner with friends, chores around the house—a world that's safe and predictable.

World Two: back rooms, murder plots, guns, thugs, drugs, mobsters, rubouts, hit men, Italians and Albanians, warring families and clans. A world of extortion, gambling, intimidation, robbery, and murder.

He's trapped in the machinations of a vicious cabal, not knowing what awaits him or the people he loves.

He thinks back to the mantra he heard as a kid: *like father like son.* The predictions from everyone who knew him—that he'd become a violent man who'd resort to brutality and bloodshed, as did his father. That he'd succumb to the indelible stain of genetics, the traits painted on his DNA—now etched into his soul.

And because he now lives with a foot in each world, one thing is certain: the brutal acts he committed at Snapper Pond are sucking him away from the safety of World One directly into the abyss of World Two.

And there's no way to extricate himself from the hell his life has become.

He's hypervigilant; it's now reflexive.

And he's doing it right now: the goon scan.

Roddy's gaze crawls over the room, trying to spot a wiseguy, some tough-looking, steep-jawed thug who reeks of criminality. He takes it all in, from the tables near the wine rack to those tucked under the staircase leading to the private room upstairs. He's like a scent hound, sniffing out anyone who looks ethnic, maybe mobbed up. Ever since McLaughlin's, he can virtually smell Mafia types, the Russian Bratva crews, and the other low-life scum with whom he's now entrenched, guys mired in crime.

He drains his glass of Barbera, knowing the wine should taste fruity with a hint of strawberry, but it might as well be mud. Nothing tastes good anymore—the whole world's gone sour.

He used to think the worst that could happen to Danny and him would be they'd be nabbed for Grange's murder, be hauled off to prison for a very long time, even life for first-degree murder.

But right now incarceration in some hellhole seems like the least of his problems. Roddy's not naive enough to think this thing with Cellini will ever end well.

If he's lucky, he'll be the only casualty. His wife and kids will be spared. But himself? No way will they let him live, no matter what he does or doesn't do with that guy Merko.

Once they have no use for him, forget about it. He ends up in a city morgue or, more likely, in some landfill.

He signals the waiter for another glass of wine.

More laughter from that same table—drilling through his skull. Another glance across the room.

They're not gangsters.

And very soon these Bronx mobsters will sink their claws into Danny.

And what should he do about Danny?

If he tells him, it'll send him over the edge.

Dan's cut from a very different bolt of cloth. That's why he never shared his plans for Grange the night he drugged that dirtbag and enlisted Danny's help getting him into the car. For all Danny knew, they were taking the fat slob home. It was only while they were headed upstate on the Taconic, with Kenny Egan in the backseat, slamming his fists into the comatose gangster, that Danny saw Roddy's scenario unfolding.

It was wrong to have involved Danny.

Dan's strict Catholic conscience would never have allowed him to be part of a murder plot. And Roddy knows Danny's suffered mightily since that night at Snapper Pond. He didn't stop Roddy, and even egged him on to finish off Kenny once Dan learned Kenny not only was part of the extortion plot but had nearly killed Angela by driving her off the road.

The second glass of Barbera arrives. Roddy's tempted to guzzle it, but he can't get buzzed. He has an early day in the OR tomorrow—some complicated surgeries for which he'll need a clear head and sure hands.

And he's got to stay sharp to hear whatever bad news Danny has in store.

Danny's voice on the phone made it clear: something's come up.

Danny's voice is always a giveaway—begins warbling, an uncontrolled quivering that says, *I'm worried and I gotta talk to you real soon, Roddy.*

They don't talk on the phone or e-mail or text about Snapper Pond. Never. They only discuss it in person softly, *sotto voce*, in a public place—at a mall or in a restaurant like Rocco's, with the clatter of dishes and the babble of diners in the background, preferably with music playing on a sound system, where no one can hack into, tap, or overhear what's being said.

Yes, he's become paranoid about surveillance systems, too.

These days, everything's hackable, discoverable, explorable— e-mails, texts, phone calls, even your driving route—because of ubiquitous closed-circuit TV cameras with 24-7 microchip video feeds, like when you're headed upstate to dispose of a blubbery, liver-lipped mobster and extortionist, one John Gargano masquerading as John Grange.

No, when it comes to discussing what went down at Snapper Pond, they talk up close and personal, face-to-face—no high-tech go-betweens.

In a digital world, it's impossible to keep anything secret.

But the most important secrets are those he keeps from his wife.

Chapter 6

Danny Burns enters Rocco's. He sheds his overcoat, thankful for the restaurant's warmth.

There's a bone-chilling nip in the air for this early in November. And the wind is horrendous, cutting right through him like a knife. He feels like a frozen tree limb about to crack on a frigid winter day.

The drive on the Cross County Parkway took maybe ten minutes, but it seemed like an hour to make the trip from his office in Yonkers. He's so primed, he's ready to explode if he doesn't tell Roddy what he learned only a few hours ago.

The coat check girl hands him his ticket, and rubbing his palms together, he scans the room, spotting Roddy at that same rear corner table tucked into a dimly lit section of the room. Whenever they meet at Rocco's, Roddy always gets there first and sits at that recessed table, away from the crowd and out of earshot.

It must be his army ranger training, which has him primed to scope out danger and be on the alert for the safest place to talk.

It all began when they were seventeen and Roddy was arrested for burglary. It's because of that botched crime, instigated by none other than Kenny Egan, that Roddy straightened himself out and eventually became a doctor. Dan's mother, Peggy, and Roddy's teachers implored the judge to go lenient on this poor kid who, despite his awful circumstances, was a good young man and smarter than any other kid in the class. The judge listened, and Roddy was given the choice: either enlist into the army or be sentenced to a prison term.

The army set Roddy straight in so many ways, and he eventually became a doctor. But ever since Snapper Pond, Dan realizes a darker part of his best friend has never really changed.

They greet each other with the usual hugs and backslaps. There was a time when being with Roddy was the most comfortable thing in the world. After all, they'd known each other from their toddler days, playing in the sandbox. That's what Ma told him a million times. He recalls speaking with Roddy about those days.

"I don't remember a thing about that time," Roddy said.

"Funny, I remember it very well," Dan replied.

Of course, Roddy must've buried his memories of back then. It had to be sheer misery, living with his mother, a drug-addicted petty thief. And there were no baby pictures. There was only the criminal legacy of his dead father and his mother's lowlife friends coupled with her drug-addled negligence. That was part of the soil in which Danny and Roddy's friendship grew.

But lately there's been more than a subtle shift in their relationship: in some ways, a chasm has opened between them.

They used to get together and shoot the breeze about anything; or they'd dine out with their wives—a great foursome. Their friendship was based on a solid footing.

But since McLaughlin's and Snapper Pond, there's been a change in their bond, one that neither wants to openly confront.

But Dan also knows this: just as when they were kids, he's much too dependent on Roddy. Years ago it was Roddy defending him by fighting off the neighborhood bullies and always coming up with a way to get out of trouble.

Now he leans on Roddy for emotional support. Dan knows he finds it hard to take decisive action, to really man up.

He's always blamed his asthma for what was actually his way of being in the world.

But maybe tonight a new chapter will begin between them.

For once Danny feels the news he'll share with Roddy may start getting them on an even keel. Maybe it can all be put behind them. And maybe Dan will shore up Roddy for a change.

"Roddy, I've got some good news . . . *finally*," Dan says as he sits across from Roddy. Dan's voice bubbles with excitement. The waiter has trailed Danny to the table, so he turns to the guy and orders a dry martini, straight up with extra olives.

Roddy remains expressionless until the waiter retreats toward the bar.

Then his piercing blue eyes laser in on Dan's. Though he's closing in on forty-seven, Roddy still has that taut, tensile, strong appearance of the street fighter he once was.

But something about Roddy looks different tonight, and it's troubling: deeply etched worry lines cover his face, and his brow is lined by furrows. His skin has a bluish skim-milk-pale hue— or maybe it's the lighting—and he looks drained, sleep-deprived, friggin' fatigued.

Danny considers asking what's wrong, but he's so jacked, he *has* to tell Roddy what he's learned. His breath quickens, coming in short minigasps; damned asthma better not kick in like it does when he gets too excited. It's tough to keep his voice modulated, but if he focuses on his breathing—slow and steady, in, out, just stay aware of each breath—and if he doesn't let his nerves take over, he'll be all right.

Can't let anyone overhear him. Dan's eyes dart from table to table. The place is crammed and the ambient noise level will mask his words. And Pavarotti's belting out some Neapolitan love song on the sound system. Thank God for music—nearly every restaurant has a soundtrack these days—it masks conversation.

"We're in luck, Roddy," he says, just above a whisper.

Roddy leans closer and turns his left ear toward Danny as he stares nonchalantly at the wine rack across the room.

"I said, we're in luck."

Roddy turns his head to Dan; his lips form a pale slash.

"The president of the Lake Rhoda Homeowners' Association called. The condo project's blocked."

Roddy's eyebrows rise. "Really?"

Dan nods. "The Columbia County Conservation Society got involved and hired some hotshot lawyer. It's done: the county's declared Snapper Pond a nature preserve. There'll be no development anywhere, now or in the future. No backhoes, no bulldozers, no condos, no golf course. Nothing. Nature wins. Into perpetuity, as the lawyers say."

The corner of Roddy's lips turn up as he peers into Dan's eyes.

Dan leans across the table and closes in on Roddy's ear. "There'll be no dredging anywhere *near* Snapper Pond. Nothing gets dug up," Dan rasps in as low a voice as possible. "Those guys're gonna rot in that hole . . . till they turn to dust. The gun, the shell casings, and that stupid ring of Grange's, too."

Dan glances around the room again.

Roddy nods and leans back in his chair.

Dan would never have expected such a low-key—really sort of muted—reaction from Roddy. He doesn't even look relieved. Just looks wrecked.

The waiter approaches, sets Dan's martini on the table, and asks if they're ready to order.

Dan orders salmon and Roddy orders veal parmigiana.

Dan picks up the martini and watches Roddy raise his glass of wine. Dan sips, feeling the gin slip down his throat, and then warmth mushrooms through his belly. Funny how an icy drink drains its way to your stomach and moments later you feel the heat everywhere. Only one swallow and he's light-headed, almost floating.

It's not easy to contain his elation. "I swear, Roddy, I feel like I can breathe again. Maybe we'll be free of this thing. I don't even wanna *think* about that goddamned place *ever* again."

"You're good with it? I mean *all* of it?" Roddy asks in a monotone.

Danny nods his head so vigorously his teeth clack, because with today's news, he knows he'll be able to barge through the minefield of dread that's threatened his sense of well-being since that night.

Sitting amid the music and clatter of dishes with the aromas of Italian food flooding his nostrils, Dan can barely stifle the temptation to laugh out loud, to bray the way Kenny Egan used to, to get up and virtually sing along with Pavarotti—as ridiculous as that would be—because they won't end up being interrogated by the police and wind up in prison.

"Roddy, we'll be in the clear."

Roddy's eyes bore into him. Even though this is such great news, Roddy looks wasted. Jesus, the guy looks like a ghost. *Ghost* . . . Shit, it reminds him of Grange.

"Roddy, you look awful. What's wrong?"

Roddy shakes his head. "I don't know, Dan. I sometimes find myself waiting for the other shoe to drop. I just feel like we're sitting on an IED. I guess I'm just taking it one day at a time."

"I know, Roddy. I know. And let's face it, I was no altar boy that night, either." Danny leans across the table, lowers his voice, and adds, "When Kenny was standing down in that hole and admitted he ran Angela off the road, I wanted him dead. I had hate in my heart. I remember telling you to shoot the bastard, and if Kenny hadn't forced you, I'd have grabbed the gun and wasted him myself."

Dan can't get over how lousy Roddy looks. In addition to those forehead creases, Roddy's face appears taut, like his jaw muscles are quivering.

And he sees something else: for the first time ever, he notices Roddy's hair is threaded with gray at the temples.

"You sure you're okay, Roddy?"

"Yeah, I'm fine. Just some crap going on at the hospital."

"You look *really* tired."

"Forget it. It's nothing."

They talk a bit more—not about Snapper Pond, but about neutral things: the kids, Tracy's job, Angela's volunteer work, how Angela's mother's memory is going down the tubes and they're arranging for an assisted living facility, or maybe, God forbid, a lousy nursing home. They talk about the ins and outs of daily life, the trivialities of suburban living—and Dan's aware he's doing most of the talking. He knows Roddy's mind is a galaxy away.

Oh, the blessings of being able to forget.

But for Roddy, the torment goes on.

Dan knows the feeling. For months he felt like a buzz saw was whirring away, cutting him to pieces, and he was burdened by a flood of thoughts so powerful it felt like his insides would explode. Like his lungs would shut down.

Suddenly, a flash reminiscence of McLaughlin's comes to him: aproned waiters, linen tablecloths, leather chairs, bar crowds, a glitzy throng of celebrities, businessmen, Bratva gorillas and mafiosi thugs feasting at their Midtown chophouse. All the while, Kenny Egan, maître d' and managing partner, conspires with Grange to suck a fortune out of Roddy and him and barrels from table to table at Mach 2 velocity, glad-handing mobsters and laughing like a speed-stoked hyena.

Dan shoves the memory aside. These last few months, it's been easier to relegate it to the back of his mind. Like that chapter in his life never happened. And he's sleeping better, too.

But poor Roddy. He's always been the strong one, the guy who'd come up with a solution to any problem, the smartest and toughest guy in the room. The guy Dan's always looked up to.

But now Roddy looks totally bummed out. *Jesus, it's a one-eighty.*

When the food arrives, Dan watches Roddy peer down at the veal parmigiana—at the mozzarella cheese bubbling and the tomato sauce swirled on top, at the pile of spaghetti with red sauce, and next to it, a dish of broccoli rabe sautéed in olive oil and garlic—and he notices Roddy's face twist into a mask of disgust, and it's obvious the sight and smell of the food will make him heave.

Roddy closes his eyes and pushes his plate to the side.

"Jesus, what's wrong, Roddy?"

"Nothing, Dan. I'm just hoping this all passes, that it'll be over."

"You still worried about it?"

Roddy shrugs.

Not a very convincing response.

"Hey, Roddy, you're not alone." He can unload on Roddy and tell him how bad things were for him, maybe make him feel a little better. "I was all fucked up. There were times I thought I was losing my mind. I'd walk into a room and forget why I was there. Or I'd misplace my keys, my wallet, the TV remote. I'd forget phone numbers or someone's name." Dan glances about, afraid the diners at the next table can hear him. "And when the phone rang, I'd jump. I'd wonder if it was some Russian goon, or mafioso. I couldn't watch *Soprano* reruns, or *Breaking Bad.* I had the feeling my whole life was a lie.

"You know when things began turning around for me? It was when I was in the hospital, at St. Joe's, after I got shot in that bullshit holdup. I was half-awake—nearly out of it, but I knew what was going on—when the priest came into the emergency room and gave me last rites. I know you're not religious, but I gotta tell you, that did something for me. I began to accept that I'd been forgiven. That was when it started getting better for me. And now, with that condo deal on the rocks, this might just be over."

Roddy nods, but none of this seems to have penetrated.

"You know what?" Dan continues. "I've been thinking about that conversation we had when I wanted to tell Angela what we did. Man, you were *so* on the money. It would've brought her pain and worry, and like you said, she'd've been an accessory after the fact, a coconspirator. And I'm sure she'd have ended up despising you and me."

"Absolutely, Dan. You've been a solid soldier."

"Besides, I can't be a wuss," Dan says. "I gotta admit I depend way too much on Angie. Sometimes when I'm home it feels like she's the only adult in the room. Maybe it's because I grew up with no father and Ma was always there for me."

"Peggy was a saint," Roddy says. "I still think back to those days. She was like a mother to me."

"Yeah, everything was good back then. Remember, Roddy, we'd hitch a ride on the back bumper of a bus, get to my house, watch TV, and wait for Ma to get home from work?"

Danny feels a flood of warmth, a misty longing for those days.

"She treated me like a son," Roddy says. "Like we were brothers."

"That's because she knew what went on at your house."

Roddy says, "She'd cook up great stuff: stews, meat loaf, casseroles—and we'd eat like animals."

"Nothing made her happier than watching us devour her food."

Do we ever outgrow our need for mother's milk? Dan thinks.

He read somewhere that most men are just little boys packaged differently, that every man marries some version of his mother. Jesus, it's so fucked up.

Roddy leans in and says, "Look, Dan, I'm living a sham life, and I have a feeling Tracy suspects something's seriously wrong. I feel it in a hundred little ways—the way she looks at me, the tone in her voice, the way she kisses me, like it's an obligation, not something she *feels*. She's been distant—even cold—and we hardly talk anymore."

Roddy's face and shoulders seem to sag, as though some weight threatens to sink him in a quagmire of misery.

"It's taking a toll on us," Roddy continues. "On the kids, too. They're not stupid; they sense something's wrong. I swear, the only thing that keeps me focused is the OR. Otherwise, I'm living a bogus life."

Dan nods. Roddy's speaking his own dismal truth.

"Tracy's the best thing that ever happened to you."

Roddy nods.

"It's strange," Dan says. "You married what you never had. A woman who loves and cares for you. And looking back, I know I married Angela to get back what I lost when Ma died. We did the same thing in different ways."

Danny's throat tightens.

Roddy's eyes grow wet.

"You don't ever want to lose Tracy."

Roddy sighs. "You know what, Dan? The other night she asked me if I'm having an affair."

"No shit."

"Yeah, and I can't blame her. And I blew up at her. Really lost it. You know what I do to feel better? I tell myself I'm protecting Tracy and the kids by keeping it all secret, just like you did with Angela. But I can't go back to being the way things were before Snapper Pond, and Tracy doesn't want to be around me now." Roddy's voice catches; phlegm gurgles in his throat and thickens his voice. "What can I say, Dan? I'm trying to save what we have, but I think she's getting ready to leave me."

Roddy's face twists into a grimace, as though a spasm seizes him.

Dan reaches across the table and sets his hand on Roddy's arm.

Dan's at a loss for words. He knows Roddy's facing an ordeal he was spared. He can't imagine losing Angela. It's unthinkable.

And he knows something else: Roddy's a changed man.

And Dan has a feeling deep in his marrow that all the good news in the world won't bring Roddy back from wherever he's gone.

Chapter 7

The house is eerily quiet. The kids are upstairs. No doubt Sandy's working on a school project, doing her best to get superb grades. Eleven years old, and she already knows she wants to be a doctor; she's going to emulate her father.

But Tom's probably playing Call of War—whatever he needs to work off the testosterone bubbling through his brain circuits. Or looking at porn. There's no firewall against that. No matter what parental controls they install—crap like Net Nanny or WebWatcher—the kid uses proxy sites to get around them. A supersmart kid.

And if Roddy confronts, corrects, or counsels him? The kid shrugs. But at thirteen, that's his job: to drive his parents crazy.

In the kitchen, Roddy inhales the lingering aroma of Tracy's beef stew. It smells delicious, a lot better than the veal parmigiana at Rocco's. Funny, now he feels like eating. There's something about Tracy's cooking he can't define. It's not only delicious, but it's also comforting—it smells like home.

But there's little comfort at home these days. There's been an uneasy truce for months, until his outburst in the shower the other night. Now their rupture is open and raw.

On the drive home, Roddy rehearsed what he'd say to try to patch things over. Buy some time, hope things will mellow out. He never thought this could happen to them. Tracy and the kids are his entire world, but he's brought their marriage to this break-ing point with a cavalcade of secrets and lies.

And now Cellini has him buried even deeper in deception.

He makes his way to the den. Tracy sits on the tuxedo love seat.

As Roddy enters, she glances at him and sets a magazine on the end table.

But he can tell she wasn't reading it. She probably picked it up when she heard him come into the house. Her eyes are wet; she's on the verge of tears.

"Hi, honey. Danny says hello."

Can he gloss over her simmering anger, pretending he doesn't detect it?

He sits next to her, sinks into the cushion, and senses her body go taut.

Her forehead creases in a burgeoning scowl. She shakes her head subtly, but it's there: a negative vibe.

His legs tighten.

"Honey, I want to apologize for the other night when I—"

"Roddy, we need to talk."

Glacial coolness he's never encountered until recently—since his worry and preoccupation with what happened at Snapper Pond. But the other night might have been the last straw for her.

"Yes, I want to talk, too," he says. "I know I've been—"

"I have to say something before you tell me you're tired and have to get to bed because you have a full day in the OR."

The edges of the room darken.

"Fine, honey. I just—"

"Roddy, I just can't get past certain things anymore."

She stands, paces for a moment, and then stops and sits on the love seat facing him.

He waits for more. His body pulses.

"Are you having an affair?"

"*No*, Tracy. *Never.*"

"Are you telling me the truth?"

"Yes. I *swear* it's the truth."

At first she says nothing, just looks beyond Roddy. Then, in a voice sounding distant, she begins. "You know, when you said you were meeting Danny for dinner, I didn't believe you." She inhales deeply and looks at him with a piercing gaze. "I was on the verge of calling Angela to find out the truth, but I didn't. I realized right then that our relationship has gotten to the point where it no longer matters whether you're actually doing what you said you were going to do. I can't believe anything you tell me. It hit me very hard, but I realized I no longer trust you. I need to be apart from you."

"Honey, *no*. I'm sorry I've been so . . ." He stops midsentence, shaking his head.

"You've been *what*?"

"I know I've been preoccupied, but there's not another woman. I'd never . . . You have to believe me."

"And there are other things."

"What other things?"

"Last February Danny was shot in his office."

"Honey, the cops investigated. It was a holdup."

"Let me finish, Roddy." She fixes him with those green eyes. "You told me that after the restaurant closed, Kenny went back to Las Vegas. But then the story changed—after Danny was *shot*, you said Kenny had *disappeared*. *Not* that he was back in Las Vegas. You said he *vanished*, as though people just vaporize into thin air."

Tracy's words sound muffled—as though she's talking underwater or his ears are clogged.

His thoughts swirl. She's nailed it. What can he say? She's onto something; the half truths and evasions are coming back at him full circle.

Tracy's had months to cogitate about this, and she's band-saw sharp. She's cobbled together the moving parts in his intricate bundle of lies. He was making it up on the fly, and she's onto it—she knows the pieces don't fit. She sees the whole picture.

He's always thought of himself as someone who told the truth, but now he's so accustomed to lying, it's become second nature. His entire life is a pack of lies.

And now that life is shredding.

"Then, Roddy, you tell me the police said Kenny was gambling and had lots of debts, that some mob people probably got to him." Her voice gets pitchy. "And *then* you tell me—after Kenny 'vanished'"—and she makes air quotes with her fingers—"it's possible the same mob guys might be coming for you and Danny because you were all partners."

Tracy's lower lip quivers. Her voice turns thin, reedy. "And you *then* tell me—*after* Danny's been shot, not before—that you think it's best for the kids and me to go to my sister's house in Nutley and stay there. That we could all be in danger."

"Trace, I didn't want to scare you. I—"

She gets up and starts pacing again, crossing her arms in front of her. "You didn't want me to *worry*?" Tears form at the corners of her eyes.

His life is breaking into a million little pieces. Everything's being shredded, discarded.

McLaughlin's, Grange, murder, Cellini—and now Tracy.

The unbearable weight of secrets. Of vile undisclosed things I can never share, because by doing that what little is left of my life will explode.

Tracy's eyes laser in on him. "Roddy, back when that happened, I asked if you trusted me . . . if you *ever* trusted me . . . and I have to be honest with you. I don't think you're capable of trust, the kind that needs to be there between a husband and wife. Maybe it's because of your lousy childhood. But you know what? That's no excuse. There was a time when I felt you *did* trust me. But not now."

She keeps pacing, looks down at the floor, and it's clear more is coming. But he must say something.

"Trace, what can I . . . ? How do I . . . ?" But the words won't form. He begins the sentence without knowing how to end it, and then realizes he cannot.

With her arms still crossed in front of her, she stares at him, shakes her head, and says, "And something's really clear to me. I haven't been living with the man I married. I don't *know* you anymore. Something's happened, and you won't share it with me."

She stands stock-still, staring at him.

"You used to talk about your day at the hospital, about people, your OR team, about the kids, the house . . . anything. But not now. You've become secretive, or maybe you always were and just hid it from me. Since that restaurant deal, you've been remote. Your mind is somewhere else."

"Tracy, it's the hospital, the politics, and I don't know what's going to happen."

"I don't buy that, not for a moment. The Roddy Dolan I married would've been asking for advice. You've never done anything professionally without discussing it with me. But you haven't said a word about the hospital, or whatever's on your mind. It's like there's a big secret in your life.

"And don't think I haven't noticed how you get up in the middle of the night and sneak downstairs. I've followed you into the den a few times. I've watched you sitting in the dark . . . and then you go to the breakfront, open a bottle and pour whiskey into a glass, and guzzle it like some alcoholic sneaking drinks in the night. Then you sit on the couch and wait—for what, I don't know—bent over, holding your head in your hands."

Her voice is flat, but her eyes flash.

Tracy's always had great antennae for deceit. She can sniff out the subtlest shading of the truth.

"Honey, I've had things on my mind," he says, but it's anemic, a pathetic stretch, and she won't buy it.

"What sort of things?"

"Oh, the hospital, the staff changes. I—I guess I'm wondering where I'm going professionally."

"You guess? You *guess*? Roddy, you're lying to me." She shakes her head, squints at him, and wrinkles her nose. "Something's happened in your life . . . in our lives, and you're keeping it a secret."

She stands in front of him, pursing her lips. "The Roddy Dolan I married is gone. And I don't know where he went." She gazes at him with eyes glittering as tears gather on her lashes. "I can't go on this way."

The weight of her sadness hits him like a mallet. It's sorrow so deep, he feels guilt for having brought it on her. Dread envelops him.

"Honey, from now on, it'll be different . . . better. I mean it."

"Oh, please don't say anything, Roddy." Her voice quivers as tears well in her eyes. "Trust is the foundation of any marriage. You don't have it, and you've taken mine away."

He gets to his feet, goes to her, and reaches out, but she moves back and shakes her head. "No, Roddy. This isn't the time for sweet talk."

"Tracy . . ."

"We need to think seriously about where we're going."

"Honey, what're you saying is not . . . I—"

"Roddy, we need to separate."

Chapter 8

The Regency on Parkway Road in Bronxville is one of the few rental complexes available in an ever-expanding community of condos and co-ops. Three stories high, the block-long construction has a pseudo timber-frame look reminiscent of Roddy and Tracy's Tudor-style home, only a mile and a half away.

Roddy walks through the model apartment with the rental agent. A short, pixyish-looking woman with blond hair, her expression virtually screams, *Now, you can join the other divorced and separated people in this place.*

"We cater to short-term tenants," she says. "People waiting for their homes to be remodeled, or renting until they find something to buy."

Short-term, like my life may be right now. And while I'm still alive, it'll be dinner with the kids on Wednesday nights. On alternating weekends, one and then the other will sleep in the second bedroom. But Tom won't want to spend a weekend here.

A placard on a credenza reads, Furnishings by Carter Rentals. He slips a business card into his pocket.

"They have a move-in-ready package," says the agent. "You can have the place fully furnished in a few days."

Three days later—or maybe four; he's lost track of time—Roddy stands in the living room of his furnished two-bedroom apartment. The place is a real downer with new—and inferior—construction, plasterboard walls, beige and off-white fabrics, low-pile carpeting, mass-produced lamps, and pedestrian bathroom and kitchen fixtures. The furniture has a cheap look, like it's been bought from Overstock.com, and it's made from particleboard. The place has a utilitarian—strictly functional—and very decorated look.

It radiates transience.

Tracy wanted him out, so here he is, in an apartment denuded of anything resembling the home he's loved for years. He feels uprooted, emptied, hollowed out, missing all he cares about—Tracy, Tom, and Sandy.

It'll be hospital cafeteria food, takeout, and meals at a local diner—the place on Kraft Avenue in Bronxville—because he has neither the time nor the inclination to shop and cook.

"No, Roddy, we can't make things better right now," Tracy said. "We need time apart . . . time to think about the future. And *you* need to get your priorities straight."

When Sandy learned they were separating, she broke out in convulsive sobs.

"It's only for a little while," Roddy whispered, but she kept crying.

Tom feigned indifference, but Roddy could tell he was shaken. The kid used to come home from school talking about how this or that kid was all screwed up because the parents had separated. And now it's happening to him.

It had been coming for months, and its roots were planted the evening Kenny Egan showed up at his office with that sales pitch about becoming a silent partner in a restaurant. And now that poisonous plant is bearing its toxic fruit: his marriage is in ruins. And Roddy's spirit is lost in a dark and broken place.

For months he'd sensed the trajectory their relationship was taking. There were mornings he awakened from a dream-filled sleep and reached over to luxuriate in the velvety feel of Tracy's skin only to be met by rumpled sheets.

Her side of the bed was empty, and he heard her downstairs in the kitchen, rattling around, getting ready to leave for the library.

She didn't have to leave so early for work, and he wondered if she could no longer tolerate making small talk over their morning coffee.

She'd spend hours on her laptop or cell, her brow furrowed as she sent e-mails or texted or read the newspaper—she didn't look at or talk to him—and he recalls having felt shunted aside, locked out.

When he tried to kiss her, she gave him her cheek or pulled away from his embrace. And her smile was distant, reserved, as though she was merely indulging him.

All so different from their life together before that restaurant disaster, when he'd never even heard of McLaughlin's.

And now he's living alone.

It's an overwhelming sense of loss, a crushing emptiness, as though he's been gutted. He misses Tracy and the kids like they were bones ripped from his body. He's reminded of the days back in medical school, when he had a long-dead father and a sick, drug-addicted mother who died of liver failure during his second year, when he subsisted in a one-room, run-down, roach-infested scholarship apartment, feeling alone, adrift, and unwanted.

But back then there was hope. There was a future.

And now what little future awaits him is dictated by Cellini.

It's Friday evening, after a grueling day beginning at seven a.m. in the OR, with back-to-back surgeries: two hernias, a gallbladder procedure, and a bowel resection on a cancer-ridden woman. Roddy's feet ache from standing all day, but the OR has been a lifesaver. It engages him in something other than ruminations about his empty life. And worries about Cellini.

Yesterday he'd called Tracy's cell phone twice while she was at work, but both calls had gone to voice mail. That had never happened in all the years they'd been together. She always answered her cell when the call was from him.

The third time he called, she answered. In clipped tones, she said, "Roddy, I can't talk now. I'm busy."

He won't text her. He hates textual intercourse. He wants to *hear* Tracy's voice, wants a real conversation, not some half-assed digital dialogue.

Using a plastic fork, he picks at his takeout chicken salad. Sipping from a bottle of Bud, he wonders if he has enough interest to turn on the TV. The last thing on earth he wants to watch or hear is the news. All bad, all the time.

Living in this mausoleum of an apartment, surrounded by divorced tenants, his kids getting older, soon striking out on their own, he's drowning in a wave of loss.

Dan hasn't mentioned being contacted yet by Cellini. When they latch on to him, Danny will panic. He'll lose it completely. But he can't tell Dan what's going down.

Roddy knows he violated something elemental in his friendship with Danny. He never should have dragged him into that murder at Snapper Pond. It probably ruined Dan.

And he knows because of it something has died between them.

Sure, Dan will always be his accountant, financial adviser, and godfather to his children, but they can never return to the way things were.

His relationships with Tracy and Dan have been poisoned.

Probably for as long as he lives.

Chapter 9

The surgeries sustain him. They're the only sanity left in his life.

The operating room with its gleaming tile walls, Skytron lights, retractors, scalpels, hemostats, and curettes—all the paraphernalia—along with the nurses, assistants, interns, and residents, keep him grounded, focused.

The OR team is family, the only one he has now. The surgeries are more than his work—in some cases, they're life and death—and they soak up mental energy, so while he's focused on cutting, probing, and coagulating, he can leave behind the disarray of his life.

But the day is done. At six in the evening, Roddy, still wearing surgical scrubs, sits in the doctor's lounge. Aching feet, a spent feeling, and a sense of accomplishment are the usual residuals of a day in the OR.

But not this evening. Not when Cellini, DiNardo, and Vinzy are in his life.

It's been days since Vinzy's tried calling him. But the time will come—and what will he do?

He's on tenterhooks waiting for his cell phone to display a call from Carmel Medical Associates.

Yes, the mob has snared him, the way a hawk's talons clutch a helpless hare. Everything's in jeopardy—his family, his home, his very life.

An icy thought clutches him: they kill people. It's part of their business model. How many bodies have they dumped in the Pelham Bay wetlands, or the Staten Island Greenbelt, or the salt marshes of Jamaica Bay? And of course there're the New Jersey Meadowlands, home of a hundred bodies, no doubt, including Jimmy Hoffa's.

Even if Cellini doesn't really believe Roddy and Danny killed Grange, he's got them by the short hairs. He can simply tell the Staten Island mob Roddy and Dan were involved in Gargano's disappearance. That's all the Brunettis would have to hear—they'd come for both of them.

And if Cellini gets his way, he'll corner Dan, who will have no choice but to crunch the numbers and make cash vanish into the ether.

If he warns Dan about that night at Geppetto's, Danny's anxiety will kick in so hard, a mucus-laden riot would erupt in his lungs. Even more crucial, Dan's soul could never deal with the evil that's in the offing. So he's got to figure out a way to make certain Cellini and DiNardo never follow through on their plans for Dan.

Focus, focus, think, Roddy tells himself.

Nearly every one of the interns and residents—all the medical students and junior associates he's taught over the years—has told him he's a clear thinker. He sees his way logically and rationally through problems and doesn't let the static of unanticipated complications upend him.

How many times has he had to act quickly and interrupt a surgery to stop an out-of-control bleeder, or resort to extreme measures to resuscitate a patient whose heart stopped in the middle of an operation? He can't count how many times his quick thinking and nimble reaction to an unforeseen complication led people to say, "Roddy, you're so quick with your decisions, you could be an emergency room physician."

He has time—maybe a week or two before this guy Merko's surgery—to consider his options. If he moves deliberately, as though it's a chess match, he can sort things out.

So, think . . . think . . . think.

When Cellini made his proposal—no, it wasn't a proposal; it was a demand—Roddy neither committed nor refused. Though he thought he'd explode—and didn't give a shit about those thugs or what they might do to him—he kept his cool. He tamed the beast, the Mad Dog.

That monster is buried.

"Sit on it and we'll get in touch," Cellini had said.

So here he is, sitting on it.

Except he's not sitting; he's marching back and forth in this lounge like a caged beast.

But life is always filled with choices—some good, some bad—and the choices you make have consequences and eventually lead to more forks in the road. And when it's time to negotiate those forks—to make a decision—you choose a road to somewhere. There are always choices to be made.

Roads to be taken.

Is there any clear or sensible choice in this situation?

Choice one: stall for time. Make Cellini and DiNardo think he's in on the deal, and then—what?

What happens when Merko's admitted to the hospital? How does he handle that?

Does he go to the police? Not an option.

Choice two: tell Cellini to fuck off.

Will Cellini contact the Brunettis?

Will Roddy get clipped?

Dan, too?

Or, since they know he lives in Bronxville—and they've pinpointed exactly where he lives on Clubway—will Tracy and the kids be in danger? Are they already in jeopardy?

What did DiNardo say?

"I'm sure the Brunettis would be . . . Let's just say they'd be very upset to learn that a top-notch Westchester surgeon named Roddy Dolan, a guy livin' in Bronxville—a guy with a wife and two kids livin' in a nice house on the edge of the Siwanoy Country Club . . ."

Telling Cellini to fuck off—not an option.

Choice three: play along, do nothing but wait, hope it'll all pass?

Wishful thinking.

Not an option.

Choice four: play along but be like a politician, pull strings. Have Merko's surgery canceled, rescheduled, or better yet, arrange for it to be done at a hospital where Roddy's not on staff. Where he's not a player.

But he's not on the hospital's administrative board and has no say over who's treated at Lawrence Hospital. And he has no say and no sway at any other facility.

He's only a surgeon on staff at Lawrence Hospital.

There's no administrative solution.

And Merko's surgery will be done where he or his doctor want it done.

So, choice four—manipulate the choice of hospitals? Not an option.

Choice five: go along with Cellini and DiNardo. Become an assassin. Shoot a slug of K-Dur into Merko's IV tubing and bring on a quick and painless cardiac arrest—sudden death. You're awake and a moment later you're gone. The world goes black. You see, hear, and feel nothing. The endless sleep.

No can do.

Impossible.

A choice he could never live with. Not now, not ever.

It goes against everything he is.

And something else is very clear: whether he does Cellini's bidding or not, there's no possible version of the world in which he survives this situation.

Either way—to kill or not to kill—once it's over, the mob will have no use for him.

He gets clipped.

Choice five—not an option.

Choice six: go Entebbe on these bastards. Get an Uzi or an AR-15—from someplace, God knows where—burst into Geppetto's when they're in that back room, and spray the place with so much lead it'll be a rain of death. Like Tony Montana in *Scarface*. Cover the walls, tables, and everyone with a barrage of nine-millimeter slugs, put the whole fucking bunch out of commission.

Back when he was a ranger he had plenty of training in the use of a mind-boggling variety of weapons. There was barely a rifle or pistol he couldn't break down, reassemble with head-spinning speed, and use with lethal efficiency.

But those days are long gone. He's not a ranger at Fort Benning or Fort Bragg, and he's not finishing ranger training, parachuting into Florida's Camp Rudder and wading through snake-ridden swamps. He's no longer a special-ops soldier.

He's an upper-middle-class Westchester surgeon with a wife and kids, living the good life, decades removed from the reckless conceits of youth.

And even if he could get his hands on an arsenal, could he stomp into a restaurant and in a cold-blooded frenzy blast away, blitz the room like a low-flying A-10 Warthog strafing retreating Iraqi forces, slip the weapon into automatic mode—fire twelve hundred rounds a minute—and fill a bunch of goons with body-blasting bullets? Could he fire deadly two-second bursts, swivel the weapon, rake the room, demolish everything, and take them all out? Could he ratchet up enough rage and unfettered fury to blast away and watch flesh fly and blood spray?

And what about witnesses? Waiters, kitchen staff, and those old patrons in that front room. They'd see what he did. Could he be so merciless, so indifferent to their lives that he'd slaughter them, too?

Not a chance.

Could he be an out-of-control madman willing to kill anyone in his path?

Don't kid yourself. That's not an option. It's not only a prescription for mass murder, but it's also suicide, because some thug will manage to whip out a pistol and fire back.

And even if he survived such a horrific massacre, Roddy's final days would be spent in a maximum-security prison, caged in a rabid hellhole, locked behind cinder block, steel bars, and razor wire, and he'd never survive among the tattooed gangbangers, shit flingers, crack addicts, psychotics, rapists, iron-pumping sociopaths, and remorseless murderers—scum-of-the-earth, dope-smoking psychos who'd shank you for a nickel, just like what happened to his father in Attica.

Prison would be the final chapter in the squalid life of the Mad Dog, a guy who as a kid never avoided a fistfight or a boxing match—the ball-busting, brawling king of the Sheepshead Bay streets—a guy who never got beyond his own violent past.

And what about Tracy, Sandy, and Tom?

What happens to them if he dies or goes to prison?

The lives they have now would be over. They'd be devastated.

As he looks around the deserted doctors' lounge, one thought crackles through his mind: how does he deal with the darkness that's turned his life into a fetid pile of garbage?

Chapter 10

Back in the apartment, Roddy's overwhelmed by the soulless-ness of the place. If it had been done by a high-end decorator with furnishings from Bloomingdale's, it would still feel barren, impersonal. The tan, beige, and off-white fabrics covering the couch and chairs and the cheap-looking, low-pile grayish carpet-ing—the blandness of it all—make it seem so generic, it could be a model apartment.

His thoughts drift back to his family.

First an image of Tracy: as usual, he sees her facing away from him and sees the lovely nape of her neck, the arch of her back. She turns her head to look at him. Her emerald-green eyes widen, beckoning him. A half smile spreads over her lips. Strangely, her look is both seductive and innocent. Her blond hair—usually in a ponytail—shines in the overhead light, the way it did when they first met in the hospital library so long ago.

He was foraging through the lower shelves trying to find some obscure medical journal when she jumped down from a library ladder like a pale angel who suddenly entered his life. And it seemed he forgot the world. In that moment there was only her. Nothing else. It was years ago, and yet not very distant—only yesterday it seems.

And right now she's so close he inhales the fragrance of her hair. He's overcome with the wish to nuzzle the skin of her neck, so smooth, so redolent of *her*. That unique scent of hers. He sets his hands on her shoulders, feeling the warmth of her body. She turns to him. He's mesmerized by those green eyes, so bottomless, so alluring, they consume him. With the backs of his fingers, he strokes her cheek. God, how he loves her. More than anyone or anything on this earth. His body hums with joy, with the promise of things to come.

Tracy, my love, my life.

Has he ever told her how aware he is of all she does for him and the kids—for their home, their lives? She works at the Sarah Lawrence College library; chauffeurs Sandy to playdates and soccer matches; drives Tom everywhere; shops for the freshest ingredients, avoiding processed foods; cooks up a storm; and does a thousand things to make their lives better.

She's not high-maintenance: cares little for clothes, jewelry, or cosmetics; doesn't crave high-end vacations in thousand-bucks-a-night hotels on Anguilla; avoids budget-busting gyms or spas, won't enroll in SoulCycle like half the women she knows, yet stays in shape; is beautiful, smart, and practical; and has a surplus of emotional intelligence, and always sees the hidden sides of so many things that escape him.

She's his anchor, his everything. Hers is a love he can feel, see, sense in everything she does—for the kids and for him. If he believed in God, he'd think Tracy's a gift from heaven for his having survived his past. Has he ever made clear how deeply he loves, respects, and needs her, how meaningless life would be without her?

If she knew what he did that night at Snapper Pond, whatever love she has left in her heart for him would dissolve.

When he telephoned the house, Sandy answered, sounding whiny, her voice warbling. He could tell she was holding back tears.

"When are you coming home, Daddy?"

"I'm not sure, honey. Mom and I will talk about it."

Tom was his usual thirteen-year-old self—matter-of-fact, non-committal, nonchalant. Like it would cost him something to show some feelings.

And then a brief interlude with Tracy.

"Yes, Roddy . . ."

There was no "honey" or any expression of endearment.

A few words went back and forth, feeling forced, uncomfortable. She was as impersonal as his apartment.

He goes to the refrigerator, grabs a bottle of Bud, snaps off the cap, plops down onto the couch, and sips the brew. It has no taste—it's as dull as the apartment, as lacking in palatability as the hospital food.

It's me, not the food or the beer.

His life feels most empty at night, when he lies in bed alone, when Tracy's absence is palpable. No sound of her breathing, no warmth of her body—just a suffocating loneliness as he lies in the dark listening to his heartbeat throb through the pillow.

Except for the brief period when Tracy and the kids were in Nutley, he hasn't slept alone for sixteen years. The absence of life's most basic routines heightens the emptiness: no TV sounds from the den, no aroma of freshly brewed coffee or the smell and sound of sizzling bacon in the morning, no doors opening or closing, no music bleeding through Tom's bedroom door, no science questions from Sandy.

Only silence.

He leans back and closes his eyes, trying to shut down his thoughts. *If only I could empty my mind.*

Glancing at the coffee table, he notices something: it's that little matchbox from the restaurant—the small rectangular box with a picture of Geppetto carving the wooden Pinocchio.

The sight of it sends a shudder through him. He doesn't recall having put it in his pocket. He must have been in some altered state. Yes, he'd been in shock—lacking cognizance—when Cellini and DiNardo had clobbered him with their plans for Merko; it was so unreal, he'd been in a fog.

His reverie is interrupted by a *ping* from his cell phone.

A look at the screen.

Another update to download.

He presses Remind Me Later and sets the phone back on the coffee table.

A moment later his ringtone, "Musetta's Waltz," sounds from the device. He's tempted to ignore it, but it could be a resident calling about some post-op problem.

He reaches for the cell on the coffee table and sees Vinzy's face on the screen.

Crunch time.

Vinzy's using FaceTime.

Fighting the urge to power off his phone, he holds it up. "Yeah, Vinzy. What do you want?"

He keeps his voice neutral, though heat flames in his cheeks. It's the fire within, smoldering, ready to erupt in a rage-filled inferno.

This conversation will be unlike all the others over the years since medical school. There won't be the usual "Vincenzo," and Vinzy won't call him Rodney. No friendly banter, no good-natured back-and-forth about their respective ethnicities—not anymore.

The so-called friendship is dead.

"Roddy, I finally got you. I wanna talk."

"Talk." Voice even yet cold, unforgiving.

"I wanna talk face-to-face, where we see each other, we're not just voices comin' outta phones."

"We're face-to-face, so talk." It's impossible to stifle the bitterness in his voice.

Vinzy's face—narrow, dark, curly hair, black eyes—appears distorted on the cell phone screen. And a sweat sheen glosses his forehead.

"Look, Roddy, what happened the other night . . . I had no choice."

"You had no *choice*?" He feels coiled, cobra ready, as though he could lash out with a power punch and shatter every bone in Vinzy's face.

Blood rushes in Roddy's ears.

"Listen, Roddy, these guys are the last remnants of the Bronx mob. They're losin' ground to the Albanians—to the Russians, too—and they just wanna hold on to the few gigs they got left, you know, the video and card games, a few numbers rackets, that's all."

"What about you, Vinzy? What are *you* all about?"

"Roddy, you came from the streets. You know how it is."

"Tell me how it *is*, Vinzy. Tell me how the *streets* are."

"Hey, Roddy. I know you a long time. You can't pretend you're somethin' different from what you were."

"That was a long time ago. And you're still stuck in the cess-pool of your past. Right?"

"I wouldn't say that."

"So what would you say?"

"I've stayed in touch with people from my past."

"You mean *friends of yours*?"

Vinzy shakes his head, looking like he's wincing, as though Roddy can't understand his position. Then a smirk creeps over his thin lips.

"So you're mobbed up, right, Vinzy?"

"I just keep in touch with people I know from a long time ago."

"So, you fucking lowlife, here we are, years after med school, and you violate my confidence? You tell these guys about me, things you said you'd never tell anyone?"

The words pour out in a hot torrent, like lava.

"You rat out my wanting a piece for protection. And my mentioning something about a friend's gambling debt to some

guy named Grange? And these mafiosi add up the numbers—
which they got all *wrong*—and then I'm invited to dinner by an
old medical school buddy—a bullshit artist who says he wants
to rehash old times—but before I know it, I'm strong-armed by
these hoods into a scheme to . . . I don't even wanna mention it.
What the fuck are you all about?"

"Roddy. I had no choice."

"No *choice*? You mean someone put a *gun* to your head and
made you mention me—just like that, out of the blue?"

He can barely catch his breath as the words cascade past
his lips.

"Whaddaya mean 'I had no choice'? You gotta be shitting me.
You had no *choice*?"

Spittle collects on his lips. His pulse throbs and his left hand
clenches into a fist. He's furious, so filled with righteous indignation, it's like a grenade will go off in his chest. He's lying like a rug
about Grange. But what choice is there?

"It doesn't matter if you had nothin' to do with Gargano,"
Vinzy retorts. "All that matters now is that Cellini *wants* you,
Roddy. You're his man."

Vinzy's speaking the truth. Roddy *is* Cellini's man, the ticket
to controlling the Bronx gambling clubs, maybe more. The
Gargano link and the threat to use it—whether Cellini believes
Roddy was involved or not—is Cellini's leverage, and Roddy's
chin deep in shit.

But he can't go down without a fight.

"Cellini can go fuck himself."

"Look, just like I know you, I know Carmine Cellini. You don't
wanna fuck with him. *Ever*. He means business."

Vinzy's eyes widen. That sweat sheen on his face virtually glows.

"He's an old-timer," Vinzy continues, "a relic, but he's tough
and he's smart, and he's a dangerous man. This is his last shot at
controlling certain enterprises."

"Go ahead, try to tell me you're not into that crap."

"Whatever . . ."

"Don't *whatever* me, you son of a bitch. You've fucked my life."

"Roddy, I only want you to realize what's best for you . . . and for your family. These guys don't mess around."

"And you're *threatening* me, right? And my *family*." The words pour from his mouth in a rush of temper. "You've not only dragged me into this, but you're saying if I don't do what Cellini wants, I'm toast. Or my *family's* in danger, right?"

"I'm tellin' you what's in your best interest, that's all."

"As a *friend*, right?" Acid crawls up his gullet, sears his throat.

"Call it what you want, Roddy . . . as a friend, an associate . . . an acquaintance . . . someone who knew you when we were students."

"Some goddamned friend."

"Roddy, I don't want to get into a pissing match with you. I called so we could talk face-to-face, like two mature men. I'm just saying that *I* have no choice and *you* have no choice. We're in this together."

"Don't go buddy-buddy on me. That's bullshit. Cellini never heard of me until you opened your fucking mouth."

"That's irrelevant, Roddy."

"Not to me it isn't. Why'd you bring me up?"

"What's important now, Roddy, is what you do for Carmine Cellini, not why this happened. I'm only tryin' to tell you—"

"I'm in this shitstorm because of *you*."

"Blame me all you want, Roddy. But Cellini wantsa know if you're on board. What do I tell him?"

The acid in his gullet turns to bile, hot as magma. His throat is seared by a fiery upsurge from his stomach. His hand squeezes the cell phone so tightly it creaks.

"Tell him I'm doing what he said to do. I'm *sitting* on it."

His thoughts spin in a frenzied shuttling—past, present, Cellini, Tracy, Tom, and Sandy, the Brooklyn streets, Kenny "Snake Eyes" Egan—and Danny Burns.

My life's an insane asylum.

"Oh, and another thing . . . Tell Cellini to forget about using Danny Burns to cook the books."

"Why?" Vinzy's eyes widen.

"He's a shitty accountant. A real loser. He fucked up big-time with the restaurant. Tell Cellini to get someone else to hide his . . . to do his accounting. Burns'll fuck it up."

"Okay, I'll tell him."

"Make sure you do. Otherwise the IRS will come down on you in a heartbeat."

Roddy has to bad-mouth Danny. He's gotta keep him out of this disaster.

"Burns is an audit waiting to happen. He got me audited up the ass. And if you even *think* about bringing him on board, you can *all* go fuck yourselves. You can count me out. I don't care about the consequences."

"Okay, I'll tell him. But what do I tell Cellini about *you*?"

"Like I said, I'm sitting on it."

"Well, don't sit too long. The surgery's comin' up soon."

"One more time, Vinzy . . . I'm sitting on it."

"Don't make me call you again."

"You know what, Vinzy, if we were in the same room right now, I'd break your fucking neck."

"See, Roddy. You haven't changed. You're the same guy you were back in Brooklyn . . . and in the army. You're a tough motherfucker. Nothin's changed."

Roddy pauses, wondering if he should add another acid-laden insult to those he's already hurled at Vinzy's face. But what will it accomplish?

"I'll let you know what I've decided."

"Don't take too long, Roddy. Cellini's an impatient man."

Chapter 11

It's nine in the evening. For the hundredth time Roddy runs through last night's conversation with Vinzy. All he's managed to do is stall for time.

Time to do what?

There's nowhere to go, nothing he can do. Stalling won't solve a thing.

All his life he's made choices, decisions—some very bad ones, and some very good. As Roddy looks back, it always seemed one choice was preferable to another, leading to a better outcome than the other.

He inventories the good decisions.

Going into the army when the judge gave him the option between army service and prison.

Going Airborne, then on to ranger school. Learned plenty of hands-on skills, met all kinds of people, saw things he'd never imagined he would, built self-confidence.

Discovered he loved the field surgery he learned as a US Ranger—got a huge charge out of sewing up injured soldiers in the field.

Decided to go to college, then medical school.

A whole new world.

A new life.

Becoming a surgeon.

Meeting and marrying Tracy.

A new way of being in the world.

Then the kids.

And the bad choices?

That's all he's been thinking about ever since Snapper Pond.

Too many of them. Beginning with Kenny Egan and that restaurant, and then Gargano masquerading as Grange.

How do I get out of this swamp?

Think, think. Use what you know about life.

Stop sinking into the quicksand. Get beyond fear.

You're smarter and tougher than Cellini.

Everything you've ever been through is waiting to be tapped.

Your past, the present, your skills, your abilities.

Snap out of it and get to work.

"Musetta's Waltz."

Shit, the cell phone.

His insides drop.

It'll be Vinzy. What now?

His heart thrashes. His pulse quickens.

A glance at the screen.

The readout: it's Ivan Snyder, his partner.

"Yes, Ivan?"

"Roddy, I need your help."

"What's up?"

"I'm stuck here in Manhattan and there's an emergency, a patient I've been working up. He's had some vague abdominal pain for a day or so, but early this evening it peaked. It's a small-bowel obstruction at the duodenum. It could be an adhesion from a gallbladder operation ten years ago."

"Yes, I understand."

"He's got abdominal cramping and projectile vomiting. He's running a fever—a hundred and one—sweating profusely, and has tachycardia; his heart rate is one fifty. He has a prior history of diabetes and coronary artery disease, and I'm worried he'll go into cardiac decompensation. It's a serious small-bowel obstruction."

"Got it."

A complete SBO, a life-threatening situation.

"The bowel will strangulate."

"Where is he?" Roddy asks.

"At Lawrence Hospital."

"Is he on an NG tube?"

"Yes, and despite nasogastric suction and decompression, he's blocked."

"They do X-rays?"

"Hold on, Roddy. I just got a text."

A pause.

Even though it's nearly nine in the evening, Roddy's thankful for this interruption. It derails his thoughts of Vinzy and Cellini.

"Roddy, they did plain radiographs, flat and upright. They also did a CT scan, and it's a complete obstruction at the duodenum. And the resident says the abdomen's distended."

"Lab tests?"

"Done."

"Good."

"He's being prepped as we speak."

"I'll get over there right now."

"Patient's name is Merko, Edmond Merko. He's scheduled for elective knee replacement, but that's on hold."

A galvanic shock seizes Roddy. His skin prickles, and the hairs at the back of his neck stand on end.

This is it. Crunch time.

The OR is blindingly bright. The tile walls gleam in the fluorescence.

He's scrubbed and ready. Always remembers every step of proper aseptic technique. No *C. difficile* or MRSA in this place.

Not with Roddy Dolan on a case. These bacterial infections can kill a compromised patient. And Merko's vulnerable.

Merko.

Prepped.

Unconscious.

Defenseless.

Cellini would salivate over this situation.

Roddy's favorite nurse, Claire Copen, is there, scrubbed, gowned, capped, gloved, ready to assist.

Roddy recognizes the aria playing on the OR sound system— "Nessun Dorma" from Puccini's *Turandot*, Plácido Domingo belting out the aria. It always moves him, making his scalp prickle.

A while back he asked them to change the music from mournful adagios to Italian operas.

Now, after Geppetto's, he's not sure he wants to hear Puccini, Verdi, Rossini, and all the rest. Even the mention of their names pumps his blood pressure to stratospheric heights.

But there's a more important consideration right now: Edmond Merko.

"Claire, you're working this late?"

"Only because I heard from Ivan and he said you're on this case, Roddy. Anyone else and I'd be outta here." They laugh.

The chief resident, Howard Welsh, laughs, too. He's a good resident. In a couple years, he'll be a top-notch surgeon. Maybe even join Roddy and Ivan's group.

A third-year medical student is in attendance. A good-looking kid.

Roddy's body hums as a vibratory sense of anticipation courses through him. This is it—surgery—the one intact domain in his life, the one that keeps him sane.

And he's about to operate on a man he's been ordered to murder.

Cap, gown, mask, surgical booties, everything's on; he's ready.

"Blood pressure's good," says the anesthesiologist.

"Induction?" Roddy asks.

"Yup. Propofol . . . He's under."

"This guy's diabetic and has coronary artery disease," Roddy says. "Let's just use Propofol, nothing else. That should keep him under while I do this laparoscopically."

"I'll stand by and be ready to open him up if you can't do it that way," says Welsh.

"Fine. What're you using for IV fluid?"

"Dilute Ringer's lactate with potassium," says Claire.

He thinks of K-Dur. Pure potassium. Amazing coincidence. Could anything be more surreal than this?

Potassium, a heart-stopping element, if used improperly.

And it's being dripped slowly into Merko.

A flash of Cellini, then of that back room, the cigar and cigarette smoke, the thugs.

I'm sure you can think of lotsa ways to put a sick guy like Edmond Merko out of his misery . . . you know, a little somethin' in his IV . . ."

"We'll monitor the IV very carefully," says Claire.

"Yes," Roddy says. "Too much potassium could set his heart into an arrhythmia."

"What's the pulse ox say?"

"Good oxygenation . . . ninety-seven percent. Heart rate's good at eighty," Claire replies. "EKG looks good. We're all set."

Roddy looks down at Edmond Merko. He's unconscious, lying on the table in the Trendelenburg position, perfect for maximum access to his abdominal organs. He's been draped and prepped.

He's a huge man, obviously tall and probably a good fifty or sixty pounds overweight, just as Cellini said. He's an immense human being.

Merko's belly has been swabbed with Betadine. His eyes are covered with surgical tape, a nasogastric tube protrudes from his nose, and an endotracheal tube exits his mouth, should resuscitation be needed. The tube is taped to the side of his face.

Roddy's thankful the man's face is obscured by the operative paraphernalia. It's better not to see the face of the man he's been ordered to kill.

Merko's on the table, partly covered, draped, not talking, seeing, or hearing, completely insensate. It's good Roddy never met him preoperatively; it makes all this impersonal.

For a moment Roddy feels like a butcher standing in his shop.

Or maybe in a slaughterhouse.

But it's not a butcher shop or a slaughterhouse.

It's an OR, with monitors beeping and IVs dripping, with tubes and instruments, a defibrillator, respiratory ventilator, electrosurgical generator, infusion pump, and suction pumps, and Roddy's a physician—a man practiced in the art of healing—and there's the Hippocratic oath and the admonition he's heard all his professional life: *Before all else, do no harm.* And even though he's killed two men, Roddy knows he hasn't got the heart of a murderer, and in some nascent but profound way, he knows his soul is at stake in the matter of Edmond Merko.

Where do I fit on the scale of right and wrong?

For a man like Edmond Merko—a huge man, obese, saddled with diabetes and whose cardiac status is questionable—any surgery is risky. Even the slightest glitch could be lethal.

A film of sweat forms on Roddy's forehead.

"Okay," Roddy says, turning to the medical student.

A teaching moment.

"We're doing this laparoscopically. I'll make three small incisions, maybe a half inch wide and then infuse carbon dioxide into the abdominal cavity to inflate it and give us room to see what's going on. Then we'll insert trocars and the laparoscope . . . and we'll watch the monitor. We'll go step by step, and when we find the adhesion, we'll lyse it very carefully. Why do we have to be careful?"

"Because you don't want to rupture an artery if the adhesion is vascular," the student answers.

"Exactly," Roddy replies. "Anything else?"

"Because you don't want to puncture the small intestine."

"Exactly. And most likely any adhesion will be sticking to a blood vessel or it'll be right next to it. What happens if the small bowel is punctured?"

"Peritonitis and the possibility of sepsis. Even death."

Death . . . what Cellini has ordered me to orchestrate.

"Absolutely. Tell me what you know about small-bowel obstruction."

The student launches into a description of the condition while Roddy makes small incisions.

The abdomen is inflated; the trocars are inserted.

Roddy's hand is steady. He slips the laparoscope into the abdomen. They watch the high-resolution monitor as Roddy manipulates the instrument through the abdominal cavity. The LED light within the endoscope casts brilliant light on the organs and connective tissue. Everything glistens—fascia, liver, duodenum, all of it. As charted in Merko's history, there's no gallbladder.

It's always felt strange to Roddy—watching high-tech instruments weave their way through the abdomen guided by his hand, yet he's watching on a monitor as though seeing it from afar. Like watching a TV program.

My life is insane. I've been ordered to murder this man in cold blood, here in the hospital, and what am I doing? I'm looking around his insides because he could die if I don't fix whatever's about to kill him. And I'm watching it all on a television screen.

"See that white, fibrous band there?" Roddy says, tilting his head toward the student while eyeing the monitor. "It's constricting the duodenum, just like Dr. Snyder suspected. It's bulging and discolored. In another hour, there's a good chance strangulation with tissue death or rupture of the gut would have happened."

The student nods.

"Blood pressure's still good," says Claire. "EKG is normal."

"Now we want to lyse that adhesion and free the duodenum from it."

"Pulse is slowing," says the anesthesiologist. "Wait . . . wait . . . the heart's beating erratically. We have atrial fibrillation now . . ."

Roddy stops and waits. "Let's see if it normalizes."

"I'm worried the anesthesia and probing of the abdomen might be too much for this patient. He could go into cardiac arrest," says the anesthesiologist.

"Is the defibrillator ready?" Roddy asks.

"Yes," replies Claire.

If this man dies on the table, certain people will be happy.

And then Cellini will have no more use for me.

Roddy's underarms are soaked.

"The rhythm's back to normal," says the anesthesiologist.

Roddy gets the signal to resume.

"Okay. Now we go through the trocar with a blunt-tipped scissors and very gently we tease apart the adhesions from the vascular attachments. We go carefully. We don't want to create any bleeders in the abdominal cavity."

Roddy takes his time, separates the adhesion from the blood vessels and surrounding tissue, and cuts away the fibrotic band of tissue and slips it out of the abdomen through the trocar.

"Are we done yet?" Roddy asks.

"No," says the student.

"Why not?"

"You want to see if there are any more adhesions."

This kid's sharp. Knows his shit.

"You got it, young man. What's your name?"

"Winslow. Don Winslow."

"Well, Don, I can tell you're gonna be a fine physician."

Roddy glances up at the chief resident. Welsh smiles and nods his head. It was only a few years ago when Welsh was a fourth-year medical student and Roddy spent hours teaching him surgical procedures.

Roddy moves the laparoscope with its miniature camera and light throughout the abdominal cavity, looking for more adhesions.

None.

"Let's go over the anatomy of the abdominal cavity," Roddy says to the student.

You never truly learn from a textbook. In the army, it was called OJT—on-the-job training. He could never have learned the ins and outs of a 50-caliber machine gun, or an M-16 rifle, or how to break down a .45 semiautomatic pistol, how to infiltrate enemy lines, or how to close off a sucking chest wound or rappel down the walls of a ravine from books or lectures.

It's an old story: you learn by *doing*.

So, what's he gonna *do* about Cellini? Roddy thinks.

Roddy and Winslow review all the visible structures and their connections.

"So now we close," Roddy says. "Don, tell me about possible postoperative complications."

The student launches into a tsunami of possibilities, all of them right on the money. Yes, the kid's as sharp as a scalpel.

"You interested in becoming a surgeon?" he asks.

"Yes," answers the student.

"Well, Don, when it comes time to apply for a residency, I'd like you to come see me."

Winslow nods and smiles.

Roddy says, "Howard, you'll close, right?"

"Of course."

Welsh begins suturing the small holes in Merko's abdominal wall.

"Skin to skin in under thirty minutes," says Claire. "As usual, great work, Roddy."

"Let's monitor him carefully," Roddy says. "He's a high-risk patient and could decompensate postsurgically."

"We don't want that to happen," Claire says with a quick smile.

Roddy turns and shoots the medical student a thumbs-up.

He leaves the OR.

Chapter 12

It's almost midnight. Roddy glances at the clock on the wall in Edmund Merko's private room on the surgical ward. His patient's sleeping comfortably, snoring like a chain saw—sleep apnea, no doubt, in a guy so overweight. The big man is definitely compromised.

All went well in the recovery room, and things are stable here.

Merko's vital signs are good, and his IV is running at a slow drip. Merko's doing well and should have an uneventful night.

Roddy heads for the parking area near the emergency department. On his way in, he left his car with the valet rather than park in the garage section reserved for physicians. It was a quicker way to get to the OR.

Merko's gonna make it.

But now there's Cellini.

"Don't make me call you again."

Vinzy's words from last night trumpet in his ears.

Roddy sits behind the wheel. His hands grip the steering wheel so tightly, his knuckles pop as rage courses through him.

Instead of killing the man, I saved his life.

If that Judas Vinzy were here, Roddy knows he would literally kill him.

I've already killed two men. I know I could do it again.

In a heartbeat.

But that's gonna get me nowhere, Roddy thinks. *I've gotta come up with something. If not, I'm history. And my family's in danger.*

Moments pass, and he puts the car in gear and heads toward home.

Traveling the empty streets through the center of Bronxville, he realizes one thing: temporizing with Cellini won't do any good.

"Don't take too long, Roddy. Cellini's a very impatient man."

By now Vinzy's words from their last phone call have lost their power to derail Roddy.

It occurs to Roddy that there must have been a progression of hidden events leading to the desperate situation in which he's now trapped. And there are people involved about whom he knows nothing. These underworld groups must have informants in all sorts of places—the police, politicians, the courts, even in hospitals. Yes, *hospitals.* The Bronx mob has contacts at Lawrence Hospital.

No doubt Cellini learned about Merko's scheduled knee surgery and assigned Vinzy the task of taking out the Albanian.

But Vinzy has no connection to Lawrence Hospital. His only base of operation is his Medicaid clinic on Arthur Avenue. Vinzy couldn't do the job, but he knew how to get it done.

He passed it off to the one guy he knew with a staff appointment at Lawrence Hospital. He had his patsy: an Irish guy named Roddy Dolan who'd asked him for two favors. Now it's time to have those favors returned.

I'm their man. Their assassin.

How do they know so much about me? About Tracy, the house, the kids?

Jesus, what a stupid question.

Vinzy knows plenty about him from what had been their casual friendship. And in today's world nothing is private. Tom's on Facebook, probably every day. Twitter, too. And Snapchat, whatever the fuck that is. Who knows what he shares with friends and so-called friends on Facebook? You can have a thousand "friends" on Facebook. A click and you're friends. Another click and you're unfriended. Disposable. And people who aren't your friends can access your page.

With social media, anyone's life can be an open book.

Even if you don't have Facebook friends or tweet, people can learn plenty about you.

Roddy's on staff at a well-known hospital, one affiliated with New York–Presbyterian Hospital and Columbia University. The hospital's website has photos and a brief professional bio of every physician in each department. He teaches medical students, interns, and residents, has a private office, and owns a home in Bronxville. All that information is available online.

The office of Dolan, Snyder, and Campbell has its own website. Online reviews are available on Yelp, Zocdoc, Healthgrades, and a rash of other Internet sites. Some even provide the partnership's estimated annual income and the number of people it employs. Multiple listings with his name are online for anyone to see. And each of the three partners are on LinkedIn; it's almost mandatory if you network professionally.

Or just Google him, or look for a hit on Yahoo! Only a few months ago, Ivan hired an IT guy to ensure their practice has search-engine optimization for anyone looking for a surgeon in Westchester County.

In this digital age, virtually everything's accessible by letting your fingers do the walking—over a keyboard.

No more Yellow Pages—those are relics of the past.

These days there's very little privacy.

If you know someone's address, whether you use Zillow or some other real estate site, you can learn how long someone's lived in a home, how much they paid for it, and what their annual realty taxes are. It's just a few clicks away.

And Vinzy knows Tracy works at Sarah Lawrence. Her daily routines are available for all to see if you take the school's virtual tour of the library.

It opens with her seated at the reference desk, welcoming the online visitor with her glorious smile.

And the kids—Sandy made the honor roll; her name is posted in the local paper at the end of each school year, and you don't have to be Sherlock Holmes to learn more about her and her family.

It's all available, all the time, all online.

On Parkway he comes abreast of an Avalon housing development, a large complex with more than a hundred apartments. He'd briefly considered renting there but opted for the smaller Regency. No matter how luxurious it may be, living in close quarters with too many neighbors reminds Roddy of growing up in that Sheepshead Bay, Brooklyn, basement apartment. He thought he'd put those days permanently behind him: the sounds of neighbors arguing, the slamming of doors in the hallway, the stale cooking odors permeating the hallways, the uncollected garbage, and the inevitable march of roaches parading through the apartment.

Yeah, living in a private house has its own hassles, but they're nothing like apartment living.

He never imagined living apart from Tracy, Tom, and Sandy, but now he's headed to an apartment, back to a life lived amid strangers, separated by thin walls in a cheaply constructed building.

The street widens. The Avalon complex is on his left; a parking lot is on his right.

A pair of headlights appear in his rearview mirror. They seem unusually bright.

Now they're even closer. And intensely bright.

The inside of Roddy's car explodes in a blinding white flare. He can barely see. Dots and specks form on his retinas. The guy behind him flashes his brights. On, off, on again.

High, low, high, low. Intermittent brilliance bursting with strobe-like intensity.

Roddy's doing the speed limit, but he steps on the gas pedal. The speedometer needle shoots up to forty-five.

A red cherry light goes off on the dashboard of a sedan behind him.

An unmarked police car.

Roddy wasn't speeding, but he's being pulled over. Why?

Can't be a cop. Unmarked police cars have lights inside the front grille. And there's no siren.

He comes to a stop sign, rolls through it, and picks up speed.

I'm being tailed. Gotta be Cellini's guys.

The car behind follows and moves in, closer. The cherry light stops swirling.

The distance between the cars is now small. Roddy looks into the rearview mirror and sees the silhouettes of three men in the vehicle behind him. He stomps on the accelerator and speeds away, but the car behind him closes in.

Again the high beams, then low beams, then the brights.

Should he find a side road or driveway to pull into?

Not a good idea. He'd be cornered.

He's driving at a steady forty-five miles an hour. He hits the hazard light button, hoping the flashing lights alert someone he's in trouble.

A sudden *thump.* His car lurches forward, and the seat belt tightens on his chest.

They've kissed his rear bumper. They'll run him off the road.

Another look in the rearview mirror.

Two cars are behind now him; another one follows the first.

Good, a witness.

He slows down.

The car bumps him again, and he's thrown forward. The seat belt catches his chest, this time with a sharp tug. He clutches the steering wheel.

The vehicle two cars behind honks its horn. He wants the cars ahead to pick up speed.

Roddy thinks about hitting the accelerator again but decides to slow down.

He decelerates to fifteen miles an hour.

The next stretch of road has an unobstructed view in the opposite direction.

The second car pulls out to the oncoming lane and speeds ahead. His right front fender is alongside Roddy's left rear quarter panel. The driver hits the gas and pulls alongside Roddy.

He stays adjacent to Roddy for a second, blows his horn, keeps pressing it, speeds up in a honking rush, surges ahead, and pulls back in front of Roddy. But instead of pulling away, the vehicle slows and the brake lights brighten.

The car comes to a stop.

Roddy has no choice but to apply the brakes.

He pulls up to the car in front of his. He's too close to pull around it and speed away.

The car at the rear pulls up right behind him.

He's sandwiched between two cars.

It's a setup. He's trapped. Now he wishes he had a piece.

Roddy squints and peers ahead.

Two men get out of the front car. Silhouetted by Roddy's low beams and flashing hazard lights, they stand on either side of their sedan. One man holds a pistol in his right hand. Their car's exhaust fumes billow in undulating clouds.

The men wear dark leather jackets and jeans.

They stand there waiting.

Roddy keeps his hands on the steering wheel. *Don't move a muscle.* His heart somersaults in his chest.

Do I get out of the car and run?

A glance in his side-view mirror.

The driver's door of the car behind opens. A man emerges and stands there for a moment. Black leather car coat, knee-length, open at the front, flapping in the breeze. He leaves the driver's door open and strides toward Roddy.

A glance in the right side-view mirror. Front and right rear passenger doors open.

Two more men get out of the vehicle.

Five men. Three behind, two in front.

He waits, hands on the steering wheel in a death grip. He doesn't move a muscle for fear they'll think he's reaching for a piece—for sure they'd shoot him; maybe they'll waste him anyway.

Cellini might have had enough of Roddy's ducking him.

He can't do a thing. Just wait. And hope.

The three men move toward him. The driver of the car approaches on the left. The other two men move along the passenger's side of his car.

The driver bends at the waist and makes a rolling motion with his hand.

Roddy lowers the window.

The guy leans forward, his head nearly in Roddy's car. His breath smells of cigarettes and garlic.

"I hear you're a tough guy," he growls. His eyes gleam in the ambient light. Breath vapor pours from his mouth.

Roddy says nothing. Stares at the guy. Medium height, solidly built, slicked-back hair, closely set eyes, Roman nose. Reminds him of toughs he knew in Brooklyn.

Any attempt to resist will be a losing battle. Can't even count on a surprise punch to the gut; there are too many of them, and they're armed.

I'm toast.

"You a tough guy?" the thug asks.

Keeping his voice steady, neutral, "No, not really."

"You're not *really* tough?"

Roddy's armpits dampen. His heart beats an insane tattoo.

There are no right words here. Just keep your mouth shut. Speak only when spoken to.

The hood moves back two paces. "Step outta the car, tough guy."

Roddy exits the car. He stands stock-still; a searing ache in his forearms travels down to his fingers, now cramping from having clutched the steering wheel so tightly.

The other two move around the front of his car and stand next to the guy facing him.

A sideways glance to his right: the other guys wait beside the car ahead of his.

He's facing three men. All young, in their twenties or thirties. Men with hard faces, men who would think nothing of beating him to a pulp.

It's hopeless. Can't do a thing.

One guy holds a tire iron.

Another wears brass knuckles.

This is it. He's due for a beatdown.

The driver steps closer. "You see, Doc, we can get to you any-where and anytime. Understand?"

"Yes."

"Say, 'I understand.'"

"I understand."

"We know where you live. We know where you work—the hospital and your office. We know who your partners are. We know where your wife and kids live. We know where your wife works. We know your friends. You understand?"

"Yes, I understand."

The man nods. His eyes narrow. "If we come for you again, you won't get off easy. Understand?"

"I understand."

"You know why we're here?"

"Yes."

"Why're we here?"

"Because I haven't said yes."

The man nods. "So, is it a yes or a no?"

"It's a yes."

"I don't think you mean it."

"I do."

"Say it again."

"Yes."

"Maybe we gotta convince you."

Roddy shakes his head.

It's about to happen.

"You want it to be *you* or someone you care about?"

"If anything happens . . ." A choking sensation closes off his throat. He coughs.

"Yeah? What the fuck're you saying? If anything happens . . . ?" The thug steps closer, so close his cigarette breath is overpowering.

"If anything happens, it should be me. No one else."

"We'll see about that," the guy says, nodding his head. "Just remember, until you do what you agreed to, no one's safe. Understand?"

"Yes, I understand."

The guy motions to the others, and they return to their cars.

The thug stands in front of him, staring long and hard; his presence—up close, encroaching on Roddy's space—is a threat; then he moves back, turns to his right, and makes his way back to his car.

With a throttling roar, the first sedan peels away, fishtails, and then races into the night.

The vehicle at the rear backs up and pulls into the oncoming lane. The engine roars, and the car speeds away.

Roddy watches the taillights—evil red eyes glowing in darkness—as they recede, get smaller in the distance, and disappear.

Butterflies flutter in his chest. Palpitations. Severe, like something inside him is quivering, about to burst. He's light-headed and feels faint. It's supraventricular tachycardia. He can't breathe.

He sucks in air, then presses his lips together, closes his wind-pipe, bears down—the Valsalva maneuver—and his heart slows. He inhales deeply but still can't get air. He sucks in again, holds his breath, blows out, in and out. Again. *Steady . . . slow down, calm yourself.*

But suddenly the world spins, the night washes white, and yes, he's gonna fall to the roadway because his blood has dropped to his feet, so he grabs the side-view mirror, bends over, and looks down. The asphalt wavers. He clutches the door handle and holds on.

Seconds go by. It seems like minutes pass. He waits longer and closes his eyes. The feeling's gone.

The road is desolate. He stands alone in the chilled night air and rubs his hands together as breath vapor plumes from his mouth. He's cold to his core.

He's gotta do something. But what?

Chapter 13

Edmond Merko sits with the head of his hospital bed angled up at forty-five degrees. "Don't you worry, my darling Masiela," he says to his wife. "The doctors fixed me up. I'll be going home tomorrow. They want to be sure my heart doesn't make trouble."

"Edmond, my love, you're not a young man anymore," Masiela says. "You can't eat all that *sujuk*. That's why you had this trouble."

"Ach . . . what would I do without my sausages?" He waves his hand. "What will be will be. Isn't that right, Victor?" he says to his son.

Victor shakes his head. "No, it isn't, Dad. You have to take care of yourself."

"Edmond, you almost *died* last night," Masiela says, stroking his forehead. "You must lose weight."

Peering into her sad-looking eyes, Edmond Merko feels love for Masiela so deep it nearly leaves him breathless. "Okay, darling. I promise . . . I will lose weight."

"I don't want to lose you, Edmond."

"I will be around for a long time."

"Promise me."

"I promise. I will live forever."

He laughs and peers at Victor. "Isn't that right, my son? I'll live forever." He pinches Masiela's cheek.

"It's not a joke, Dad."

His wife plants a kiss on his forehead. "Victor, see if you can convince your father to be sensible."

After Masiela leaves, Edmond Merko lies back in bed and regards his son. "Okay, so last night I ate a big meal—*sujuk* and potatoes with cabbage, and I had that delicious Bulgarian cheese."

"And that's when the pain started, isn't it?" Victor asks.

"Yes."

"And the doctor said you were dehydrated from vomiting, so you have to stay in the hospital."

"Yes, with this stupid tube dripping liquid into me."

"Dad, you should lose weight for Mom and for the family."

"It's more than a family, Victor. It's our clan."

"That's old-world stuff, Dad. We're in America, not Albania."

Edmond Merko's thoughts drift back to the small village of Corovode in Albania at the mention of his homeland.

Pressing the button, he raises the head of the bed. "Victor, let me tell you about the old world, something I've never told you . . ."

Victor cants his head and says nothing.

"Come, sit down near me."

Victor pulls a chair to the bedside and sits.

"You know that when I was a boy we lived in Albania, in the mountains. Ah, the air was pure, and you could smell wildflowers every spring. And the streams flowed with melted winter snow. One day, when I was fifteen years old, I was pitching hay in the barn while my father and brothers were mending fences in the far pasture.

"We separated our land from the land of the Gjokaj clan. There were disputes and threats. I must admit, they went both ways.

"I had finished my chores and was walking to the outer pastures. I looked up and saw them coming over the crest of a hill—four men from the Gjokaj clan. With shotguns. And one man carried a satchel.

"Papa and my brothers ran for their weapons, but it was too late." He pauses as the memory sears him. "Victor, my son, I watched those Gjokaj men aim their shotguns and saw my father and brothers get torn apart."

Victor's face appears horror-stricken. "I never heard this."

"I never told you, and I have forbidden your mother to say a word about it. But I'm telling you this now for a reason."

"Why now?"

"Let me tell you the rest of the story," Edmond Merko replies, inhaling deeply. "I ran like the wind toward the house, and the Gjokaj men came after me. When I was near the house, Mama opened the door, saw them coming, and rushed back inside for a shotgun.

"But it was too late. A gasoline bomb set the house on fire. There was black smoke everywhere, and my mother came out the front door coughing and gagging. They shot her dead."

Victor gasps. His eyes bulge.

"My son, I cannot tell you the horror I felt. Like a frightened rabbit, I ran into the woods even as they shot at me. I knew they would never let me live.

"They came after me, so I tramped through a thick forest. I ran until my legs could no longer hold me. But still they came. I could hear them shouting and talking. I was desperate, and when I saw a fallen tree that was hollow, I crawled inside.

"I lay in there holding my breath. Soon I heard footsteps. They were thrashing through the bushes, searching for me. It seemed like forever, but they finally went away.

"By nightfall I was shivering from cold and fear, still inside the log. I was terrified a wolf or bear would come as I lay there, knowing I was alone in the world. I knew there was no choice but to face a very different life from the one I loved.

"In the morning, half-frozen, I made my way through the woods. I came to the highway leading to the port city of Durres on the Adriatic Coast. A truck driver stopped for me and took me to the city. I wandered through the streets and sneaked into a Communist military compound. I stole clothing and changed in a bathroom. Then I left through a back door.

"I found a café, where the owner hired me for kitchen work. He let me eat and sleep there.

"A week later I went to a government office and got a passport. When I had saved enough *leks*, I got on a ship leaving for Bari, Italy.

"As you know, Victor, I spoke Italian, as do many of us Albanians. I got a kitchen job in a pizzeria and worked in Bari. The owner let me eat food I prepared in a sweltering kitchen, where I also slept.

"I decided to go to America and join my cousins. So I got a job as a deck boy on a freighter going to Mexico. The crew members—Italians, Albanians, Slavs, and Greeks—treated me well.

"At Altamira, Mexico, I left the ship and hitchhiked north. At a place called Modelo, I changed my money to dollars and then climbed onto a flatbed truck carrying heavy equipment. I lay beneath a tarpaulin as we crossed over the US border at a place called Brownsville, Texas.

"I hitchhiked through America and finally got to the Bronx, where my cousin Nikola and his family were living. As you know, he left Albania with his family because the Communists controlled everything. Nikola took me under his wing and got me a social security card and a false birth certificate. So I became an American citizen."

"You were never naturalized?" Victor's eyes widen.

"That is correct, but you must never tell your sister or anyone else. Only you and your mother know this."

Victor nods.

"And . . . as they say in America, the rest is history. Nikola gave me a start in his import-export business. He died of a heart attack when he was fifty. I was thirty-five when I took over the business. Before that your mother and I had met at an Albanian club. Oh, she was so beautiful, and shy, and we courted in the traditional Albanian way.

"By the time you and Liza were born, the business was a great success. I owned three warehouses and the two apartment buildings on the Grand Concourse. And we moved from the apartment on Perry Avenue to our house in Eastchester."

"Yes, I remember when we moved."

"We've all done well in the American way. Eliza will be a doctor, and now that you are finishing law school, I want to talk with you about your future."

"My future is with Merko Imports and Exports. I'll be your attorney."

"No, Victor. That will not be your future."

"But that's what I want to do."

"I told you my story for a reason, my son. Just as I had to make my way in the world on my own, you will do the same."

"But, Dad, I want—"

"Listen to me, Victor. I will say to you what you always say to me. We are not in Albania now. We are in *America*. We are not in the old world. Here it is not the custom for a son to follow his father's path into business. Here you will be on your own. You will be a lawyer in a big New York law firm, and I will help you find a fine position. But you will not work for our company."

"But—"

"When you finish law school, you will join a big law firm."

Watching his son's face drop, Edmond Merko understands Victor's disappointment, but it's the best road for his beloved son.

"Victor, for years you've heard people talk about me and the company."

"Yes, but they're just ugly rumors."

"But they are spoken by people of influence."

"By people who are jealous."

"Perhaps so. But they are hurtful, these rumors and accusations. You cannot begin a career with the stain of rumor on you."

"But, Dad, I don't—"

"That is the final word."

Victor bows his head.

"Now, my son, my soon-to-be lawyer for a big New York City law firm, give your father a hug and a kiss and be on your way. I feel tired and I must rest."

When Victor is gone, Edmond Merko thinks about his journey in America. He's never told Masiela the truth about his career. And the kids know little about his business dealings.

When Nikola took him into the Merko clan's operations, he was fifteen years old. Many cousins and distant relatives were part of the organization—one that smuggled contraband into and out of the country.

Edmond Merko devoured books. He watched television and listened to the radio to improve his English. He ran errands, taught himself bookkeeping, and mastered the clan's business dealings. At eighteen he got a driver's license and began driving a box truck to Michigan. Each week he picked up five hundred pounds of marijuana smuggled into the United States over the Canadian border and drove it to New York City. Another crew member, Elvis Sadiki, would drive a sedan behind the truck in case the police pulled Edmond over. The emergency plan was for Sadiki to smash his sedan into the stopped police car and claim he fell asleep at the wheel. Meanwhile, Edmond would speed away.

And then came a fateful event, one that ensured Edmond Merko's future in the clan.

One night, carrying five hundred pounds of product, he was driving toward a drop-off point on Whittier Street in the Bronx.

It was a deserted roadway fronted by warehouses and a truck depot. Elvis Sadiki's sedan was a few hundred feet behind.

Suddenly, a parked car swerved onto the road, blocking his way. Edmond knew it was a hijacking. He jammed on the brakes, waiting for what would happen. Two men jumped out of the car, one with a shotgun, the other holding a pistol. They moved toward him, one on each side of the truck.

Acting on raw instinct, he reached down and pulled out his pistol. He rolled down the window, holding the gun below the sill. The shotgun-wielding hijacker approached on the driver's side; the weapon pointed at Edmond. The other man approached on the passenger's side.

Elvis pulled his sedan up behind them.

The hijacker with the shotgun glanced toward Elvis's headlights.

At that instant Edmond raised the pistol and shot. The man's face and head exploded with red mist, bits of skull, brain, and hair.

The other hijacker turned and dashed toward his car. Edmond leaped from the truck, ran after him, and in the beam of the truck's headlights, shot him in the back. The man slammed against his car's fender and slipped down to the pavement. Dead.

Edmond and Elvis rummaged through the hijackers' pockets, found identification—they were Albanians from the Malota clan—and then dumped their blood-soaked bodies on the sidewalk, parked their car, and took off.

Had the sight of that shotgun returned him to that fateful day in Albania? Was he exacting revenge for the massacre at Corovode? There was no way to know.

When Elvis described the hijacking to the clan members, Edmond was suddenly more than a trafficker—he was a decisive and fearless young man.

Over the next few years he became Nikola's second-in-command. "We all admire how smart you are," Nikola said. "Your reputation is known by all the clans." And Edmond concluded early on that it was best to avoid violence, if possible. Smuggling marijuana, cocaine, ecstasy, weapons, counterfeit sneakers, and other contraband was profitable, but it occurred in a cauldron of threats and violence.

"Nikola," he said, "we must find legitimate businesses to be fronts for our operations."

But he couldn't convince his cousin to change the clan's operations.

When Nikola died suddenly, Edmond became head of the Merko clan.

Edmond Merko knows by hiding thousands of kilos of marijuana in tractor trailers carrying legitimate cargo, the clan has made more money than he could spend in three lifetimes. And yes, the drugs are stashed in his Bronx warehouses, waiting to be distributed throughout the city and suburbs. Millions upon millions of dollars—all in cash—are made, and Edmond Merko pays a cadre of accountants and lawyers to launder money through shell companies.

But it's now more dangerous, with these young Albanians who lack the discipline of the old-timers, which at age fifty-five includes him.

And these young men like Alex Dushku are worrisome. Some years ago, Dushku formed the Corporation, a ruthless bunch. They established ties with the Gambino crime family. Before long, Dushku was battling the Lucchese family for territory in Queens, the Bronx, and Westchester County.

One night fifteen Corporation soldiers burst into a Gambino gambling parlor called Jungle Fever. They overturned gambling tables, grabbed fistfuls of money, and pistol-whipped the patrons. "Gentlemen, the game is over," one of the soldiers sneered as the others shouted, "*Shqiptar* are here"—meaning *Albanians*—"all Italians out."

Even worse, these young ones—eighteen- and nineteen-year-old kids—will bring the wrath of the FBI and the NYPD onto the Albanian community. And they deal in human trafficking. He thinks of his daughter, Eliza, being kidnapped and forced into the sex trade. It turns his stomach.

So Edmond Merko now directs his clan toward less violent activities: betting parlors, restaurant linens, and food supplies. There's a huge market in automotive parts and garbage hauling. They can move into the Hunts Point Food Distribution Terminal in the South Bronx—all low-profile operations. All nonviolent.

Of course, some ventures risk clashing with the Italians, but there's a place at the table for everyone.

His second-in-command, Baki, told him, "The Italians might make a move against you, Edmond."

But gang warfare is far too reminiscent of what happened to his family.

"We must avoid war at all costs," he said to Baki.

Certain customs still apply: payoffs to politicians, police officers, judges, and city officials and maintaining contacts with South American banks.

Ah, yes, his pockets are deep enough to hold many greedy men.

And, of course, he has paid informants on his payroll—in the other Albanian clans, the Russian Bratva, and even a spy in an Italian family. Money can erode a man's loyalty to his clan. That's why Edmond Merko makes certain his clan members are well paid. But he's sure of one thing: his son will never be part of a criminal enterprise.

Edmond Merko wonders if it had not been for a single event—his family's massacre—would he still be a dairy farmer living in the hills of Corovode?

So here he is: a wealthy, respected man of great appetites, one who gorges on Albanian fare like stewed meat and onion—*chumlek,* his favorite. Yes, he eats like a bear and drinks too much Albanian Kallmet, a glorious red wine.

Living well means that despite a cruel and indifferent world, Edmond Merko commands his own fiefdom.

But his appetites have made him gain weight, and this blockage formed in his belly. And he needed an emergency operation, which, thanks to God, was a success.

So now he's lying in bed, waiting to talk with the surgeon who saved his life.

Chapter 14

Roddy stops at the surgical ward's nursing station. His legs ache; his eyes feel gritty and sting.

He didn't get a moment's sleep last night. He lay awake for hours, his thoughts endlessly replaying what had happened, from the irony of his doing Merko's surgery to being intercepted by thugs itching to beat the crap out of him.

The only reason he got off without his hands being broken or his brains smashed was because Cellini wants him to do a job.

Otherwise he'd have been left like a splattered squirrel in the middle of Pondfield Road.

He visited Merko at seven in the morning. The man was sleeping soundly, so he listened to his belly with a stethoscope without waking him.

Now, two hours later, he'll see him again. Roddy goes to the laptop, types in Edmond Merko's name, and peruses the record. The man is doing well. No postoperative complaints. No complications. His IV is still in place and hasn't infiltrated, and a nurse thinks she heard bowel sounds—a good sign peristalsis has returned. The man has good physiologic reserve, which is surprising given that he's diabetic and so overweight. If Roddy hears normal bowel sounds when he examines him, Merko can begin eating soft food today. If all goes well, after lunch he can be discharged.

After typing orders for the nursing staff, he walks down the hall and knocks on Merko's door. Waiting for a response, Roddy feels an adrenaline surge. He's wired, not knowing what to expect. His patient won't be unconscious on an OR table. He'll be awake and alert, in his own private room.

A deep baritone voice says, "Come in . . ."

Roddy enters the room.

Edmond Merko lies there with the head of his bed elevated. His scalp is shaved, and despite a two-day growth of dark stubble, he sports a neatly trimmed black beard. He looks like a modern-day version of a Viking.

It's so strange to now face the man who last night was lying on an OR table, insensate and intubated. A man whose insides Roddy was exploring through a laparoscope, whose guts he watched on a TV monitor. He feels that way about every post-op patient when he talks with them while making rounds. It's almost as though the dead have awakened. Merko appears robust, red-cheeked, and very much alive.

The Albanian smiles and extends a huge hand, pointing a thick index finger at Roddy as he enters the room and shuts the door. The man's smile is an engaging one, the look of someone who feels comfortable with others.

Roddy's first impression is that Merko's an affable man, one of hearty appetites. There's something expansive about him, even more than his enormous size. He exudes kinetic energy and looks like a man others would gladly follow. And Roddy knows he heads up a lethal criminal enterprise.

"Ha. You are Dr. Dolan, I presume?" Edmond Merko pushes a button, and the head of the bed rises a bit more.

"Yes, I am, Mr. Merko. How are you feeling?"

"I feel wonderful, thanks to *you*." Merko's smile becomes a grin. "I was told it was you who got rid of a . . . what do you call this thing . . . an adhesion?"

"Yes, that's what it was. It was scar tissue from your gallbladder surgery, and it closed off your small intestine."

"Please, Doctor, sit . . . sit . . . Let's talk," Edmond Merko says, waving at a Naugahyde chair in the corner of the room.

"First let me listen to your belly," Roddy says, taking out his stethoscope.

Roddy sets the diaphragm of his stethoscope on Merko's abdomen, listens, and hears good bowel sounds. "Completely normal," he says. "The obstruction is gone and things are moving. You can have lunch today, though I can't really recommend the hospital food."

Merko laughs as Roddy moves the chair closer to the bed and sits down.

There's a knock on the door. "Yes . . . ?" Merko calls.

The door opens. "Housekeeping," says a plump woman poking her head through the opening. "Oh, I see the doctor is here. I'll be back in a little while."

The door closes.

"And after you've eaten and held the food down, we'll stop the IV."

The IV I've been asked to spike with a dose of heart-stopping medication.

"Dr. Dolan, you saved my life."

"I did what any surgeon would have done."

"That may be true, but I owe you my life. Dr. Snyder was not here, so it was *you*—your hands—that kept me alive."

Roddy peers at Edmond Merko, thinking how utterly insane it is to be sitting with this fellow, who speaks in a deep, robust voice—with a heavy Balkan accent—and the guy is thanking him for having saved his life.

"It must be a strange feeling, Doctor, to know you have the power of life and death within your grasp. My wife, Masiela, thinks you are a god, a savior."

At the mention of Merko's wife, thoughts of Tracy blitz through Roddy's head. She's at the library for a day's work. And she won't pick up her cell if he calls. And Tom and Sandy have headed off to school.

Merko crosses his huge arms over his chest. The man is a sumo-sized human being. Even if he lost 50 pounds, he'd still weigh in at a good 230, probably more. Etched amid a tangle of black hairs on a massive forearm is a tattoo of a black double-winged eagle against a bloodred background.

Merko notices Roddy staring at the tattoo and raises his arm.

"This is the symbol of Albania," he says, holding out an arm as thick as a thigh. "We are a very old-fashioned people. Do you know, Doctor, that many Albanians believe sickness comes from poor eating, or oppression? Some of us believe it stems from evil." A rumbling laugh emanates from deep within his chest.

What kind of evil lurks behind this man's ingratiating smile?

"I don't think your problem came from poor eating," Roddy says, smothering a smile.

Another robust laugh from Merko. "So, Doctor, are you going to tell me I must lose weight?" His eyebrows arch as a grin burgeons on his lips.

"I won't tell you what you already know. You're aware of what to do to live a long life."

Merko nods again, smiling. "So you will not nag me like my wife does?"

"Not at all. *You* know what you must do."

Merko's lips purse. He peers out the window, seeming pre-occupied. "Tell me, Dr. Dolan, being a doctor . . . is it a good life? I mean . . . are you content with what you do?"

"Yes, very content. What makes you ask?"

"I ask because my daughter, Eliza, is a second-year medical student at Johns Hopkins."

Merko's mention of medical school brings images of Vinzy Masconi to Roddy, first at the dissecting table in Gross Anatomy—amid the reek of formalin and slowly rotting cadaver flesh—then another, a more chilling memory of him sitting with Cellini at Geppetto's, in that rear room with those thugs, maybe the ones who stopped him last night on Pondfield. It all seems like a dream, floating in the nimbus of memory.

"And I am very happy for her," Merko adds. "I want her to be a success in life and to be better than her father . . ."

Merko pauses and looks contemplative, as though he's lost in thought.

"Tell me, why did you say you want Eliza to be *better* than you?"

"Ah, every child should rise above the parents, do you agree?" Merko's unruly eyebrows rise again. "I say that because I'm in the import and export business . . . and . . . it is filled with trouble, and the people I deal with are very difficult."

"What do you import and export?"

"Oh, electronics, ladies wear, shoes, many, many things."

"And the people you deal with, what's difficult about them?"

"Greed rules them."

Once again Merko looks pensive, gazing off to nowhere. Then he turns to Roddy and says, "You know, Doctor, I think about death more than I would like, much more often than a man my age should."

"What makes you think that way?"

"I think it goes back to my having almost died as a boy, when I was fifteen. Each day of your life after such a thing seems like a gift, as though you cheated death and worry that maybe it will come back soon for you."

"How did you almost die?"

"Ach, I do not want to talk about it."

Roddy nods.

"I doubt you can imagine how bad life was back in Albania, with the Communists and the clans always at war. It was not like America, where you can live in peace and prosper. Life there was cheap, and people ran wild. If they had a grudge against you, they took matters into their own hands."

Roddy stifles the urge to again ask what happened when Merko was fifteen years old. The less he knows about him, the better.

Turning to Roddy, Merko says, "I learned very early in my life that human beings are the most vicious of all beasts. And death always waits for us. You never know how or when it will come— in the day or the night, quickly or slowly—and of course, it will someday take you."

Merko shoots Roddy a quick smile and then grunts as though some insight crystallized in his mind.

"And last night I was close to death once again. It was like a claw dropped from the sky and was squeezing the life out of me. And here you are, the man who saved my life," Merko says with a sweep of his hand. "And I must thank you for the gift you have given me."

"If it hadn't been me, someone else would have done it."

"Maybe, maybe not. It is a matter of fate, is it not . . . ? One thing leading to another in ways one can never foretell. But it was *you* who saved my life, and I am grateful to you."

"Seeing you doing so well is the best thanks any surgeon could ever have."

The man seems genuinely grateful. Illness and a brush with death does that to people: makes them see the doctor as a savior, the one who plucked them from the station of last resort—the undertaker's table.

"Dr. Dolan, let me try to repay you in my very small way."

"Please, Mr. Merko, there's no need . . ."

"Ah, where I came from, a man must show gratitude to another who has saved his life. If he does not, it is a great insult, and I try never to insult a fellow traveler."

"Traveler?"

"Yes, Doctor. We are all travelers. And I never forget that in this life, we are just passing through. We are all too busy with the day-to-day nonsense of our little lives, the things that barely count. But we are just passing through this world."

"Well said."

"Doctor, I own a restaurant in the Bronx, on Jerome Avenue and a Hundred and Ninety-Ninth Street. It's called Tirana, which is the name of the capital of my homeland, Albania. It is a lovely place with music and dancing and very good food, if I do say so. It is my greatest pleasure to go there and dine with my wife, Masiela. Tirana is a home away from home for us—and in some way, listening to the music and dancing makes us feel like we are young again."

"That's lovely," Roddy says, thinking of Tracy and the times they ate at the cheapest restaurants they could find, when he was a poorly paid surgical resident and she was a librarian's assistant. How they'd scrimped and saved, cut coupons from magazines, and looked for bargains in Upper East Side thrift and consignment shops when they began furnishing their Manhattan apartment. And when they couldn't find something appropriate at a thrift shop, they bought the cheapest furniture at the Third Avenue Bazaar. But those days are long gone, as are the days of their lives in Bronxville, and all they'd built together.

He fights off a wave of melancholy.

"May I extend an invitation to you and your wife to dine at Tirana as my guests?"

"I'd be happy to take you up on that."

Be careful. Just accept the invitation and then forget about it. Fuck the Albanians and the Italians.

"Please, Doctor, this a genuine invitation. All you must do is telephone when you make a reservation and tell the receptionist you are Mr. Merko's honored guest."

"I'll do that, Mr. Merko."

"I am very pleased. Just remember the name . . . Tirana on Jerome Avenue in the Bronx."

"I'll remember."

Chapter 15

"**M**usetta's Waltz." Roddy nearly jumps when the cell phone plays the melody. He used to love that aria from Puccini's *La Bohème*. Now he loathes it.

It won't be Tracy or the kids. It's seven o'clock on Friday evening, and Tracy's with Sandy at the ice-skating rink. For some reason, there's no signal available there. And Tom never calls. He's rebelling, something that will go on for the next six years, or longer.

Tentatively, with his scalp dampening, he reaches for the phone.

A quick glance at the readout. It's Vinzy.

"Yeah?"

"Roddy . . . we gotta talk."

"I have nothing to say to you."

"Listen to me, Roddy, because I'm not foolin' around. Carmine's pissed, *really* pissed."

"Nothing I can do about that."

"He knows a certain someone was admitted into the hospital last night and he knows you were there, too."

Roddy's been expecting this call ever since those thugs ambushed him on the way home from Merko's surgery. But how much does Cellini actually know about last night?

"We told you, we have contacts. We can access every admission."

"So why're you calling me, Vinzy?"

"Don't play dumb, Roddy. Like I said, we know you were there last night, too."

"So what?"

"Listen to me, Roddy. You don't wanna fuck around with Carmine Cellini any more than you already have. He wants to see you . . . *now*."

"*Now*?"

"Within the hour. You know where he'll be."

"I do?"

"Same place. He's there every night."

"Look, Vinzy, we gotta talk . . ."

"Not on the phone. In person. *Be* there."

"Forget it, Vinzy. I have an early day tomorrow."

"Roddy, if you know what's good for you, you'll be there in a half hour. If you're not at Geppetto's, I can't guarantee your safety. Or *anyone's* safety, if you get my meaning."

Same red awning. Same painted, highly glossed wooden Pinocchio sitting on the inside windowsill.

Recollections flood him as he approaches the restaurant's front door: memories of seeing the Disney movie *Pinocchio* as a kid, of the fox and the cat ambushing Pinocchio. He could never have imagined the story would now fill him with such dread.

As he enters Geppetto's, his body feels like a taut wire. There's a storm brewing in his head, but he's gotta keep a lid on it. He can't go volcanic like when he was a kid. Those days are gone.

Same situation as last time: the restaurant's nearly empty. Only a few patrons are dining, even though it's prime dinner time on a Friday night. They're much older people who look like they're from the old country—most of them dressed formally. A few old guys have cloth napkins tucked into their shirt collars. Very old-world.

One thing's certain: the place can't earn its keep with this sparse a crowd. No doubt it's a front for Cellini's operations, whatever they are. He's gotta run more than a few local card games. He's probably into garbage hauling, restaurant linens, and video gambling.

Who knows what else? Nothing legal, that's for sure.

The same wiry little waiter approaches him. Franco's the name, if he recalls. Roddy moves past the guy, strides down the side aisle, slides the pocket door aside, and enters the back room. A smoky haze fills the air.

A pang of alarm seizes Roddy.

Six hoods sit at two tables closest to the door.

He recognizes one guy sitting at the near table—the greaser who threatened him on Pondfield last night. Same slicked-back hair, same leather car coat. The thug smirks, nods knowingly at him, and even winks. The other men eye Roddy with hard stares. He can almost smell testosterone in the room. Threat and peril pervade the place.

He slides the door closed, looking toward the left rear corner table.

Sure enough, Cellini, DiNardo, and Vinzy are there, seated in the same order as the night he was first here. They must be in this back room every night. It's their version of a headquarters.

Cellini sucks on a cigar. A cigarette dangles from DiNardo's lips. Three espresso cups sit on the table.

No doubt they've had dinner. Looks like a nightly ritual. Cellini must own this place.

Merko owns an Albanian restaurant; Cellini owns an Italian restaurant.

Roddy's skin prickles as he walks toward the table.

This time Vinzy doesn't get up to greet him. There's no smile, no back slapping or handshake, none of Vinzy's bogus bonhomie. Just cold stares from Cellini and DiNardo. Vinzy casts his eyes down.

Fucking snake. Reminds him of Kenny "Snake Eyes" Egan, inveterate gambler and con man. And former partner in a failed restaurant. And a guy rotting six feet under at a hellhole called Snapper Pond, upstate, New York.

"You're late," Cellini snarls.

"Traffic was bad."

Roddy sits, facing him. Clasps his hands on the table to keep them steady.

Stay calm. No confrontation, no static.

He's again reminded of sitting across from Grange in McLaughlin's back room, where he endured vile threats to his wife and children.

But Cellini isn't a lone wolf like Grange was. He's got soldiers.

And Roddy's been conscripted.

Vinzy looks pale, sweaty. He's a sniveling coward. Once again, he can't meet Roddy's stare.

"I hear you had a traffic stop," Cellini says, toying with his cigar.

Roddy nods. *The less said, the better.*

"I heard someone was at the hospital last night . . . an emergency."

"Right."

"You knew about it?"

Roddy nods.

No use trying to lie. They know Merko had surgery. I left the hospital late, and they must know I operated on him.

"You see him?"

"Yeah . . ."

"And you didn't do anything?"

"I operated on Merko."

Cellini's eyes go ice-cold. It's a stare that would wither most men.

"I had no choice. It was an emergency. I got a call from the hospital and had to go in. His doctor wasn't available."

"*You* did the surgery?"

"Yes."

"And you didn't touch his IV?"

"How could I? Other people were in the OR. The nurse, a resident, a medical student, the anesthesiologist. I wasn't alone with him."

"Carmine," Vinzy says, leaning toward Cellini. "He couldn't do a thing in the OR. Whaddaya want from the guy?"

"What about later?" Carmine asks. "Were you alone with him after the surgery?"

"Only briefly, but the IV was already stopped. The resident decided to stop it because Merko was doing well. By the time I saw him in the morning, the IV was out."

He can't know I'm lying. Or does he? They have contacts at the hospital. A file clerk? An administrator? A nurse? Or maybe . . . yes, that cleaning woman who popped in while I was with Merko.

"I couldn't do a thing," he says. "The man was wide awake and talking. It was an emergency admission, completely unexpected. It wasn't planned in advance like the knee surgery was."

"What do you mean *was*?"

"I looked at his record on the computer system," Roddy says, keeping his voice even despite the thrumming sensation in his chest. "His knee surgery's been put off. An overweight man with diabetes and a heart condition isn't a good candidate for elective surgery after what happened. They'll make sure he can handle another surgery before they put him under again."

"What was his emergency?"

"A blockage of his intestine."

"What'd you do for him?" Cellini's eyes narrow.

"I cut away an adhesion causing the blockage."

Cellini's eyes flicker in the room's light.

Vinzy says, "That means they make a few small incisions in the abdomen, Carmine, and they use a small instrument to—"

"I know, Vinzy," Cellini says through the side of his mouth. "I wasn't born yesterday."

Cellini's eyes drill into Roddy. The man projects glacial coldness. He sets the cigar between his teeth, then wraps his lips around it, sucks inward, and blows a puff of smoke across the table. It billows into Roddy's face.

The cloud is thick, smelling acrid. Roddy holds his breath and feels his legs tighten. An insane impulse surges through him—like an electric charge—to shoot a fist into the man's throat, to crush his trachea. Roddy's shoulders hunch, and his jaw muscles tighten. His clasped fingers tighten. He hears and feels his knuckles crack.

Stay cool. Don't go Mad Dog. If I do, I die.

Cellini slips the cigar onto the edge of an ashtray. The saliva-ridden tip is chewed, nearly flattened. Roddy's eyes burn from the smoke.

Cellini peers over Roddy's shoulder. "Albie," he calls.

"Yeah, Carmine . . . ?"

"Why don't you and the boys check out the front room. See how business is tonight."

As though given a military order, the six men get up and move toward the door.

"Hey, Albie," calls Vinzy, "will ya tell Franco I'll call in his refill tomorrow?"

"Yeah, sure, Vinzy," Albie calls back as he and the others move into the front room and slide the door closed.

Only the four of them are left in the room. Cellini's eyes laser on Roddy, and then he says, "Lemme lay it on the line for you, Doc."

Roddy meets his stare despite the gust of dread clutching him. He holds steady and doesn't avert his eyes or show submission. It's a badass stare-down, like back in the days when he was a Brooklyn brawler.

"I'm through listening to your bullshit, Dolan. We know *exactly* what happened at the hospital." Cellini leans forward; his jaw juts and his eyes narrow. "You're walkin' a very fine line and you haven't gotten the message, have you?"

Roddy's about to answer, but Cellini goes on. "Merko's gotta go. I mean *go*. And it's gotta be sooner rather than later. You find out who his knee surgeon is and when it's gonna get done . . . a few weeks, a month, whatever. I don't give a damn. And you *do* it."

Roddy feels pressure behind his eyes—it's a pulsing of blood—and they feel like they're bulging.

Roddy nods. His skin feels hot.

"You get on your horse and do what you gotta do, 'cause I'm tellin' you, you're lookin' for trouble and it's gonna happen. We're not negotiatin' here . . . This isn't some goddamned Arab bazaar. I set the terms and they're clear: either you do it—and I mean *soon*—or there'll be consequences. Very serious ones. Or maybe you need somethin' to happen—to someone, anyone you care about—so you'll know I mean business."

Cellini stares fixedly at Roddy. His eyes convey malice so deep Roddy nearly shudders. And Roddy feels everything in his world—all that's been and all that will ever be—is drifting away from him, funneling down a black hole.

"I don't need to be convinced."

A drop of sweat caterpillars down the midline furrow of Roddy's back. His armpits are clammy.

"You sure?"

"I'm sure."

"Maybe you *do* need convincing, like maybe somethin' happening to your wife or one of your kids."

Fear prickles the hairs on the back of Roddy's neck. These aren't idle threats or bravado-laden taunts he heard in Manny's pool hall or John's Bar back in the Sheepshead Bay neighborhood. This is the real thing—mob thugs menacing him and, far more ominous, threatening his family.

"You need to be convinced?"

"No, I don't."

"Don't make somethin' happen—somethin' very unfortunate—that you'll regret for the rest of your life," Cellini rasps. He points a gnarled finger at Roddy.

"No need to do that. I'm on board."

"Are you playing me?"

"I'm not. I hear you loud and clear."

"You sure?"

"I am."

Cellini nods. "Good. Because playtime is over. No more games. You do what you gotta do or you'll have nothin' to show for this but a lifetime of regret. *Capiche*?"

Out on the street, the air chills Roddy to the marrow of his bones.

He and Vinzy stand beneath Geppetto's awning. An icy wind kicks up and whistles down the street.

"I'm sorry I got you into this, Roddy."

"Yeah, sure . . ." Roddy tries not to sound too scornful, but he can't stop himself. Inside his coat pockets, his hands ball into fists. He stamps his feet, not so much against the cold, but to release the strain in his body. His insides burn, and his muscles are strung so tightly, they hum, feeling like they'll tear from their tendons.

It's the same raw feeling he had as a kid before a boxing match or a street fight—a superheated fury, a Mad Dog buildup coursing through him. So he'd live up to his boxing nickname Mad Dog Dolan—and it feels as though a burst of toxic rage will detonate into violence. It's the brute force that earned him his canine moniker, when he got into street fights even at age twelve, and for the five years afterward. His reputation was solidified at sixteen, when in a Golden Gloves middleweight match—even though he wore eighteen-ounce gloves—he pummeled an opponent so brutally, they carted the guy off to Bellevue for the night.

Roddy "Mad Dog Dolan," the Brooklyn brawler who never stops punching.

But he forestalls the squall of temper and won't let it explode, and it contracts around his heart like a boa constrictor in his chest.

Can't let it happen like it did with Grange and Kenny.

And he's not in the boxing ring, can't go Mad Dog. Not now.

He won't revert to the Roddy Dolan he was back then.

Control, control . . . that's the key. Keep calm. Think it through. You can get out of this.

"Ya gotta understand who you're dealing with, Roddy. Carmine's old-school. He won't tolerate insolence."

"Oh, I see . . . He's a man of *respect*, huh? Like we're in some cheap B movie?"

"I know you think it's bullshit, all this Cosa Nostra crap, but listen to me: Carmine'll stop at nothing to get what he wants. He carries out every threat. He'll think nothing of hurting you . . . *or your family.*"

Even on the dimly lit street, the whites of Vinzy's eyes show above his dark irises.

"Lemme tell you, Roddy, if you don't do exactly what he wants, bad things're gonna happen. Believe me, very bad things. You can count on it."

Chapter 16

Edmond Merko leans back on the sofa in the sunroom. He loves this house, especially this glass-enclosed room. He sits contentedly as the low November sun warms him through the expanse of glass. He had a light lunch of tomatoes, cucumbers, green peppers, and olives dressed in vinegar and oil, with a pinch of salt.

He gazes at Masiela sitting nearby, reading. Hers is the beauty of kindness and understanding, the loveliness of empathy, of giving. It's a gift given only by a woman who loves you with her whole being. A woman's true beauty is found not in her looks but in her heart and soul.

"My sweet," he says, "I do think I will lose weight. I so much enjoyed that salad instead of having meat. I feel lighter already." He laughs.

"Edmond, if you starve yourself all day, you will gorge on food and wine in the evening. And I think your doctor, that very handsome man—Dr. Dolan—was right when he told me that if you lose weight, you will not only improve your health, but your knees will get better, too."

"Ah . . . Dr. Dolan," Edmond Merko says, stroking his beard. "A man of modesty and, I sensed, one of inner strength. You know what impressed me about him? He didn't kiss up to me as so many men do. Many men respond to me in a more open way—they reveal too much about themselves. But not Dr. Dolan. I sensed that he's a man of courage, of principle. And I invited him to join us at Tirana."

"Did he tell you to lose weight?"

"He did, without lecturing me. But I will do it for you, my love."

"I love that thought, Edmond, but you must do it for yourself. We are not getting any younger, and I want you to live a long time, so we can both take pleasure in our children, in their accomplishments."

"I have been thinking about that. It is now clear to me that I have not had time to—as they say in America—smell flowers. I would like to change that."

"Work has always been important to you, Edmond."

"Since the other night, I've been thinking about my life. About *our* lives. It might be good to change things . . ."

"Change? How?"

"Perhaps I will retire . . ."

Masiela gets up and sits next to him on the sofa. "Retire? But you have built such a wonderful business. It won't run by itself."

"We can sell the business, the buildings, and restaurant. Baki could take over. He knows the business."

"Really?"

"Yes, my love. There's so much I have taught him . . . things I never talk about because it would bore you. I could simply hand it all over to him."

"Are you sure of this, Edmond?"

"Masiela, we have more money than we will ever need and more than the children could ever spend. Life is too short. I would like to get out of the business."

"But what would you do?"

"You have relatives in Albania, and now that Albania is a democracy, we could return there. We could still travel back here to see the children."

"Edmond, let me ask you something." She hesitates.

"Yes, my love?"

"Will you go back to take revenge on the Gjokaj clan?"

"No, no. That would never be the reason."

"Are you sure?"

"Yes. If I wanted to take revenge, it would have happened long ago. I have gone on with my life, and we have succeeded together. We have a lovely home and two fine children. And we have a wonderful life. Perhaps that's the best revenge. As for the Gjokaj clan . . . sometimes it is better to forgive and forget than to take revenge and remember."

Chapter 17

Half dozing on the couch, Roddy is jolted awake. It happens as he's drifting off. It's a shocklike feeling, a sudden thought or an image jabbing at him just as he's sinking away, dropping into the realm of oblivion. Like a blow to the belly, it takes his breath away. His heart feels like it's quivering in his chest.

It must've been something about Cellini.

It's Saturday night, and the plan had been for the kids to spend the weekend. But Sandy came down with a cold, and according to Tracy, Tom didn't want to come. He can almost hear the kid complaining: *It's boring. I have better things to do than sit around with him.*

Tonight Tom has something planned with his friends—a bunch of overprivileged kids— probably hanging out at the New Rochelle Mall or smoking dope in somebody's bedroom while the parents are at a party.

He thinks back to when he was thirteen. It was so different then, but was it really?

True, he and Danny didn't have a pot to piss in. Rather than hang out at a mall, they'd snag a booth at the corner luncheonette near Sheepshead Bay—Leo's—order a Coke, and smoke "loosies" until Leo would kick them out for monopolizing a table. Then they'd hang out on the street corner or hop onto the back bumper of a bus and ride it all the way to Surf Avenue in Coney Island.

They'd head to Astroland and then watch the men hit baseballs at the Bat-A-Way concession. Then they'd wander over to the Cyclone, slip the operator a buck, and ride the roller coaster all afternoon—standing as the car careened around sharp curves even though it was against the rules.

But they felt just the way he imagines Tom and his friends do now: they were immortal and felt—despite having no money— anything was possible.

Now he's alone in this sterile apartment, facing the impossible.

Vinzy's called three times today. Roddy let the calls go to voice mail.

He hasn't played back the messages: he can't stomach hearing Vinzy's voice and knows why the bastard's calling. Cellini's using that lowlife to tighten the vise around Roddy's head.

And it's working.

He thought more than once of turning off his phone, but he's on call this weekend, and there could be an emergency.

An emergency. Like the other night with Merko. For God's sake, why'd the guy get obstructed while Ivan was in the city? Isn't Roddy already in enough of a mess with Cellini and his crew?

Did I really believe those mobsters didn't know I operated on the guy they wanted me to kill?

His cell phone erupts with "Musetta's Waltz." It sends a pang of dread through him. That lousy tune again.

He glances at the readout: it's Tracy's cell.

What does he feel? It's so strange. A surge of joy and a pang of dread.

But mostly joy.

Maybe she's calling to say she and the kids are accepting his offer to take them all to breakfast at the City Limits Diner in White Plains tomorrow morning. The four of them always enjoyed outings there for waffles, pancakes, eggs—the works. Of course, Tom would *have* to order a scoop of vanilla ice cream on top of his waffles.

And how many times over the years had they met Dan and Angela with their kids on a Sunday morning for that place's gargantuan breakfasts?

Yes, it's Tracy. His heart jumps and then races. A sense of relief floods him as he answers.

"Hi, honey." He hopes she can hear in his voice how happy he is to talk with her.

"Roddy, come to the hospital. It's Tom. He's been in an accident."

A needle of dread pierces him.

"What kind of accident?" He rockets up from the sofa as every pore in his body opens, and he dampens with sweat.

"He was skateboarding across Clubway and was hit by a car."

"And he's at the hospital?"

"Yes. Hurry, Roddy. Get over here. *Please.*"

Muffled sobs come through the phone.

"Is he in the ER?"

"No. He's in the OR. Ivan Snyder's working on him."

Roddy's heart rate surges to a throbbing drumbeat.

He must have internal injuries, Roddy thinks, grabbing his coat. His legs go weak. They feel as though they're melting. He stumbles toward the door.

"Where are you now?"

"In the waiting area on the surgery ward."

"I'll be there in five minutes."

It's so strange: walking along the hospital corridor, not as a surgeon making pre- or post-op visits, but as the father of a patient. No, it's more than strange; it's otherworldly.

Fear and worry—pure dread—nag at him like a drawing pain, one far worse than anything physical. And it's mixed with a sense of disbelief.

He's like all the mothers and fathers, husbands and wives he's seen in the waiting room, people whose faces and voices brim with terror for their loved ones. And that's exactly what he's become—a frightened parent reeling from a disaster having befallen his child.

Is there anything worse than this? No, never.

That spike of dread is now a gnawing sense of the world gone wrong, of everything upended, the future unknown.

Or gone.

No future.

Only his past failings.

Is it Cellini? Or just an accident?

He feels that sickening adrenaline surge in the pit of his stomach. It radiates into his chest, his guts, everywhere. It's pure fear for his child, along with a sense of the world as treacherous and unknowable, a grotesque gathering of tragedies.

Tracy is in the waiting room.

When she sees him, she jumps up from the chair and rushes to him. She throws her arms around him and sobs. "I'm frightened, Roddy. I'm *so* scared."

He circles her with his arms. "Have you spoken with Ivan?"

"Very briefly," she whispers. "He said Tom's lost lots of blood and he has to look inside. He said, 'I have to open him up.'" She stifles a sob and buries her face on his chest.

"You want me to scrub and go in there?"

She looks up at him with tears in her eyes. "Ivan said he doesn't want you anywhere *near* Tom right now." Her fist goes to her mouth, shaking. It presses against her teeth.

"Do you know what happened?"

"Just a little, but Scott Williams saw it. It was a hit-and-run."

"Scott saw it? So, it was in front of the *house*? On Clubway?"

"Yes. Tom was coming home on his skateboard when he was hit. I didn't have time to talk with Scott."

Roddy's thoughts churn. No coherence, just a rushing sequence of fragments—disjointed, and he can barely corral them into a linear sequence.

Hit-and-run, in front of our house, on a dark, nearly deserted street, after that last threat from Cellini. And those guys in the cars. Maybe something will happen to someone I care about? Holy shit. It's unbelievable.

He's overcome by a feeling of helplessness coupled with an incandescent fury at the calculated cruelty of others.

It's all my fault, my doing. If I'd never done what I did, none of this would have happened.

Tracy's shoulders shake. She again buries her face against Roddy's chest.

Those bastards might as well drive a stake through my heart.

"This can't be happening," Tracy says, sobbing. "It can't be real."

"Honey, Ivan's the best. Tom's in great hands."

"Why? Why did this happen?" Tracy moans. Her body trembles.

He shakes his head as his thoughts swirl in an insane loop of possibilities. But it's achingly clear: it's all his fault.

"This shouldn't happen to us," she whispers.

"Trace, we don't get to choose."

"What if he dies?"

"He won't die."

"How do you know?" She pulls away from him. Her eyes widen.

"Ivan won't let Tommy die."

Do I believe that? What do I believe? God, my whole life is torture. And Tom, my son, my flesh and blood. Our flesh and blood. How do you deal with the death of a child?

"My God, he's so young," Tracy whispers.

"Honey, try not to think that way."

"I can't help it. He's too young to die."

"Ivan will do everything possible."

"Is Ivan religious?"

"I don't know. And religion won't save Tom. Ivan's hands will. Trust me and have faith in Ivan."

"Faith is a good thing, isn't it?"

She sounds so desperate. As desperate as I feel.

"Yes, it helps," he says, thinking back to Danny and his need to confess, to fall on his knees in contrition.

"Roddy, I—I want to have faith in God, but I don't know why God would let this happen."

He clutches her coat sleeves, not knowing what to say.

"Oh, Roddy. I'm so scared. Please hold me."

He embraces Tracy, rubs and pats her back, keeps his eyes closed, and wants to pray but feels it's futile. He's descended into a chasm of hopelessness.

Pure despair.

It could be an hour later, maybe two, or even three.

Time is gone, lost in a sea of heart-thrashing, dread-filled preoccupation, Roddy is waiting while hoping, yet filled with fear, sitting, standing, pacing, sitting again, holding Tracy as his thoughts swirl in eddies of self-recrimination. He castigates himself for all his wrongdoings, for not being sensitive to the boy's needs, for not appreciating Tom's world—the kid's music, his hip lingo, his shitty attitude, his computer games and digitally driven interests in violent competitions like Postal 2, and other diversions the kid uses to dissipate his adolescent hormonal urges, stuff he never tried to understand.

Roddy berates himself for everything he's done in the past: his youthful excesses, the street fights, beating his mother's abusive boyfriend, Horst, to a bloody pulp when Roddy was fifteen and knew he could finally expel that cruel bastard from her life—and his own—and he upbraids himself for killing Grange and Kenny, for being a lousy friend to Danny, and for how he breezed through his early years never thinking of consequences or costs.

He thinks of his father—a man he never knew, a man whose violence led to robbery and prison and being shanked in a penitentiary shower, where he lay dying in a pool of blood and shit—and he wonders if he'd known his father, would things somehow have been different.

He recalls his mother—a drug addict—who carried on with vile men who abused her, men who mocked and beat him, and her boyfriend Horst, who locked him in a closet for hours and taunted him, laughing as Roddy trembled in the darkness. And he remembers the drunken beatdowns, the incessant shrieking, cursing, threats, and intimidation; he has memories of the cops showing up, the arrests, his running to Danny's house, and the foul rot of his life during his first seventeen years. Until the army rescued him, he was doomed to live amid such depravity but for the grace of Peggy Burns, who showed him the only kindness he knew in his early life.

But the past is no excuse; he can't escape the sordid reality of this moment, and Roddy blames only himself for the morass his life has become, for the harm he's done in the past, and for any wrongs he'll do in the future.

It's a tidal wave of self-blame.

I've brought on the undoing of my family's life. Cellini's in our lives because of what I've done. How will I ever live with myself?

And then he wonders: *how much can I regret? How much remorse must I feel?*

How deeply can he mine his own wrongdoing and how much can he torture himself by focusing on the ugly ore of his own sins?

What's my name . . . Danny Burns?

Tracy paces and wrings her hands. Her shoulders shake.

Except for the two of them, the waiting room is empty.

This surgery's taking way too long, and there's an ominous sign Roddy knows all too well: no one has come out of the OR to give them an update. Usually, a nurse in scrubs appears—however briefly—to tell the patient's relatives everything's going smoothly. But when no one ventures out to the waiting area with a status report, it means there are complications, or things are going badly or were very dire in the first place. And the silence of the waiting room is ominous and feels deadly.

He can't let Tracy see the fear brimming within him, the doubt and dread threatening to intensify to the point where it'll crest and erupt in sheer panic. He can't let it show on his face or his body. He's gotta stop pacing, can't fidget, can't look like he's ready to break into a million pieces.

So he sits on the couch beside her and holds her hand as his heart pounds and his body thrums and he feels like he's standing at the edge of a deep chasm.

If only he could slip beyond the locked doors and make his way down to Surgical Suite 3, where the most serious trauma cases are taken.

What if Tom doesn't make it, and what if this is just the start of a reign of terror about to descend on Tracy and their daughter?

He can't hold back the tears any longer. They flood his eyes and course down his cheeks. Tracy turns to him, and they embrace. They hold each other tightly.

Enough self-pity. Tom's in the OR and you're ruing your own shitty self. Think of the kid, what he's going through, the troubles he's had in his young life, a life too short to be over. And Tracy—the horror of a mother contemplating the death of her child.

Ivan, still wearing his green scrubs and surgical cap, enters the waiting room.

Roddy leaps to his feet and joins Tracy as they rush toward him.

He tries to read Ivan's expression. His partner's narrowed eyes and tightly clenched jaw send a tremor of dread through Roddy.

He's been in this situation before, but from the other side: a surgeon about to deliver bad news to a family.

He knows exactly what Ivan's thinking and how he feels.

Roddy knows what's coming next: an attempt to sound earnest and compassionate, to show empathy and concern, to remind them that Tommy has youth on his side, but all the while the surgeon's noncommittal face betrays a dismal prognosis. God, he's been in this situation scores of times—but never as the parent of a patient.

In the space of mere seconds, all hope drains from Roddy's soul.

And then Ivan's words, "We're very fortunate . . ."

Roddy feels sudden lightness in his chest, and Tracy's stiffened body visibly relaxes.

"They got Tom to the hospital very quickly," Ivan continues. "He lost a great deal of blood, and if he hadn't gotten here so soon, well . . ." He pauses midsentence. "Fortunately, there was no significant head trauma, only some bruising of the face, but that's just cosmetic. There was a good deal of internal bleeding. He had a ruptured spleen and a laceration of the liver. We did a splenectomy and repaired the liver tear. He's been given plenty of plasma expanders and packed blood cells, and he's still on an IV. He has some rib fractures, but they'll heal just fine. He's in recovery now."

"A lot of internal bleeding? Give it to us straight, Ivan."

"My only concern is . . ." Ivan hesitates and then coughs.

It's coming now . . .

"The blood loss?" Roddy asks.

"Yes, there was a period when Tom's brain wasn't perfused quite as well as it could have been, but he certainly was oxygenated, to some degree."

To some degree?

A surge of nausea rises from Roddy's gut, and his balance seems off, as the waiting room darkens and starts spinning. He knows what Ivan's alluding to, but he's not so sure Tracy grasps the implications.

Ivan continues: "We can't know if there'll be any long-term consequences." He clears his throat. "It's speculation right now, nothing more. But I want to give you the full picture. We'll have to wait and see."

Roddy's insides plunge. Then comes an aching sadness so deep, it feels as though a vapor seeps into his brain, fogging everything over. Tears again brim in his eyes; the room blurs.

Tracy stares at nothing, wide-eyed, silent.

Does she understand what Ivan's implying?

"Can we see him?" Roddy croaks through a clogged throat.

"I think it's better if you wait awhile. He's still heavily sedated and won't be able to talk intelligently. We'll have a clearer picture in a few hours."

Tracy's bewildered look tells Roddy she's not processing Ivan's words. They're floating past her in a perceptual haze of motherly worry.

From years of Roddy's descriptions of patients with extreme blood loss—leading to compromise or even death of brain cells—Tracy should know Ivan's referring to potential brain damage.

But Roddy's having told Tracy about those patients occurred under vastly different circumstances, when he was talking casually about his day in the OR, doing surgery on patients. It wasn't personal and lacked the impact of such a horror befalling someone they love.

It wasn't about their son, Tom.

Tom's having been hit by a car is something that happens to other people; it involves the fates of strangers, told dispassionately with the shelter of distance—and you learn of it from accounts in the *New York Post* or *Daily News* or the *Bronxville Daily Voice*, or stories reported while you're watching the six o'clock TV news, not from a doctor who's looking into your eyes and talking about your own child, your flesh and blood.

My God, I'd do anything to turn this around, to let our son live a normal life.

Roddy slips his arm around Tracy's shoulder, pulling her close to him.

Ivan pats Roddy on the shoulder, turns, and leaves.

Tracy pulls away, peers into Roddy's eyes, and asks, "What was Ivan saying?"

He tries to calm himself, but the possibility of Tom living a brain-damaged existence scalds through his thoughts like an electrical storm. He struggles to keep it together, to not fall on his knees and roar his despair at the unfathomable evil that's befallen his family.

"Please, Roddy. Tell me the truth."

"Ivan's trying to prepare us for the possibility that the internal bleeding might've caused a decreased flow of oxygen to the brain." Roddy's voice seems so small, and his words passing his lips are baffled, distant. He feels robotic, derealized.

"Meaning what, Roddy?" Tracy's voice sounds pitchy, and her breathing comes in short, shallow bursts.

He doesn't want to lie to her again, but how does he tell Tracy there's a possibility of a lifelong disability for Tom?

"There's a remote possibility of permanent damage," he hears himself whisper.

A gasp erupts from Tracy's throat. Then muffled sobbing as she buries her face in her hands.

He embraces her tightly, wanting more than anything to change everything, to hold on to the people he loves with greater fervor than ever before.

But there's nothing he or anyone can do.

Chapter 18

Time is lost, just gone—seconds, minutes, hours—they blend in an ether of ambiguity.

It's pure terror.

Light streams through the waiting room's window. It's dawn.

Roddy's thoughts turn to Sandy; Tracy's sister Colleen has come in from New Jersey to babysit.

He does his best to assuage doubt. Won't Tom's youth—the near-boundless capacities of a young and healthy constitution—prevail over bodily insult? Didn't he read somewhere about a team of Uruguayan rugby players whose plane crashed in the Andes? Yes, and there was a movie about it, too. The crew and passengers were trapped for weeks in a snowbound mountain pass, far from civilization. Many died of starvation while the survivors had no choice but to eat the flesh of the dead.

When they were rescued, it was learned that most of those who survived the two-month ordeal were teenage boys. The physical resources of the young are enormous.

But as desperate as he is for a glint of optimism, what awaits him and Tracy is a fearsome possibility. Can they live with what may be? They'll have no choice, and they'll do whatever they can to make the best of it.

"How do we deal with this?" Tracy asks, her voice trembling.

"One minute at a time, my love. One minute at a time."

"Will we have to let him go?" Her eyes widen.

"Tracy, try not to think like that. Let's wait and see."

If he dies, I'll only be able to stagger through the rest of my life. And if that happens, my life will be forever poisoned.

"I can't bear the thought of outliving my child . . . our child," she says. "I'm too weak for this."

"No, you're not, Trace. You're the strongest person I know, and we'll get through this."

Finally, at Tom's bedside, he looks down at his son.

Despite the wreckage, the bruising and swelling of his face, Tom's underlying comeliness is evident.

My beautiful broken boy. How I love you . . . how much you mean to your mother and me. I wish I'd told you how much I love you.

Love will always be there. These feelings will never fade.

Tom's not pale—not anemic—though he's always had fair skin, a legacy of the McDonald side of the family, inherited from his mother. His face looks distorted. The area around his eyes is swollen, and the skin is purple, shiny. His blond hair is a tangled mess.

His chest rises and falls; his breathing is steady, even. He's not on a respirator. A good sign. The IV is running smoothly and the urinary catheter is working; the collection bag is filling.

The monitors beep steadily. The red and green neon numbers—despite their portentous implications—are strangely comforting to Roddy. They're digital readouts of a young and very strong heart.

But did that heart pump enough blood to Tom's brain to keep it functioning normally?

Not until Tom is awake and alert—only when they can communicate with him—will they know what's in store. How desperately Roddy needs—even craves—reassurance, and how urgently he looks for any sign of improvement.

Tracy reaches over the bed rails, strokes Tom's hair, leans over, and kisses his forehead.

The boy stirs, mumbles in a whispery voice, but doesn't open his eyes.

Roddy feels his heartbeat through his jaws, in his teeth. He grips the bed rail tightly.

Tracy takes Tom's hand and kisses it.

Roddy watches her gaze down at their son, drinking in the sight of him.

Clearing his phlegm-filled throat, Roddy leans in toward the boy—only inches away from Tracy—and with the hum of anticipation ramping through him, gently says, "Tom, can you hear me?"

Nothing. No movement. His son's eyes remain closed.

Roddy's breathing comes in shallow gulps, and the room momentarily bleaches white.

"Tom, Mom and I are here. Can you hear me?"

Roddy notices a slight stirring: the boy's mouth twitches, his eyelids flutter, and then all goes still.

"Tom?"

Nothing.

"Tom, we're here."

Tracy holds the boy's hand, gently massaging his bruised fingers.

Tom's lips part. There's whispering; it's incoherent word salad. A hodgepodge of sibilant mumblings.

With that strange mélange of verbiage, Roddy tumbles through a dark void, imagines the worst, wonders how he and Tracy will deal with a brain-damaged child, and questions what the future will hold for them all.

"Tom, it's Dad. We're here."

"Dad . . . ?" Tom whispers in a slurred voice.

The kid's drugged, still brain-addled from the anesthesia.

"Dad? You here?"

Roddy's heart somersaults as a burst of joy blooms within him.

"Yes, Tom. We're here."

"Dad, everything hurts."

"I know. It'll pass."

Roddy's breathing is strident in his ears. Euphoria threatens to erupt; Tom is making sense, but Roddy doesn't want to jump to a premature conclusion. There must be something more convincing.

Tom's eyes remain closed.

"Tom . . . ?" Roddy whispers.

"Dad, I love you."

Tracy gasps and then sobs. As she holds Tom's hand, hers trembles.

"And we love you, Tom," Roddy murmurs in a warbling voice, nearly choking. "We love you so much."

"I know, Dad. I really know that."

A burst of ecstasy overwhelms him, and he feels his heart expand to the point of nearly bursting. It's pure elation. Tom's life won't be blighted; there will be a future, and he's certain the boy will recover. Completely.

Roddy watches as Tracy kisses Tom and then strokes his hair while whispering in his ear.

She must be saying something funny because a slight giggle erupts. Even though Tom's eyes stay closed, the corners of his lips turn upward and it's definite: he's smiling. Then he nods and chortles, and it's clear he's processing—understanding completely—whatever Tracy is whispering to him. And that smile is the most beautiful thing Roddy's ever seen. Tears form in his eyes, and he welcomes how they cascade down his cheeks.

Those tears will cleanse and wash away the heartache that gripped him only moments ago.

Now, for the first time, he truly understands the powerful emotions he'd witnessed so many times in the past, but always as an outsider, as the surgeon onlooker watching someone else's miracle blossom before his eyes. He could never have imagined what it feels like when someone you love is released from the clutches of death or from a life-altering disability. It's inexpressible unless you've lived through it, and Roddy's certain he and Tracy have. Tom will be spared a life of infirmity.

Roddy wants to seize this moment, hold on to it forever. Life has never felt more precious than it does right now, but the reason his son was so close to death pushes forward.

If it weren't for him, this would never have happened.

And will Tom be the last victim?

Cellini will stop at nothing to force Roddy's hand.

Gazing at his wife and the son he almost lost, Roddy knows he's trapped in Cellini's plot.

He can never share with Tracy his involvement in what led to Tom's injuries. And since she won't know this was more than a random hit-and-run, he can never convince her to leave with the kids and go into hiding.

Tracy turns toward Roddy, reaching for him, and he holds her close.

"Our boy's going to be fine," she murmurs. "We're all going to be fine."

How can he tell her that's not true?

Chapter 19

Monday evening, eight o'clock. Two days since the hit-and-run.

Roddy just got home with Sandy from the hospital.

He'll be staying the night caring for her, while Tracy sleeps on a cot in Tom's hospital room.

Home, not the apartment at the Regency, but *their* home.

The house they first decorated together with furnishings from estate sales and little odds and ends they found in thrift shops. The house that over time became filled with family photos, books, children's drawings, and mementos of their vacations.

The last two days have taken a toll on everyone, and although she normally begs to stay up until nine thirty, Sandy heads upstairs to bed as soon as they get back from the hospital. Seeing her brother doing so well has given the child enough peace of mind to get some sleep.

Roddy's alone in what is his house, yet isn't.

He thinks he must be feeling the way every divorced or separated man feels standing in the foyer of what had once been his home.

He enters the kitchen, grabs a Bud from the refrigerator, and twists the cap off. A crown of foam forms on top of the bottle. He takes a pull. The sight of the breakfast nook, just off the kitchen, fills him with a longing for the simple things he misses so much but used to take for granted.

They ate dinner there—together as a family—just about every evening.

He can hear Tom's refrain at the dinner table that he'd rather be having KFC or McDonald's than his mother's cooking. He can see Sandy, sitting opposite her brother, asking Roddy endless questions about science. He hears the laughter, bickering, and teasing and longs for the easy, casual way they all talked about their days at work or school.

He wanders into the den, settling on the sofa next to where Tracy usually read a novel while he watched TV. He always marveled how she could tune out the noise and concentrate on her book. He once asked her why she didn't read in the living room, where it was quiet.

"I want to be with you," was her reply.

How terribly different things are now.

He tries closing his eyes, but he knows he's too jacked to fall asleep.

Thank God Tom is making progress. He's being given pediatric doses of Tylenol with codeine for pain, and it supposedly dulls him, but the kid's as sharp as ever. The neuropsychologist said Tom's doing so well that based on two interviews, it won't be necessary to test him for cognitive defects. The kid is completely intact.

Roddy wonders if he's wrong to keep everything from Tracy. Did he really believe he could shield her and the kids from the nightmare that began at Snapper Pond?

Would it be unfair to unburden himself completely now—to tell her everything? If he does, she'll leave with the kids, maybe go to her sister's place in Nutley again. But would that keep her and the kids safe? Probably not.

And it *would* guarantee the end of their marriage.

There's no good answer. It's an untenable situation.

Earlier that day, he spoke with Detective Bob Carol of the Bronxville PD.

"Yes, it was a hit-and-run," Carol said. "Your next-door neighbor, Mr. Williams, saw it. We've alerted all body shops in the area to be on the lookout for any vehicle with front-end damage, especially one where the owner's paying in cash or where it's not covered by an insurance policy."

Roddy knows the police can do nothing else about the incident. Cellini's crew won't be taking the car to any body shop other than one they control.

He should speak with Scott Williams.

Certain Sandy's asleep, Roddy locks the front door, turns on the alarm, and makes his way next door.

Scott and Alice Williams have lived next door for five years. She's a bond trader on Wall Street and he's a corporate attorney working out of a White Plains law office.

Masters and movers of the universe. People who work in the money fields, harvesting the crop every day.

Scott's a good guy. He and Roddy have had a few beers together at a few neighborhood barbecues.

Roddy waits after ringing the Williamses' doorbell.

"Roddy, come in," Scott says, opening the door. "How's Tommy doing?"

"He's pretty banged up, but he'll be all right. Tracy's with him at the hospital."

Scott says Alice is working late and asks if Roddy wants to stay for a while.

"No thanks, Scott. I've gotta get back and check on Sandy. I want to thank you for being on the ball and calling nine-one-one."

"Hey, no problem, man."

"I also want to ask you about the accident."

"Let's talk in the den," Scott says as he leads Roddy to the clubby-looking room just off the entrance foyer.

They settle into leather chairs, facing each other, separated by a huge oaken coffee table.

"It was around eight o'clock," Scott begins. "Alice noticed the front porch light was flickering and then went dead. I wanted to wait until morning to change the bulb, but she kept nagging me to do it. So just to get her off my back, I grabbed the stepladder and was standing on it and taking the glass casing off when I heard this sound."

Scott pauses in his account to stretch his lanky frame.

"It was a loud, squealing noise, like when a car is racing. You know, we've had problems with some kids dragging on Clubway, so that's what I thought it was.

"The next thing I knew, I saw this car going really fast.

"It was too dark to see anything clearly, what with the porch light being out . . . Anyway, it was all a blur. And then I heard a *thump* and saw something go up in the air and land off to the side. I could tell it was too big to be a dog or a small deer, but I didn't know what—I mean who—got hit. Geez, I'm sorry, Roddy . . . Christ, I'm talking about your Tommy."

"That's okay, Scott. Please go on."

Scott says it was too dark to make out any details of the car and apologizes for not being able to help more than he has.

"Hey, Scott, that's fine. Anything else you remember?"

"I'm not sure about this, and I didn't tell the detective because I didn't want to speculate about it, if you know what I mean."

"Of course, but please, Scott, speculate for me."

"I can't really be sure, but I have the feeling that car wasn't coming down Clubway from a distance. There wasn't any drag race going on, that's for sure. It was only one car, not two.

"I just have this feeling—call it an impression—that the car was parked on Clubway, a little distance from our house. And . . . what I think I heard was the sound of peeling rubber, like when a driver hits the gas from a standing position."

The edges of the room blur.

"Scott, am I putting words in your mouth if I interpret what you're saying as there's a possibility that car may have been lying in wait?"

Scott's face turns bone white. "I don't want to mislead you, Roddy, but that's certainly a possibility."

Chapter 20

It's almost nine p.m. Back at the house. Sandy's sound asleep.

A hot sensation sears through Roddy and infuses him like snake venom, a poisonous invasion seeping through his arteries, leaking into each capillary, and saturating every cell. He's electrified with tension.

Were they lying in wait? When they spotted a kid crossing the street, did they assume it was Tom and run him down?

A thousand thoughts rampage through his head, an insane stew of sights and sounds, recollections, and ruminations so swift, there's no coherence.

Moving from room to room, he can't sit or stay in one place; his pace quickens, and his thoughts are jumbled. He goes to the refrigerator, grabs a beer, snaps the top off, chugs it down, and paces back and forth; he trudges upstairs, then down, steps outside, where the night air feels cold, and then returns to the den, where he finishes the beer. A booze-borne calm settles over him as he eases onto the sofa, leaning forward with his head down—the sofa where he sometimes sits at night in the dark, where Tracy saw him drinking whiskey as he cogitated about the evil that's engulfed his life—and he ponders the horrors that have beset his family.

He has to do something. He can't sit and wait for something else to happen.

This is the reality I'm living. Will they kill my kids? My wife? Can't let that happen.

He's so tightly coiled, he could burst from the pressure. It's a mental depth charge—and it could explode with the blasting power of TNT.

And the pressure's building, nearing ignition point.

He has to dissipate the energy.

Otherwise he'll go Mad Dog on the bastards.

If it were daytime, he could work this rage off by changing into his running shoes and sweats and jogging along one of Siwanoy Country Club's walkways. He'd lope along at a steady pace for who knows how long, as though he could go on forever with his legs and arms pumping—the way the rangers and paratroopers did at Fort Bragg—and he'd find himself in that eerie zone of otherness, floating in some weird firmament where mysteries lie hidden, even secrets from himself.

But not now. He can't run through the country club on a cold night.

The moment's heat feels like voltage powering through his body, as though he's ionized.

Yes, that's it—he's electrified.

He tramps upstairs to the spare bedroom they converted into a minigym, turns on the Precor treadmill, programs it for four miles an hour, and starts walking.

He increases the speed and breaks into a jog. With the rhythm, his mind roams; the movement—the kinetic freedom of running—dampens the inner fury. The motion brings on a flow of dreamlike thoughts and weird images, often sequential, sometimes not.

The pumping of his arms and legs, his steady breathing, the treadmill's motor hum, its spinning cylinders, and the moving belt make the horror recede.

Increasing the speed and raising the treadmill's incline bring changes: he's breathing deeply, his muscles move synchronously, and his heart pumps harder and faster. Blood washes through his brain, drenching it with nourishment, and there's an outpouring of neuro-peptides, a surge of adrenaline and serotonin, even dopamine.

Minutes seem like seconds, time contracts, and the muscle burn is so delicious, it feels like he could go on forever.

There was Sergeant Dawson's roared mantra back during ranger training—a chant the men called out in the sweltering heat, when they dripped runnels of sweat, when their chests heaved and their muscles ached from exhaustion.

Pain is only weakness leaving the body.

It all streams now: Vinzy, Cellini, DiNardo, Geppetto's, the threats—it's a flowing river of thought—and the kinetic energy brings something to consciousness. A nascent plan lies sub-merged in some mental recess, and Roddy knows something will crystallize—somehow, when he least expects it, a random sight or sound will trigger a connection.

There will be a plan.

And when the veil lifts, he'll think it through, just as Tracy would in her methodical way, and he'll do what he can to make it work.

He presses two buttons on the panel. The belt slows, and the incline lessens.

He gets off the treadmill.

Only now does he realize how depleted he is, how weak his legs feel.

Scott Williams's words were chilling, but Scott isn't certain about what he saw. He had no clear view in the darkness. Scott shared a conjecture realized after the fact, when distortion may fill in the blanks, so it boils down to little more than an inference, something so indefinite, Scott doesn't dare tell the police.

Perception and memory are always fallible.

Is Roddy backing off his deduction about Cellini? Is he even contemplating such a malevolent scenario—the near death of his son at the hands of mobsters—so frightening, Roddy can't acknowledge that reality?

He can't jump to a conclusion about the hit-and-run. That would be the way of Roddy Dolan from the streets. The Mad Dog of years ago would act on instinct and fly into a fury at an adversary. He must suffocate that creature and then bury it.

There's one way to pin it down.

He'll make a telephone call.

Chapter 21

It's nine forty-five in the evening. He's back in the den. Sandy is sound asleep in her room.

Roddy presses the speed dial. He hears the phone ring twice.

"Yeah, Roddy . . ."

"Vinzy. I haven't heard from you in days. What's up?"

In a reedy voice, Vinzy says, "I've been busy."

"Busy with what?"

"Ah, you know . . . the clinic. Lotsa paperwork."

A pause. The silence expands. He can *feel* Vinzy's tension through the phone.

"What's up with you, Roddy?"

"You hear about my boy?"

"Your boy? Tommy? What about him?"

"You didn't hear about his accident?"

"Accident? No. Whaddaya talkin' about?"

Is this feigned ignorance?

"He was hit by a car near our house. A hit-and-run."

"No *shit*. My God, that's terrible."

"I thought you had contacts at Lawrence Hospital. How come you didn't know about it?"

"Uh . . . like I said, Roddy, I been busy as hell."

Play it close to the vest; see what happens.

"But, hey, I'm sorry to hear that," Vinzy says. His voice sounds high-pitched, not his usual timbre.

Vinzy says, "How's he doing?"

"He's not out of the woods yet."

"Here's hoping he gets well. *Completely* well."

"Hey, Vinzy, give me some FaceTime."

"Yeah, sure, Roddy. Sure . . ."

People's voices give them away—a warble, a quiver, a change in pitch—but it's easier to read signals in a face-to-face conversation. Visual cues add to the mix: a slight twitch, a quivering of the lips or chin. And the eyes are a big giveaway: a shifting gaze, a few blinks, all coupled with a lie or an evasion, can tell the story.

Vinzy's face materializes on the screen. Same angular features, but he looks feral—like a distorted version of a ferret.

His face looks tight, controlled. A sweat sheen covers his cheeks.

"So, Vinzy, you telling me you had nothing to do with it?"

He studies Vinzy's face—looks for fissures in his facade. Vinzy's chin drops. His eyebrows look like they're meeting his hairline. It's a wounded look, like he's personally affronted; it's exaggerated denial.

"*What*? Roddy, what the hell ya talkin' about? *Me*? Ya gotta be *kiddin*'."

"No. I'm asking you a question and I want an answer. Did you have anything to do with it?"

"I'm offended you'd even ask that. What the fu—"

"I'm asking because Carmine threatened me and my family. You said he carries out every threat, that he'd think nothing of hurting me or my family. Those were your exact words, and I want to hear from your mouth that you had nothing to do with it."

"Roddy, trust me. I had nothin' to do with it. *Nothin*'."

"Don't shit me, Vinzy."

"I wouldn't, Roddy. Believe me, I wouldn't do that."

"You wouldn't do what, shit me or lie to me?"

"Ah, c'mon, Roddy, either one."

Roddy waits, watching Vinzy's pumped-up vehemence: Vinzy's mouth twists, his lips flatten, his eyes narrow, his brow furrows, his nostrils flare with righteous indignation, and his voice is overripe with rebuttals. Vinzy chews on his lower lip, unaware he's doing it.

Telltale signs of nerves, of lies, of evasion—like the cops say, a tell.

Sergeant Dawson always said, "Corner the enemy, and then let loose with your fire."

"Don't lie to me, Vinzy. You're one of Cellini's crew, and I hold you responsible."

"Roddy, I'm not part of any *crew*, believe me. I'm *not* a mobster. C'mon, I'd never be in on something like that."

"What about Cellini?"

"I got no idea. But you agreed to do it ... you know, that thing. Nah, not Cellini."

A pause. Vinzy's virtually snorting. His eyelids flutter like a hummingbird's wings, and his eyes dart from side to side. Evasion.

"Hey, Roddy, do you *actually* think I'd have somethin' to do with that kinda thing?"

"Swear to me."

"*Jesus.* I swear on my mother's grave, I had nothin' to do with what happened to your boy."

"Who did?"

"I have no idea. None." He shakes his head, blinking like a broken traffic light.

Roddy stares long and hard at Vinzy—without malevolence or threat; he stays calm and waits silently, like the coral snake in the underbrush at Fort Jackson, lying in wait for its prey.

A beseeching look is etched on Vinzy's face—furrowed brow, tight lips, the whole *I didn't do it* look he and Danny would assume when confronted by a teacher in the fifth grade, before being sent to the principal's office. *Who, me?*

"You have no idea who did it?"

"Absolutely, Roddy. Believe me. If I did, I'd tell you."

"What do you mean, '*If I did*'? You sound like fucking O.J."

"Jesus, you've got me confused, Roddy. I'm just so fucked up that you'd think for even one second that I had *anything* to do with somethin' like that. I'm . . . I don't know what else I can say."

"Say nothing."

"Let's get somethin' straight, Roddy. I'm as trapped in all this as you are."

"Yeah, sure."

"Believe me, I am."

Another "believe me." What did my shrink friend, Dick Simons, say? Beware spontaneous denials. And "believe me" is a spontaneous denial. Vinzy's protestations signal it's all bullshit.

"Hey, Roddy, I'd never lie to you. Never. If nothing else, for old times' sake. Believe me."

His voice is so honeyed, Roddy feels queasy.

Vinzy's face is a picture of studied earnestness. Totally disingenuous. It's a bullshit choirboy look Roddy recognizes on some politicians trying to look like they give a shit about people more than they care about monied interests supporting them.

"Vinzy, I want a guarantee that nothing happens to my family."

"I'm not in a position to—"

"No excuses, Vinzy. I want a guarantee."

"Okay, okay. I'll talk to Carmine."

"You do that. And you find out when it's going to happen."

"When what's gonna happen?"

"Don't bullshit me, Vinzy. You know what I'm talking about."

"Okay. Okay. I'll find out."

"And we'll talk about some medical issues—not over the phone, in *person*—so I don't make a mistake."

"In person? Sure. Whatever you want, Roddy."

"Because there are medical issues."

"Medical issues?"

"You're an internist. I'm a surgeon. I'll need some advice."

"I'm not an anesthesiologist."

"Neither am I, but there are things I'll need to discuss."

"Okay."

"I'm counting on you."

"You can depend on me, Roddy. Believe me, you can."

"I hope so."

"I'm still not sure you believe me, Roddy."

"Believe you? About what?"

"About your son."

"You haven't given me much to believe in, Vinzy."

"Believe me. I had nothin' to do with anything."

"Just let me know when the surgery's scheduled and then we'll talk some medicine. I'll take it from there."

"Good enough, Roddy. I'm glad you're on board. I'll be in touch."

Chapter 22

Danny enters Rocco's and doesn't see Roddy at their usual table, and he's not seated anywhere else in the room. Unless he's in the john, it's a first: Roddy's gonna be late. For all the years they've known each other, Roddy's always showed up early and cooled his heels waiting for Dan to arrive.

As Dan makes his way to the table under the black-and-white photo of the Roman Colosseum, he hopes Roddy's lateness isn't caused by a turn in Tommy's condition. *My God,* he thinks, *how have Roddy and Tracy been able to handle it?* A hit-and-run. That's what the paper said, and Angela gave him all the details after she spent time yesterday with Tracy at the hospital. The boy lost his spleen and had a torn liver, for God's sake, and he was pretty badly broken up, so he's not out of the woods yet.

Dan checks his cell: no call or text from Roddy.

An ominous sign.

Not only is Roddy never late, but he always touches base if there's gonna be a change of plans.

He speed dials Roddy's number, but the call goes to voice mail.

He tries Angela's cell, just in case she heard from Roddy or Tracy.

"Shit, voice mail again," he mutters. Then Dan remembers Angela saying she was going to Scarsdale tonight to make a surprise visit to check up on the home health aide they just hired to stay with her mother. There's never decent cell service at his mother-in-law's house.

The waiter approaches the table and asks if he'd like to order a drink while waiting for his friend.

"Extra-dry Grey Goose martini, straight up . . . with olives," Dan replies, thinking a cocktail will help calm his anxiety about Roddy's lateness.

He keeps his eyes fixed on the entrance. Each time the door opens, he hopes it'll be Roddy, but instead he sees a steady stream of the usual assortment of people who typically dine here: middle-aged couples; a few twentysomethings on their cells, texting like crazy even while being led to their tables; and one woman who's talking loudly on her cell. Damned thing looks like it's grafted onto her palm.

The martini arrives. Danny takes his first sip and waits for the balm to his brain he hopes the booze will deliver.

He's really at a loss for what to do about Roddy's lateness.

Should he try Tracy's cell?

No. That's a bad idea.

Why burden her with more worry, especially if it turns out there's nothing really wrong? Poor woman, she's already dealing with the horror of a son all broken up and in the hospital, and she's really upset with the state of her marriage. Angela gave him the lowdown after she came home last night from the hospital.

Should he call Lawrence Hospital and have Roddy paged?

If he's not here in five more minutes, I'll give it a try. But why the hell am I so worried, so damned nervous tonight? So, the guy's late . . . no big deal.

The restaurant's sound system seems especially loud tonight, and Danny's aware the Italian arias are grating on his nerves, especially the one playing now: "Musetta's Waltz," Roddy's favorite, the one he uses as his cell phone ringtone.

Just another reminder that something's gotta be wrong. Or that something's gonna go wrong. Soon.

Long ago Danny realized he has more than a healthy dose of superstitious beliefs in him. They lie there, real deep in his being.

Ma used to say it came from being Irish. Celtic people don't believe in coincidences, and that song playing now is definitely a bad sign.

It's Roddy's aria and Roddy's not here.

He's only twenty minutes late. Calm down. Don't get your balls in an uproar. You're making too much of this. For Chrissake, everybody's late once in a while.

To distract himself, Dan forces himself to look away from the door. A party of business types has just been seated at a nearby table. Eight of them, probably celebrating some deal they closed at work. One guy—a bit older than the others and sitting at the head of the table—appears to be in charge, definitely the boss. Everybody else seems to treat him in a deferential manner, like they're afraid to be themselves in his presence.

There's something about the guy's face that strikes Dan as familiar—it's more than just his cold-looking eyes and tight-lipped mouth or his closely cropped hair; thinking about it, Dan realizes the guy looks like a grown-up version of a neighborhood bully he encountered as a kid.

Not just any bully, but Kurt Bauer, the thug from Coyle Street back in Brooklyn. King of the Coyle Street Krauts.

Dan and Roddy were sixteen years old and approaching Nostrand Avenue back in Brooklyn. They didn't realize they'd crossed into the German enclave, far from their own turf in the Sheepshead Bay neighborhood.

Suddenly, they were surrounded by eight Coyle Street Krauts, the German gang always at war with the Irish.

Kurt Bauer, the leader of the group, stood chest to chest with Roddy. "I hear you're a tough guy," he snarled.

"I can handle myself," Roddy replied. He looked calm, no fear, ready to take whatever came.

Dan knew they'd take a vicious beating. His breath came in high-pitched wheezes.

"Well, tough guy, we're gonna beat the shit outta your friend here," Bauer said, pointing to Danny, "and you're gonna watch us do it."

Dan felt his bowels loosen, thought he'd shit his pants. If he did, he'd never hear the end of it from the Kraut bullies at school.

"I have a better idea," Roddy said, always the quick thinker. "I'll take on your two best fighters. If I beat 'em, you let us go. If I lose, you do your thing."

"Oh, really? I got Koenig and Schroeder here, and they'll kick your ass."

The deal was struck.

Koenig and Schroeder were high school seniors, big Germanic brutes, eighteen or nineteen years old. Both on the high school football team. Koenig was easily a two hundred pounder—a line-backer—solid and muscular, sporting closely clipped blond hair with that Aryan look.

And Schroeder was a beast—a bit on the flabby side, but freaking huge. Had to be 240 pounds at least.

At sixteen, Roddy hadn't yet filled out to become the 210-pound light-heavyweight he eventually became.

But Roddy was a Golden Gloves boxer. Even more important, he had a deep reservoir of courage.

They ducked into a nearby alley alongside an abandoned garage. The passageway was dank, and the odor of urine hung in the air. Danny was sure rats patrolled the place.

Trying to keep from shaking, Danny stood across from Bauer and the five other Germans as Roddy faced off against Schroeder and Koenig.

Schroeder moved in on Roddy, trying to grab him in a bear hug. Roddy kicked out and landed a sharp blow to his shin. Schroeder yelped and nearly fell to the ground as Koenig closed in.

Koenig swung a heavy fist—a ponderous roundhouse—at Roddy, who ducked and shot a pile-driver punch to his gut. The air went out of Koenig's lungs; he crumpled at the waist, and in a half second Roddy slammed an uppercut to his jaw. Koenig stumbled back and landed on the concrete. He rolled over onto his side, gagging, spitting teeth onto the ground as bloody saliva poured from his mouth.

Schroeder, recovered from the shin kick, lunged at Roddy and encased him in a crushing bear hug. Roddy's face turned red. The Germans shouted encouragement to Schroeder, who squeezed with his hands clamped around Roddy's back.

Writhing in the guy's arms, Roddy was lifted off the ground, but his knee shot into Schroeder's groin; the big guy grunted and his face blanched. His grip loosened; Roddy dropped to the ground and then shot an elbow into Schroeder's face. Blood sprayed from his nose. He reeled away as Roddy closed in and landed a series of cheetah-fast punches to his face.

Schroeder went down. To stay.

Roddy turned to Bauer and the others. "Who else wants to go a quick round?"

Silence.

Groans came from both guys. A delta of blood leaked onto the concrete from Schroeder's pulverized face.

Fear slithered through Danny. Mucus had collected in his lungs, thick secretions. The asthma was kicking in. He coughed. Then came tortured gasps, and his hands dropped to his knees.

"Now we're gonna kick your ass," Bauer seethed.

"We made a deal," Roddy said, meeting Bauer's stare.

"Yeah, but we're not sticking to it."

"Yes, we are," said a tough-looking German kid. "A deal's a deal. Let 'em go."

As he and Roddy headed away, Danny caught his breath and said, "Hey, kemosabe, you saved my ass."

Dan stopped walking, set his hands on his waist, and inhaled deeply; the wheezes and bubbles in his chest ebbed. When his breathing was back to normal, he asked, "How'd you come up with that idea?"

"It just came to me. They were gonna beat the shit out of us anyway. We had nothing to lose."

"But how did it come to you?"

"I think there's a secret part of the brain that helps solve problems. And when a certain little thing happens—like a word, or something you see—a plan comes to you."

"A secret part of the brain? I don't buy it."

"Lemme ask you something. You think the moon and stars come out at night?"

"Well, sure."

"What about in the daytime?"

"I guess . . . well . . ."

"Danny, they're *always* there. You only *see* them at night. It's the same with the mind. It's always thinking even though you don't know it."

Leave it to Roddy to come up with that, a weird connection between an ordinary thing and something buried down deep—the way Grange and Kenny are buried.

"Sorry I'm late," Roddy calls from a few feet away. His voice interrupts Danny's reverie.

"I was at home doing paperwork, and the next thing I know, I wake up with my head on the desk. Must've fallen asleep about an hour ago." Roddy settles into the chair opposite Dan and orders a glass of Chianti from the waiter who trailed him to the table.

"I wasn't worried," Danny lies. "I'll have another," he says to the waiter, and downs the rest of his martini.

"How's Tom doing?" Danny asks, seeing that Roddy looks like a ghost. The nap must've been the first sleep he's gotten in days. He's never seen Roddy looking so wasted.

"He's doing better every day, and he'll be home by the end of the week."

Roddy's voice sounds tired, and he looks depleted. Even more, he appears saddened, as though his soul has been beaten down. Despite Tom's progress, it's obvious Roddy's at a low point in his life.

Danny can't imagine how he'd handle it if Angela told him to move out. Where would he go? What would he do? He'd be lost, upended.

So he asked Roddy to meet him for dinner because he figured he might want to talk about it, maybe unburden himself a little bit.

For all the years they've known each other, and through all the things they've shared, Danny knows Roddy's always been very private when it comes to talking about his marriage.

And Dan respects that—it's the way he feels about his life with Angela. Some things are better left out of conversations, even with your best friend. But this separation has gotta be tough, and if Roddy feels like unloading, Dan's here for him.

The waiter returns with their drinks and takes their orders for dinner.

They both go for the veal parmigiana, and even though he's now working on his second martini, Danny suggests they share a bottle of Barolo. Worst-case scenario, he'll call for an Uber if he feels too sloshed to drive home to Tuckahoe. He wants Roddy to unwind, and he knows a good Barolo is a red Roddy really likes.

"Hey, Roddy . . . the meal's on me tonight."

"Thanks, my man," Roddy says, looking away.

Dan pretends he doesn't notice Roddy's close to tears. It's gotta be the double whammy of Tom's accident and the damned separation that's getting to Roddy.

Danny picks up his martini and sips casually, as though he doesn't register Roddy's distress, but he can't stop himself from asking, "You okay, Roddy? You look tired and you've lost weight."

"I haven't been sleeping, Dan—not since the thing with Tommy. And I know I'm not eating right. Living alone, I just grab something here and there."

"You feel like talking about the separation?"

"Not really, Dan."

"Hey, man, I understand."

A sense of awkwardness floods him, and Dan wants to quickly change the subject. It's a rare feeling to experience with Roddy. Danny recalls it having happened only once before—after the Snapper Pond fiasco—when he sensed Roddy no longer trusted him.

"When're you getting back to work?" he asks.

"As soon as Tom gets home. Till then I'm staying at the house with Sandy because Tracy stays at the hospital overnight with Tom. I visit him during the day, after Sandy's off to school. I like to be there when his doctors make rounds, and I spell Tracy so she can come home to catch up on a little sleep. She's not getting any rest on that hospital cot."

"How're things with you?"

"My business has been slow," Danny says. "It usually is this time of year, but it'll pick up right after the holidays, and even more when the weather warms up."

Small talk, pedestrian run-of-the-mill bullshit, Dan thinks. *Jesus, it's like I'm talking to a stranger, not Roddy, a guy I've known all my life.* He hardly remembers them ever resorting to trivial topics, shit like the weather or what's up at work. And that's exactly what he's doing. He's talking bullshit just to fill the silence. And he never felt uncomfortable when he and Roddy were together and didn't have much to say to each other. But he does right now.

On top of that, he notices Roddy's gaze has gone somewhere, neither at other diners nor the restaurant's decor—not anywhere at all—as though he's staring at some internal mirror and doesn't like what he sees.

"In fact," Danny adds, again just filling the silence—and knowing he wants to distract Roddy from himself—"things are so slow, Angie's got me shopping for her. Like tomorrow I'm going down to the Bronx to buy some good Italian stuff at Arthur Avenue."

Roddy seems to flinch. Dan pretends he doesn't notice, finishes his martini, and searches for something else to say.

"Yeah, there's a great pork store there, Calabria's, right near Randazzo's fish store. I gotta go to both places. Angie'll phone in the order. She doesn't trust a mick like me to make the selections. Then I'll wind up at the cheese store. Ever go to Carlo's Latticini? Right next to Madonia Bakery. The guy makes the best mozzarella in the world."

Roddy blanches, seeming to visibly recoil.

"What's wrong, Roddy? You look like you saw a ghost."

"Nothing, Dan. I'm just jumpy, with all this stress."

"Hey, Roddy, remember not too long ago we'd jump at the mention of the word 'ghost'?"

"Yeah, Dan, I remember." Roddy's voice is monotone and seems lifeless. Like *he's* a damned ghost.

"Lemme tell you, with all the shit that's on your plate right now, I'm glad we don't have that nightmare to worry about."

Roddy shrugs and nods.

"You know, Roddy, I used to think this place was where we'd come to talk about *you know what*, but now it's back to being just a great restaurant where we can share a good meal and a bottle of wine."

"Yeah."

Jesus, the guy's got no spirit. He's gotta be depressed as hell.

A waiter arrives with their entrées, and the sommelier follows, bringing the Barolo Danny ordered.

As the sommelier extends the bottle for Danny's inspection, Roddy reaches across the table and intercepts the man.

"Let's do a bottle another night, Dan. I'm too bushed to really enjoy it. It's not fair to you or the wine to waste it, not at these prices."

"I understand," Danny replies, signaling the sommelier to take the wine back to the cellar.

"I'll have a glass of Malbec instead," Dan says to the waiter. "And how about another glass for you, Roddy?" Danny asks, while the sommelier remains at the table.

"No, thanks, Dan. I'll just knock off what's left in this glass."

When the food arrives, Danny begins eating. The veal is always excellent at Rocco's, and tonight's no exception. It's so tender, you can cut it with a fork.

Dan eats in silence and then notices something.

"You haven't touched yours yet, Roddy. Everything okay?"

"Dan, it's not the food. It's me. I'm just not hungry. Hey, my good amigo, if you don't mind, I'm too tired to be out tonight. Is it okay if I have this wrapped up to take home? Maybe I'll eat it after I get back from picking Sandy up at the hospital. I'm sorry, Dan. I know I'm lousy company tonight."

"Hey, man, no need to stand on ceremony with me. But you gotta promise you'll try to eat something later. You can't afford to get sick. Your resistance is low, as Ma used to say."

"Thanks for understanding," Roddy says, signaling for the waiter.

Minutes later, when the waiter returns with his food boxed to go, Roddy pushes away from the table and reaches across to Dan. "Thanks again, kemosabe. You're the best friend a guy could ever have."

"Same here, Roddy." Danny gets up and grasps Roddy's hand. Then come the usual hugs and backslaps.

"Tell you what, why not come with Sandy tomorrow night for dinner? Angie's making pork rollatini with the meat and cheese I'll be picking up at Arthur Avenue."

"No, thanks, Dan. Another time, okay?"

Sipping his espresso, Dan realizes he's getting stronger; he's not letting that miserable McLaughlin's thing or the Snapper Pond disaster drag him down the toilet. He's a whole lot better at compartmentalizing his mind—that's what people call it— separating that clusterfuck known as McLaughlin's away from his everyday life. It's taken awhile, but it's happened. He's a lot better than he was.

He hasn't had that knot of anxiety in his stomach. It's been months since he's had a panic attack—an assault of nerves so powerful he could feel his blood pressure plummet as blood drained from his head and he'd get so light-headed he'd be on the verge of fainting. Roddy told him they were vasovagal epi-sodes, something about stress making the nerves that go to the heart slow it down so not enough blood reaches the brain. Like his heart would stall and the next thing he knew he'd be in a faint.

And something even worse would happen: everything would suddenly look like it was painted scenery on a stage, like it wasn't real, like the world was only two-dimensional and fake. And it would scare the shit out of him. It felt like he was going crazy. But those weird incidents have stopped.

Before the last few months, he was swimming—thrashing frantically—in a tidal wave of fear. When would the next attack happen? And where? Would he drop in a faint in front of strang-ers? Or in a public place like the mall or a movie theater, far from home or the office, where he couldn't get help? Jesus, there'd even been some mornings he didn't wanna leave the house.

He'd been counting on that little orange vial of Xanax, some-times ticking off the hours between doses, like a goddamned dope addict needing his next fix. It's nuts how you can love and hate something at the same time. Xanax, a lifesaver and a friggin' curse. Roddy warned him about that stuff—it can be addictive. In moments of heart-stopping anxiety, Danny would reach for that little bottle and down a pill—sometimes two—like his life depended on it.

But he's gotten beyond that torment.

From the look of things, he's doing better than Roddy. Dan's sleeping well, he has a good appetite, and the kids are doing well. He and Angie are in great shape, not separated or heading down the fuck-up trail toward a divorce the way Roddy and Tracy seem to be going.

Am I really doing better than Roddy? That's one for the books. I never thought I'd see the day when my conscience wasn't driving me crazy.

Dan knows that tonight Roddy wasn't the same guy he's known all his life. He seemed defeated, completely undone. It's strange because Roddy doesn't *do* depression. He doesn't *do* sadness or uncertainty or helplessness; he's a stranger to guilt, and he's always been sort of—well, actually, he's always been heroic.

Roddy always came through in the clutch, and he's the kind of guy Danny wishes he could be if only he'd been born with different DNA—the tough, Irish, iron-fisted, *don't-fuck-with-me* legacy of his genes. Or maybe it comes from his shitty childhood. Or maybe it's a combination of nature *and* nurture that shaped Roddy: his genetics, being Brooklyn born and bred, and a shit-ridden upbringing with that drug-addicted mother of his.

Yeah, it probably all funneled down to make Roddy Dolan who he is: a smart, tough son of a bitch, a guy who's resourceful, resilient, competent, and above all, confident in everything he does.

But if I'm more in control right now than Roddy, that's one helluva switch.

Yes, maybe Dan's not such a wuss anymore. Maybe he's getting to be more like Roddy once was. Tomorrow he's going to drive down to the Bronx and pick up some pork and bring home some balls of freshly made mozzarella. He's never tasted cheese as good as what gets made in that cheese store. It's a real treat when Angie makes her chicken or veal parmigiana, or when she cuts the mozzarella into chunks and tosses them into a steaming bowl of rigatoni with her incredible Bolognese sauce—a mix of pork, beef, and veal. Jesus, his mouth begins watering when he smells it.

Yeah, he absolutely loves Angie's pasta—always perfectly *al dente*—topped with the best homemade sauce in the world. He loves that stuff so much, he forgets about his low-cholesterol diet or how his belly might expand; he just pigs out on it.

It's so good to be married to an Italian woman.

Chapter 23

It looks just like the old Gothic-style churches in Brooklyn, "the borough of churches," as Roddy recalls having learned from Danny's mother, Peggy. He hasn't stepped inside St. Joseph's since Sandy made her First Communion here four years ago. He's left whatever religious education the kids have received to Tracy's supervision.

He thinks back to those early days with Danny, when he'd leave his mother's apartment and head off to Danny's place. Danny's ma, Peggy, would take both of them to nine a.m. Mass every Sunday at St. Andrew's on Ocean Avenue, not far from their place. She'd make sure he wore a clean, starched white shirt and navy blue trousers—which she'd bought for Roddy and kept with Danny's things—and she'd put his rumpled, dirty clothes in the wash to be cleaned while they were gone.

Roddy remembers never being able to sit still during the nearly hour-long Mass, but he loved the otherworldly sights, smells, and sounds of the church: the incense, the tinkling bells, the way a parishioner's cough would echo off the cathedral-like ceiling. Unlike Danny's, his mind was never on the priest's words. It would wander off to a stickball game he'd rather be playing, or to the special breakfast Peggy would prepare for them when they got back to Danny's apartment—fried eggs with sweet sausages and Irish soda bread or French toast with lots of maple syrup.

She'd even let them have half a cup of coffee diluted with lots of milk.

Thinking back to those days when they were just seven or eight years old, he recalls that he not only envied Danny's having a ma like Peggy Burns, but a part of him also envied Danny's connection to the spiritual world. He knew Danny felt something special during Mass, something mystical—a sensation Roddy just couldn't find within himself.

And now he stands before the massive wooden doors of St. Joseph's Church, about to go inside, hoping for what?

"Do you believe in God?" Danny had asked on their drive back home from that hellish night at Snapper Pond. After they'd disposed of Grange and Kenny. Roddy didn't know the answer then, and he doesn't know it now. All day long he's been asking himself, *How do you pray when you don't believe in God?*

But is that really true?

The evidence-based physician he's become negates the possibility of some all-knowing, all-powerful force out there who gives a shit about what happens on this earth to any one person. Impossible to believe in that. And when he was a kid in the boxing ring, he could barely believe when his opponent genuflected before the bout, crossed himself in his corner, and asked God for victory. Like God would choose one guy over another. What bullshit.

But still, something he can't rationalize or understand has drawn him to this church today. Exactly what it may be, he doesn't know. But one thing is certain: his soul is crying out for comfort, for relief from pain.

He walks into the dimly lit interior of the nave.

Late-afternoon sun radiates on the stained-glass windows, and rainbow prisms of light dance along the marble floors. The church is empty. His footsteps echo in the expanse.

He makes his way toward the altar rail. Off to the side, he sees the successive stacks of votive candles. How many times did he and Danny beg Peggy for two nickels so they could go over and each light a candle? There was the long wick you dipped into an already lit candle and carefully moved over to an unlit one, making sure you didn't catch your shirtsleeve on fire in the process.

Roddy can see from a distance that it's all electric now—you just press a tiny button to light a candle.

He kneels before the altar and clasps his hands together, resting them atop the cold marble rail. How does he begin? Not with the old, stale words of the prayers he memorized at Peggy's insistence all those years ago. They meant nothing to him then and even less now.

How do you pray? And how do you pray if you don't believe in God?

Those questions jab at him like sharp spikes.

But he knows he came here for guidance, to somehow gain some sense of the morally right thing to do, not only with Cellini, but also with Tracy.

To tell her or not to tell.

He closes his eyes and tries not to think. Maybe that's what meditation is all about. Just empty your mind and find solace in the absence of thought.

And is meditation very different from prayer? Are they different words meaning the same thing?

Try to relax and let yourself float away.

And then it happens.

A profound sense of peace envelops him. There are no thoughts, just an inner calm the likes of which he's never before felt.

As he leaves the church, walking past the doors and into the dwindling daylight, a nascent plan begins to take shape in his mind. And he knows he'll be doing the right thing.

Chapter 24

"You gotta be more controlled. You gotta execute a strategy, not attack like a mad dog." Doc Schechter's words come to Roddy, seemingly from nowhere, but they're etched indelibly in his memory.

"There's an art to boxing," his Golden Gloves coach had said again and again. "A great boxer has a plan, a road map to his opponent's weakness. Discipline and strategy, not fury . . . that's what a boxer must master."

It's been more than thirty years since Roddy's days in the ring, but Doc's voice fills his thoughts, as if the old guy were sitting next to him at the kitchen table. It's only momentary, but Roddy can nearly smell the canvas, sweat, liniment, and boxing gloves. He can almost feel the sensation of pummeling the heavy bag or hear the staccato beat as he punches the speed bag.

But above the racket of the gym, he hears Doc Schechter's gravelly voice and his admonition.

And something has changed since yesterday.

Roddy can't explain it, but since leaving the church, a calm feeling has stayed with him. Of course, part of it's got to do with how well Tom's doing, and he doesn't think he's kidding himself when he senses Tracy is feeling closer to him. Sure, once Tom gets home, things with Tracy could revert to what they've been, but right now they're drawing comfort and strength from each other.

He puts the kettle on the stove to make some tea. As he's waiting for the water to boil, he realizes he didn't reach for a Bud or pour himself two fingers of Jack Daniel's.

Yes, something's changing, and for the better. He needs to keep a clear head, not dull himself with booze.

It's very strange: he's racing against Cellini's clock, and he must devise a strategy to keep his family safe. But he's not panicked.

Yesterday he felt like a marionette on strings attached to Cellini's fingers. Pure manipulation and a feeling of helplessness. But it doesn't feel that way now; that thug and his henchmen no longer seem to have the same power over him.

An embryonic plan begins to materialize. He's far from certain what the fully formed idea will be, but he knows he's on the right track: it'll begin by using Vinzy, just like this nightmare began when that bastard used him.

It's funny how the mind works.

Roddy wasn't aware of why he'd wanted FaceTime with Vinzy. Sure, part of it was to confirm his suspicions about Cellini orchestrating Tom's accident. But there was another layer forming—a subtext, a foundation—even before he was ready to see it. And he doesn't yet realize what it will be.

But he insisted on meeting with Vinzy before Merko's surgery. Why?

There's gotta be a reason for that demand. What is it?

He knows one thing: he must go to war, but not in a traditional way. He must fight as though he's still a US Ranger.

Roddy can almost hear Sergeant Dawson's southern drawl barking out his refrain during ranger training.

"You're an elite fighting force . . . men of action and violence. You use speed and surprise to subdue your enemy. Be warned, young troopers, your enemy will kill you if he can. You must kill to survive. If you fail, you die."

Had he forgotten until this moment that he was trained for covert warfare? For infiltration? For clandestine operations?

Yes, he was trained to kill and to survive. And he must do it any way possible. It will be asymmetric warfare. One man against the mob.

His thoughts are interrupted by the sounds of Sandy practicing her violin. Yesterday the discordant notes grated on his nerves, but tonight he's amused by his daughter's lack of musical talent.

Finishing the last of his mug of Earl Grey, Roddy looks down at the withered tea bag with its string curled around the spoon. He's reminded of Doc Schechter, who always drank tea when he coached Roddy at Herbie's gym. Doc Schechter's and Sergeant Dawson's words are embedded in his being.

All for the good.

They're two men who influenced him in more ways than a superficial view would imply. Thinking back to his boxing and ranger days, he feels more confident, more in control than only a few hours before. He can master this. He can defeat Cellini, the puppeteer.

He gets ready for bed, certain he'll sleep tonight.

Things are about to happen.

Though he hasn't worked out the details, Roddy knows he'll take charge.

And he won't go Mad Dog.

Chapter 25

The driving beat of Metallica's "Halo on Fire" blasts from Roddy's cell phone.

Strange, he used to hate that song, especially when he'd hear it blaring through Tom's bedroom door. But not now. It strikes the perfect note to marshal his thoughts into action, especially if it signals a call from Vinzy.

Last night he ditched "Musetta's Waltz." Too filled with tragedy, too operatic, too Italian. A reminder of Geppetto's.

This is the first incoming call of the day, and he's ready to face whoever is on the line.

But he relaxes when the readout shows the call comes from Dan, probably touching base to see if Roddy's feeling better.

"What's up, kemosabe?" Roddy knows his voice sounds strong, more energetic than it was last night. It'll put Dan's mind at ease.

"Hey, Roddy, I'm just calling to see how you're doing."

"I'm fine, Dan. Sorry about last night."

"Hey, forget it. How's Tom?"

"Doing even better. He'll be coming home soon."

"Great news."

A brief pause. "I also called to thank you for the referral."

"What referral?"

"Got a call today from a doctor friend of yours, a guy from the Bronx, Dr. Vincent Masconi, a friend from med school."

A pang of alarm hits Roddy like a wrecking ball.

But it's only a moment of apprehension. The jolt fades in seconds. Somehow, word from or about Vinzy or Cellini doesn't have the same effect it did only a few days ago.

"He said you guys had dinner a while back and you gave him my name when he asked if you knew a good accountant. Hey, man, I really appreciate it."

"Dan, I never referred him."

"Huh?" Dan's obviously confused by the unexpected news.

"Don't get involved with that guy."

"Why not?"

Roddy hears that familiar warbling begin cresting in Dan's voice.

"He runs a shady operation, a medical mill. You don't wanna deal with him."

"If you didn't refer him, how'd he get my name?" Dan starts clearing his throat.

"He probably remembered meeting you years ago, when we all lived in the city. If nothing else, the guy's got a good memory, but he's trouble. Stay away from him."

"How do you know he runs a mill?"

"His office is an assembly line. He runs a scam operation, double billing, shit like that. If you get involved, you're looking for trouble. Big-time. Medicare and Medicaid fraud's only the beginning of it. Avoid Masconi like the plague."

"Jesus, Roddy, it's gonna be awkward. I already made an appointment for him and his manager to come to the office the Tuesday after Thanksgiving, the twenty-ninth."

Danny's throat clearing is incessant. Phlegm is building up in his throat.

"His manager?"

"Yeah, a guy named Carmine."

"Dan, listen to me. Don't take him on as a client."

"It's just a consultation."

"Get rid of the guy."

"But what am I gonna tell him? You know how I hate offending people."

Paroxysms of coughing begin as Danny tries to clear the mucus collecting in his bronchial tubes.

"Just move it back a few weeks. After a while he'll forget about it and you can kiss him goodbye."

"You're sure he's shady?"

"Absolutely. And if he asks if you talked to me, tell him no. End of story."

"Got it. And thanks for letting me know."

Pressing End Call, Roddy realizes Cellini doesn't care or didn't believe him when Roddy disparaged Dan's accounting prowess. He wants a money guy he can manipulate and control, a guy who'll do his bidding. Another puppet. He wants a mob accountant, someone who can wash money.

Either cooperate, or he'll go to the Brunetti family.

If Dan meets with Cellini, he'll bring up Gargano, and Danny will fold like a cheap tent.

And it doesn't matter whether Cellini believes he and Danny had anything to do with Gargano's disappearance. The only thing that counts for Cellini is the leverage he has over them.

And there's no doubt once Dan realizes he's trapped in a criminal scheme, he'll go Woody Allen, launch into a panic attack. The first thing he'll do is telephone Roddy and beg for more Xanax.

Then there are a couple of probable scenarios.

Scenario one: he freaks out, falls prey to that strict conscience of his, and runs to the police. In a state of mind-numbing panic, he tells them about Cellini's threat. And then, as always, one thing leads to another—that inexorable chain of events runs its course. Before the dust settles, Dan spills it all, and the Snapper Pond fiasco's in the open, rotting corpses and all.

And the flies swarming over what's left of the bodies will be cops. They'll dredge the pond and find the .45 pistol and Grange's star sapphire ring. They'll do DNA testing on the remains or whatever it takes, and before long, the whole seedy saga's out in the open. Then the wheels of justice begin spinning, and he and Dan are on the receiving end of murder one charges.

Premeditated murder.

Life in some hellhole prison with no possibility of parole.

Scenario two: bursting with anxiety, half out of his mind, Dan needs to talk to someone—he'll be so panicked he won't be thinking straight—so he'll unburden himself to a priest, or more likely, he'll sit Angela down and tell her the entire story beginning with Kenny Egan and ending with Grange and Kenny in a hole. And before long, the whole dismal chain of events unfolds.

Angela's so distressed she calls Tracy. They speak on the phone nearly every day as it is, and there's hardly a thing they don't share. Angela tells Tracy exactly what went down.

Putting it all together, Tracy realizes Tom's accident wasn't so accidental. She reasons—correctly, because she's as sharp as a well-honed straight razor—it was mob-related, that it all goes back to McLaughlin's and Kenny's disappearances. She recalls Roddy had told her the mob was coming after Kenny because he had unpaid gambling debts.

But she realizes that was all bullshit.

Tracy realizes Roddy's done nothing more than cobble together an intricate pack of lies. And it dawns on her that everything she's noticed about Roddy over the last year-plus—his preoccupation, his silence, his distance—all goes back to his having killed Kenny Egan and that mobster Grange.

Yes, it all funnels down to that step-by-step scenario of extortion, murder, and cover-up; and above all, Tracy knows her husband—that upstanding physician and pillar of the community, a guy with a checkered past who presumably buried all his dragons long ago—is nothing more than a murderer.

So this is why you had me and the kids stay in Nutley with Colleen. You thought mobsters were coming for you.

That man who came to the house and kissed Sandy was the loan shark who was extorting you?

And you and Danny killed him?

Oh my God, I married a monster.

And that's the end of their marriage.

It's the end of his life.

There's barely any time left to avert the disaster heading his way. If he knows Dan, he'll be too squeamish to cancel or postpone that meeting. Cellini will have Danny hanging on those marionette strings.

And the door's closing. It'll slam shut the moment Cellini and Vinzy meet with Danny—November twenty-ninth.

He's got to figure something out before then—crystallize a plan of action—come up with a way to short-circuit the fallout if Danny doesn't have the heart to postpone the meeting.

November twenty-ninth. Less than two weeks away.

The countdown goes on.

Chapter 26

An hour after Dan's call, Roddy is still trying to formulate a solid plan from the torrent of thoughts raging through his mind. Nothing definite or doable comes to him.

It's November eighteenth, so he has only ten days to come up with something before it all goes belly-up.

Thinking of the date, he realizes he'd forgotten completely about Thanksgiving. The fourth Thursday of November, each year, every year. This year it's on the twenty-fourth.

What's gonna happen this year?

He can't imagine spending the holiday apart from Tracy and the kids. It would be the first time he's not been with Tracy on Thanksgiving Day since they met. Once they were married, it became a standing tradition: Tracy and her sister, Colleen, would alternate hosting a huge dinner with the entire McDonald family—aunts, uncles, cousins, everyone. The women would all contribute, each bringing something special to the feast.

When he was a kid, the only Thanksgivings Roddy ever celebrated were those at Danny's house: Danny, his ma, Peggy, and Roddy. Just the three of them.

But for the last fifteen years, it's been Thanksgiving with the McDonald clan.

It's a beautiful celebration, with three generations gathered around two exquisitely set tables—the adults seated in the dining room, while the kids' table is set up in the family room. Roddy remembers the last dinner at Colleen's, before the McLaughlin's troubles had begun. The biggest problem facing him back then was dealing with Tom's whining that he no longer belonged at the kids' table.

He pictures himself standing in the kitchen, knife in hand, about to carve into a magnificently burnished turkey. The aroma seeps into his nostrils. He can hear Colleen's ex-husband, Gene, recounting the story he tells about the time, years ago, when he mercilessly hacked up the Thanksgiving bird as his wife watched him mutilate her perfectly roasted turkey. Halfway through the massacre, she grabbed the knife and called for Roddy, the surgeon. The story's become part of the family legend.

There's so much about this holiday Roddy loves: the banter, the laughter, wondering who Tracy and Colleen's bachelor brother, Greg, will be bringing to the feast this year. And, of course, there are the debates about sports and politics—sometimes veering toward no-holds-barred arguments—but the veneer of holiday conviviality covers over the petty jealousies, gripes, and minifeuds that simmer in every family.

It's a family day, with all its complications, served up with an abundance of delicious food.

Yes, some years the bird's a tad dry, and occasionally by the time desserts are served, there've been a few heated discussions, but it's a near-perfect holiday.

But what will it be like for him this year?

It's feels so familiar, yet it seems distant, out of reach. The thought of spending the holiday without Tracy and the kids sends a soul-crushing wave of sadness over him. Thanksgiving probably won't happen for him this year.

But at least Tom's alive and healing.

The cell phone sounds once again.

He closes his eyes, not wanting to look at the screen. He'll let it go to voice mail.

But he can't ignore it. A patient might be in trouble.

A glance at the readout.

It's Vinzy.

Roddy feels a momentary flush in his face.

Crunch time.

"Roddy, we got word on that patient. He's going in on November thirtieth. That's the Wednesday after Thanksgiving."

The day after Vinzy and Cellini meet with Danny.

"Vinzy, I need to talk with you about medication."

"I'm real busy these days, but lemme see . . ."

"You gotta make time for me."

Vinzy's at his desk; the sound of him flipping papers comes through the earpiece.

"Okay," Vinzy says. "I'll be at the office until eight o'clock, maybe eight thirty in the evening on the twenty-eighth. Gotta go over my books."

The day before he and Cellini meet with Danny.

"Fine, how about nine o'clock?" Roddy asks.

"Sounds good."

"I know an Italian place in Pelham; it's called Rocco's. The food's as good as Geppetto's. Let's meet at the bar at nine. They play music, so we can talk and no one'll hear a thing."

"Rocco's in Pelham? Sounds good."

"But listen, I don't want anyone associating me with your people, so don't write my name in your schedule. Just write in Rocco's. Okay?"

"No problem. Rocco's in Pelham. Nine o'clock, the twenty-eighth," Vinzy says. "And the meal's on me."

He's saying nothing about meeting with Danny the next day.

Roddy presses End Call knowing he has until November twenty-eighth; the plan's got to be set before Vinzy and Cellini latch on to Danny like leeches sucking blood.

I've got less than two weeks left, but maybe that's a gift, not a challenge.

It's all a matter of how you look at things. You're not being forced to execute a strategy overnight.

Now he's got to hope Vinzy will be alone.

And Roddy knows he can't trust that weasel.

Chapter 27

It's Thursday, November twenty-fourth, Thanksgiving Day. Tom's been out of the hospital for a few days.

Roddy's sitting with Tracy and the kids at the dining room table in their house on Clubway. The meeting with Vinzy is only four days away. It's five days before Cellini and Vinzy visit Danny. And six days before Roddy's expected to do the unthinkable.

Something more than a vague notion of a plan has begun taking shape, but the details are far from crystallized. Like he was taught in the boxing ring and later at ranger training, strategy requires knowing your opponent's vulnerabilities and targeting your attack at that weak underbelly.

He's been so preoccupied, he's scarcely done more over the last few days than grab a bite to eat. He hasn't shaved for three days. He showers each morning, and that time beneath the water stream has been where his most fertile ideas have taken shape. He simply lets his thoughts wander from one thing to another and who knows what will come?

The only place he's not fixated on formulating a game plan is in the OR. The surgery takes over, consuming him. Even when he gets a few hours of sleep, the dreams he can recall orbit around his Cellini problem.

But he's got the first step mapped out.

He knows Vinzy, including his weaknesses. People are creatures of habit, and they seldom change.

Be confident and trust your instincts about Vinzy. You've known him a hell of a long time.

Roddy forces his mind back into the moment.

He was overjoyed when Tracy asked him to come for Thanksgiving dinner. It sounded like she genuinely wanted him to be there, and not just for the sake of the kids.

Put the Cellini mess to rest. Savor every moment of this time together with the family.

The table is set beautifully with the bone china they'd purchased place setting by place setting, beginning a few years after they were married. They'd gone to Bloomingdale's in White Plains when they'd saved enough to afford to add another set.

The sterling-silver flatware gleams beneath the soft dining room light.

The Waterford crystal wine and water glasses reflect light from the crystal chandelier, casting prismatic patterns in random designs throughout the dining room.

Artfully set in runner fashion is an array of brilliantly colored silk autumn leaves, minipumpkins, multicolored gourds, and a few lit votive candles.

After all Tracy's just been through with Tom, creating a table like this takes extraordinary effort. All the kids care about is the food. Is it possible she went through all this trouble because I'm here?

The turkey is large enough to feed ten people, so there will be leftovers, just as there always have been. *Will I end up taking some back to that lousy apartment, or will she ask me to stay here and share them?* Roddy separates the thighs at the joints and carves the breast meat with surgical precision.

Tracy is blindingly beautiful. He can't keep his eyes off her. She wears her hair in an up-do, which looks ravishing, sophisticated. The room's lighting reflects off her hair, emphasizing its luster. And her milk white skin always reminds him of porcelain.

Looking at her now, he realizes he could never have *not* loved her. There was no way he could have gazed at that face and felt her nearness that day in the library and not been smitten.

He smiles at her, hoping she notices. He wants her to see the love he has for her etched on his face. A hint of a smile flashes on her lips, and she closes her eyes. Yes, she noticed. Since Tom's injury, she's softened her stance toward him. Her icy tone has mellowed, virtually disappearing.

And when she said she wanted to celebrate the holiday as a family—just the four of them at home, together, that she didn't want to go to Nutley this year—it moved his heart in a way so profound, he relives that moment again and again.

There's hope for their future, a chance they may be able to work things out.

Or is it just wishful thinking?

Tom is less surly than usual. In fact, he's not churlish at all. He's less taciturn, more caring. Maybe things are changing with him. A serious injury can do that. Except for a few complaints of rib pain, he's doing superbly, healing as only the young can.

Roddy's often wondered about himself and Tom. Some fathers seem to know what to say to an adolescent son—they find the right words, the right tone, so they can give advice without sounding preachy—but Roddy's never sure he does it well. He's never quite certain how Tom feels about him.

But the kid's words in the hospital reassure Roddy that he's been doing the right thing. Of course, you never know.

Sandy studies his technique as he carves the bird. Smiling, she looks at him with those eyes, so cobalt blue and untainted by cynicism—that'll come later when she's seen more, lived more of life—and it's obvious she adores him. She asks questions about being a surgeon. Her curiosity about things medical is bottomless. But when she asks, "How do you put people to sleep?" everyone but Roddy laughs.

An image of Edmund Merko streaks through his mind.

He shunts it aside, focusing on the pleasure of family.

Never has turkey been so succulent, and he can't recall sweet potato casserole this delicious—he detects cinnamon and brown sugar, and the marshmallow and pecan topping makes it taste like candy. Tracy's stuffing is homemade—filled with apple, cranberry, and pecans; it's a delight to the palate.

A delicate Cabernet enhances the flavor of the turkey and feels velvety on his tongue. Tracy knows wines well, especially after having taken a ten-week cooking course at the Peter Kump's Cooking School years ago. At one point Tracy raises her glass in a toast to "our family," heightening Roddy's hope that she'll welcome him back home.

If only he could slow these moments down, savor them, let them linger for a very long time.

After dinner they sit around the table and talk. Surprisingly, Tom doesn't pick himself up and head upstairs to his room to listen to ear-bleedingly loud music or play some global empire video game. He stays at the table and talks—about school, his friends, and his hopes to try out for the baseball team when high school begins next year. That's a sea of change from his usual naysaying about school and his refusal to discuss anything in his life.

Sandy's her usual vivacious self, and Tracy looks at Roddy with warmth in her eyes.

Roddy wishes this November afternoon could last forever; he hopes the evening won't come—that he won't have to retrieve his coat, say goodbye, kiss Sandy and hear her whine, "When are you coming home, Daddy?" It's her mantra.

If only he could stay with these three people and never be separated from them again—it's a longing so powerful it fills him with an ache.

Suddenly, the strangest thing happens.

A votive candle flickers and dies.

Roddy knows it's weird because there was no draft, no sudden gust of air, and the candle is only half-burned down.

"How strange," Tracy murmurs. She heads for the kitchen.

Roddy stares at the thread of smoke rising from the candle's wick.

Two images come to him in rapid succession: the stacks of votive candles he saw at St. Joseph's, along with memories of being with Danny as boys at church on Sundays; this is followed by the thought of Danny having wanted to go to church to confess their crimes at Snapper Pond to a priest.

Confess to a priest back then, or run to the police now.

If Danny's meeting with Vinzy and Cellini takes place on Tuesday, Roddy's certain Dan will panic.

Roddy's dark reverie ends when Tracy returns from the kitchen holding a butane-filled utility lighter, the one he's used countless times to light a fire in their stone-faced fireplace.

She holds the tip to the candle wick and snaps the trigger, but no flame appears.

Another snap. And another.

Still no flame.

"Roddy, you try it." She hands him the lighter.

He presses the trigger. It makes a clicking sound. A small flame appears at the tip—purple at its base, orange at the tip.

He lights the candle wick. A small white light flickers at the wick's end, and the flame dances. It reminds him of the votive candles at St. Andrew's back in Brooklyn.

And then it comes to him.

An idea.

It's as though a connection in his brain completes itself in an electrical arc and forms a circuit.

A plan.

Because of a utility lighter and a votive candle.

And a small flame to light that candle.

A plan had been taking shape beyond his awareness; after all, why had he thought of wanting to meet with Vinzy?

Seeing that lighter and the candle lit more than a flame.

It ignited a plan.

Today is Thursday, November twenty-fourth, Thanksgiving Day.

The meeting with Vinzy is on Monday evening, the twenty-eighth.

He has three days to do the groundwork.

It means taking a day off from the office and hospital, but that can't be helped. His partners can cover for him.

Three full days. Ample time, but there's no room for miscalculation.

The plan may not work. In fact, there's a big chance it will fail. Miserably.

Because disaster can lurk around any corner.

It's like doing surgery. You open a patient's belly using all your hard-won skills and experience, and you do it under the most controlled conditions possible: bright lights, aseptic technique, and sophisticated instruments, along with the most capable and highly trained people. You do your best to minimize happenstance or the random and unpredictable event.

But nothing's guaranteed. You can be resecting a cancerous segment of colon or removing a gallbladder or lysing adhesions, and suddenly there's a bleeder—an artery pops open and begins spurting blood all over the operating field, or the patient goes into cardiac arrest, or the blood pressure drops to a dizzyingly low level—and in that unforeseen moment, a routine surgery becomes a frantic attempt to save a life.

So with this plan—as rudimentary as it is— anything can go wrong. He could die or end up in prison.

But there's no choice.

Success depends partly on his ability to think things through—carefully, meticulously—to plot it out precisely and to account for a host of possible glitches. The way Tracy would plan something.

But any plan—and certainly one as dicey as this—depends partly on luck.

Variables: traffic, weather, time of day, whether a streetlight works, a passerby walking down a street, a surveillance camera, someone at a window who sees something, a police car cruising by; it can be anything—however small or seemingly inconsequential—that may determine the outcome.

His plan may fail—it very likely *will* fail—but it's got a chance to succeed, albeit a slim one.

And how does he define success?

Roddy's main objective is to keep his family and Danny's safe, permanently.

Like all soldiers, his life is expendable.

He must come to terms with the likelihood he'll die.

Thoughts of returning home and being with his family are no more than wishful thinking, not just because what's happened between him and Tracy can't be erased or easily forgotten, but it's more likely he won't live much longer anyway.

That's because of the mistakes he's made since Snapper Pond.

There's no one else to blame but himself.

One thing is certain: his mission is clearly defined.

There are three days to get everything in place, and then the plan must be executed. Forcefully.

Sergeant Dawson always said a battle plan must be carried out with precision, without remorse, with intent to demolish the enemy and to survive.

But this is no training maneuver in the swamps or forests of the Carolinas. And he's no longer an army ranger with the power and force of the US military behind him. He's a middle-aged, suburban surgeon planning to take on the mob, alone.

Danny's question asked on their ride home from Snapper Pond that dark night comes to mind. "Do you believe in God, Roddy?"

He still can't answer it, but he hears himself silently praying to God-knows-who that he'll succeed and that it will be done with the full force of righteousness—and not with the dark heart of vengeance.

Chapter 28

It's nearly nine p.m. The kids are upstairs in their rooms. Roddy and Tracy sit on the love seat in the den. They've been talking for a while now, mostly about the everyday things they used to share in this very room.

Tracy's planning to head to the Westchester Mall tomorrow, joining the throngs of Black Friday shoppers hunting for Christmas gifts. She asks his opinion about what to get for the kids, just like she would have done back when he called this house his home.

It all seems so normal, so comfortable, but Roddy's all too aware it's getting late and soon he'll have to leave.

"Tomorrow, after I get back from the mall, the kids and I are going to Nutley for the rest of the weekend," Tracy says. "This was the first Thanksgiving dinner we've had in years where I haven't been with Colleen and the family. We'll be back on Sunday evening."

"Say hello to everyone for me," he whispers through a clogged throat.

She nods and then brushes a strand of hair away from her face. He's amazed at the depth of her green eyes.

Then she says, "It was so strange, Roddy. When you rang the doorbell this afternoon, it was like you didn't live here."

Tracy's words strike him as ironic. She's bringing up his arrival when he's dreading his imminent departure.

"I *don't* live here anymore," he answers as darkness overtakes him.

"It's still your home," she says. The softness of her tone fills him with hope.

"And Tom and Sandy will always be our kids," she continues in a voice so tender he feels an ache deep in his heart.

Her reference to the kids begins to erode the optimism he was starting to feel. Too many friends have told him how they and their exes try to maintain cordial relationships "for the good of the kids."

Is this what Tracy's trying to say?

We need to stay friendly for Tom's and Sandy's sakes?

"Roddy, what I mean is this," she says, touching his arm. "We've just been through a terrible time with Tom." Her eyes grow wet. "It's the worst thing that ever happened to us, and I don't know if I could have gotten through it without you. The truth is, you held me together that first night at the hospital, and your love for Tom—for all of us—was so strong. Today, on this holiday, I'm so thankful Tom's okay and that you're here for us. I'm thankful for everything good in our lives."

He takes Tracy's hand in his. He's about to speak when she places a finger on his lips to silence him.

"Let me finish," she says in a near whisper.

"I've always loved you. That's never been my problem with us. And, yes, I wasn't sure you still had those same feelings for me, especially lately, when you'd been so distant.

"But, Roddy, I lost my trust in you, just like it seems you lost yours in me. How else can I understand whatever you've been keeping from me? To this day, there are things you haven't been willing to share. I said it before when I asked you to leave: I can't live my life with someone who's secretive . . . who won't let me into his world."

The cost of my secrets is too much to bear.

"That's not who you were when we got married," she says as tears well in her eyes. "And that's not who you were before that restaurant failed. But since then, Roddy, you've shut me out. And it was getting to be more and more obvious to me that something's wrong. And I don't know what it is." She sighs. "What I want to say is this: the decision about whether we stay together or not is really up to you."

Tracy pauses, but it's clear she's going to say more.

"If you decide to come home, from now on there can be no more lies." She shakes her head. "I've given this so much thought, especially all those nights when I stayed with Tom in the hospital. I'm willing to put every doubt about you to rest, and I won't ask you ever again to explain what's happened over the past year and a half. That's all water under the bridge. So long as there are no more secrets or lies, we can try to make it work. Maybe Tom's accident brought everything into sharper focus for me." She pauses, inhales deeply, and says, "I'm willing to try again if you are."

He nods and is about to respond when she holds up her hand.

"Give it serious thought, but please, Roddy, don't answer now. Go back to the apartment and decide what's best for you . . . for both of us."

What's happened is water under the bridge. So long as there are no more secrets and lies . . .

"You already know my answer."

"Please, I want you to think about it," she says. "We'll be back late Sunday night, and the kids have school on Monday, so Sunday night won't be a good time to talk. When you've decided what you want to do, we can talk more about it, but I don't want the kids around when we do. Why not come over on Monday night after they're asleep—around eleven? We can talk then."

Monday night. After I've done what I must do.

"I'll be here," she says. "Just let yourself in. You have the key."

Chapter 29

Danny's always loved the center-hall Colonial on Maple Street. It's unpretentious, not a McMansion, one of those statement-making behemoths popping up on every available bit of acreage in the suburbs.

Tuckahoe's a stable community, and until the last year or so, he, Angie, and the kids had an uneventful and predictable life. Before it all went excremental.

But things are turning around now that Snapper Pond's gonna stay untouched.

It's Friday, the day after Thanksgiving. He enters the house through the back door, having stuffed the trash in the outside bin.

Tons of leftovers. It'll be turkey tetrazzini and turkey sandwiches for the next two or three days. And knowing Angie, she'll use the carcass for turkey stock.

The TV is on in the den—Angela's watching the six-thirty news.

"I've got good news, honey," she calls.

As he enters the room, she hits the remote and the screen goes black.

"I just got off the phone with Tracy. She and Roddy are talking about getting back together."

Dan sits on the sofa facing her. "That *is* good news. Maybe he'll have some peace of mind."

"And maybe you can stop worrying about him."

"Speaking of Roddy," Dan says, "I'm worried about something else. He told me he had dinner with a medical school friend a few weeks back. This guy, Dr. Vincent Masconi, called and said Roddy referred him to me to do his taxes. When I called Roddy to thank him, he said he never referred the guy and told me not to take him on as a client. He said this Masconi guy runs a crooked Medicaid mill in the Bronx."

"Why would this Dr. Masconi call you if Roddy didn't refer him?"

"I have no idea. It's strange."

"How would he know to call if Roddy hadn't given him your name?"

"Roddy said the guy remembered me from years ago."

"And how does Roddy know this doctor is crooked?"

"He said he'd been to Masconi's clinic. The place overflows with patients."

"That's no basis to come to that kind of conclusion. Any clinic is busy, Daniel, especially one in the Bronx, where there're so many poor people." Angela leans forward and adds, "You know what? I think both you guys have a very stereotyped view of Italians. A lot of people do. They assume that because you're Italian, you're connected to some crime family. I don't think you'd like it if people thought all Irish were mobsters. Would you?"

"Of course not."

"Did Roddy offer any proof?"

"Nothing tangible. He said the guy does false billing. Probably tax evasion, too." Dan inhales deeply and peers at Angela.

"It's just supposition. Don't you think you ought to make that determination yourself?"

"I guess so. I have a meeting scheduled this coming Tuesday, the twenty-ninth. Roddy told me to postpone it for a few weeks and the guy'll go away. I'm up in the air about it. Should I meet with the guy and see what gives?"

Angela gets up from the Eames chair and sits beside him on the sofa. "You know what, Daniel? I think you depend way too much on Roddy. It's like, in your eyes, he can do no wrong."

"Oh, c'mon, Angie. That's not fair."

"I'm only saying what's true, and by now you ought to know it. And furthermore, if this Vincent Masconi is such a crooked Italian, what was Roddy doing having dinner with him?"

Dan shrugs. "So, you don't think I should put him off?"

"Not for a second. You *definitely* should meet with Dr. Masconi. I think you'll know very quickly if his business dealings are on the up-and-up. Roddy doesn't know a thing about financial issues. That's *your* area of expertise."

She looks deeply into his eyes. "Above all, Daniel, I think you've got to wean yourself away from always taking Roddy's advice."

"I don't *always* take his advice. He came to me to ask about going into the McLaughlin's thing."

"*Forget* McLaughlin's. You're way *past* that deal. Listen, Daniel, Roddy's not in your league when it comes to financial matters. *You're* the expert."

She grabs his hand and says, "Dan . . . look at me."

He looks into her dark brown eyes and knows she's speaking the truth.

"You've got to trust your own financial savvy. Roddy's a physician, not an accountant or financial adviser. You're smart and knowledgeable."

She pauses and strokes the back of his hand.

"Above all, you've got to be your own man. You meet with Dr. Masconi and see what he has to say."

Chapter 30

It's five fifteen on Monday morning, November twenty-eighth. The day of reckoning. The day Roddy puts his plan into motion.

His body feels heavy, as though his chest is lined with lead. All night he'd tossed in bed, desperate for sleep, which never pulled him under. Each time he began drifting off, a jagged dream—or maybe a half-formed thought—jangled him awake, and he lay there unsettled, vaguely recalling visions of brawls and blood.

Wide-awake, he lay there as a thousand thoughts careened through his brain. He'd kept his eyes closed and, in the crushing quiet of the night, heard his heartbeat through the pillow. His mind churned with images of that back room at Geppetto's and repeated scenarios of the plan. No matter how meticulous he's been in its preparation, there are so many ways it could go belly-up and he'll be killed, or worse, could end up rotting in prison.

During the night, when he didn't feel disoriented, he glanced at the bedside clock and watched the digital readout: 4:00, 4:14, 5:15. He's lucky if he got two hours of sleep.

Getting out of bed is like pulling himself out of a bog. Moving sluggishly, he feels stiff; he knows his muscles were taut during the night and now ache. Even worse, though he had no alcohol last night, he feels hungover—groggy.

He totters to the bathroom, bends over the sink, splashes water on his face, and rubs his eyes, feeling depleted. Looking in the mirror, he sees a face he barely recognizes—it's gaunt-looking and pale, with dark bluish rings beneath his eyes. A seven-day growth of beard gives him a vagrant's look—a step beyond the point when a few days ago Claire Copen, seeing his three-day look, said, "Roddy, you look like a contestant on *Survivor*."

He knows he's gotta refresh himself, so he jumps in the shower—tries rinsing away the fatigue, maybe kick-start some adrenaline to ready him for what must be done.

And what must be done will be ugly.

If he were Danny, he'd begin whispering the Act of Contrition. *"Bless me, O Lord, for I have sinned. I am heartily sorry for having offended Thee . . ."*

But prayer and incantations never made much sense to Roddy. Nor did they resolve a thing on this earth. And he must end this nightmare—if he can—and to do that, he must be relentless.

With the water temperature adjusted, he expects the soothing feel of hot water sloshing over him to form a wet wrap, a blanket of warmth to loosen his taut muscles. But the pressure's too high: the spray feels like needles pricking him. He lowers the pressure, but his skin stings beneath the pulsing stream; the water feels too hot, no matter how he adjusts the lever.

It's not the shower; it's him. He's in a state of heightened awareness, his nervous system is on alert, totally amped, and every nerve in his body is firing impulses.

Pure anticipation: he's primed.

After dressing, he makes his way to the open kitchenette. Peering out the window, he sees only darkness and hears wind streaking along the building's outer wall. It's an eerie harbinger of the unknown. Fronds of frost form a lacework on the window.

He'd watched the Weather Channel last night: it'll be a cold, windy, dreary day. The winds will be coming from the north with strong gusts up to thirty miles an hour. They won't die down this evening, and the temperature tonight will drop to the teens.

A good thing for what he intends to do.

The apartment feels unfamiliar—more so than when he first moved in—and has been this way since he spent Thanksgiving Day with the family. He knows Tracy and the kids are back home from Nutley, and it won't be long before the house is busy with the usual weekday-morning activities: the kids getting ready for school, Tracy preparing to drive to the library.

He imagines her wondering how tonight's discussion will go. He hopes she's thinking about it. His musings about Tracy propel his thoughts forward and back almost simultaneously—thinking of home for one moment, what he's about to do, the next.

Will there be a discussion with Tracy tonight? There's the real possibility he won't show up at their house.

He may be dead or arrested.

The thought reminds him of what he did early in the morning two mornings ago, on Saturday.

He wrote a longhand three-page letter to Tracy. He detailed the entire chain of events, beginning with Kenny and Grange's extortion plot, his drugging Grange, the night at Snapper Pond, and now, the developments with Cellini and Vinzy. He laid out the whole ugly story, leaving out only one thing: he never mentioned Danny having a thing to do with Snapper Pond and the killings. He described having done it alone.

If he dies, he wants Tracy to understand exactly why he'd been so troubled since the restaurant went under. Why he hadn't been his old self. No more secrets. Then she'll understand why it seemed he'd changed.

He thinks back to what he did on Saturday. That morning he went to the Chase Bank on Palmer Avenue. There he removed a wad of cash from the safe-deposit box and put the letter into the box, knowing Tracy would find it after his death.

At least she'll know I never stopped loving her. She'll understand everything. And she'll know my life became a lie so she and the kids could go on with theirs.

His thoughts return to what awaits him today and tonight.

Ivan and their junior partner Dave are covering for him today, so he won't have to worry about work.

His day is planned. And the night, too. He rethinks his itinerary and each phase of the strategy he's devised.

On Saturday, after leaving the bank in Bronxville, he made a dry-run trip down to the Bronx. He went to Arthur Avenue and the surrounding area, where he scoped out every detail of his plan. He walked it through each step of the way. He was meticulous, as if he were doing complicated surgery on a sick patient, on someone like Edmond Merko.

Now, he puts on the clothes he'll wear today—jeans, a heavy sweatshirt over a T-shirt, thick woolen athletic socks, and his walking shoes.

With time to kill, he considers turning on the TV, decides not to, and then changes his mind.

He grabs the remote, turns on the set, and starts surfing channels—but he's too wired to pay attention.

The television is no more than distant static as his thoughts stream through the plan he's concocted.

Though he has no appetite, he decides he must eat something, so he downs a piece of rye toast—it's tasteless and dry and could be sawdust. He drinks two cups of instant black coffee even though he feels queasy.

Time slips away in a farrago of tumbling thoughts, one after another, spilling through his mind. Amid these ramblings, a glance at the clock says it's getting near the time to leave.

The cold morning is a variable in his favor. He dresses warmly. He slips into a heavy overcoat he bought at a thrift shop in White Plains—for cash. No receipt. No record of purchase. No paper trail. Nothing. He has a New York Mets baseball cap he bought for cash at the Galleria, an indoor shopping mall in White Plains. He'll wear it today.

He takes out his cell phone and makes certain it's turned on, though from what he understands about cell phones, it's not necessary to have it turned on, so long as the battery's intact.

All five bars are visible—it's hooked into the telephone company's 4G network and it'll receive any incoming calls; they'll go to voice mail. He sets the phone on the kitchen counter. It'll sit there all day and into the night. If anyone asks, he simply forgot to bring it with him. It stayed in the apartment.

He must be invisible, staying out of touch. All day and into the night.

No way will the cell phone be used to track his location anywhere today or tonight. He'll be off the grid.

He's read about the police being able to track your whereabouts by following phone signals—pinging cell towers, triangulation or whatever it's called. With today's technology and GPS capabilities, there's a digital trail—a traceable record—of where you've been and whom you've contacted. It's all recorded and available through the cell phone provider. And the police can subpoena the company's records.

Siri and her satellite sisters can betray you.

No one's out of touch or untraceable anymore.

Walk around with a cell phone in your pocket and you're toast.

Thinking about his conversation with Ivan Snyder some months earlier, Roddy's glad he turned down the navigation feature option when he bought the Nissan Rogue. Ivan had purchased a Buick, which had come with the free OnStar feature during the first year of ownership. "Don't make the mistake I did, Roddy," he said. "If you buy a GM car, tell them you want OnStar disabled. That little device is part of a satellite-based GPS system. I couldn't believe it when only a few months after I bought the car, I got an e-mail telling me the oil was starting to get low. I called the dealership, and they told me that every damned function of the vehicle's monitored by an internal computer—and that includes the miles driven and the locations I drove to. It's all transmitted by OnStar or through Wi-Fi hotspots wherever you drive.

"Like it or not, when you're driving around, every movement can be tracked and logged by someone, somewhere. I'm telling you, Roddy, Big Brother's watching. You might as well have a camcorder videotaping every trip you take from the second you get in the car. You can't be invisible these days. Oh, and another thing . . . don't give the dealer your e-mail address. I'm bombarded with e-mails all the time. It's a pain in the ass."

He told Ivan and Dave he's taking the day off to try to terminate his apartment lease and return his rented furniture. And he mentioned having a hundred other things he must do, some related to Tom's hospitalization. They'd never question him about so serious a matter.

With that vague alibi in mind, he picks up the cell phone, calls the Regency's rental office—it's far too early for them to be open—and when the voice mail's outgoing message ends, he leaves a message saying he's coming in to discuss an arrangement for his lease.

Though he won't show up at the rental office, it bolsters the story he told his partners. If anyone at the rental office asks why he didn't show up, he'll say he came down with a headache and didn't feel up to doing it, a vague explanation that can't be disproven or refuted.

And his cell phone will have been in the apartment all day.

A glance at the clock. It's time to go.

He recalls when he first went to Charlie's store on Arthur Avenue to buy a pistol nearly a year and a half ago. At that time, Vinzy had told him the cheese store was a husband-and-wife setup.

"Charlie doesn't like doing gun business when his wife's working the front of the store," Vinzy said. "Your best bet is to go there on a weekday morning between eight and nine, when his wife goes to Mass at Our Lady of Mount Carmel Church. Afterward, she stops at Egidio's Pastry Shop across from the church to buy biscotti and espresso to take back to the store."

Though he didn't follow those instructions when he first went to the cheese store, he'll do so now and get there a little bit after eight a.m. to make sure Charlie's alone. Complete secrecy.

Will Charlie sell him a piece this time? Why wouldn't he? Will he recognize Roddy? It's unlikely. Wearing a baseball cap, sporting a seven-day growth of beard and a mustache, and wearing weak magnification reading glasses, he'd never be recognized as the guy Charlie saw briefly nearly eighteen months ago.

Roddy takes the elevator to the Regency's basement-level garage, gets in the car, and sits behind the wheel. He recalls the day he drove to Manhattan to meet with Danny, Kenny, and Grange in the back room of McLaughlin's—where he drugged that fat slob Grange—a day that ended with a nighttime trip to Snapper Pond.

Closing his eyes, he thinks about what he'll do later this evening. A chill overtakes him, and a tide of nausea threatens to overwhelm him, so he thinks of Sergeant Dawson's words during ranger training.

You take the fight to the enemy and show no mercy.

He has no equipment, just the heavy overcoat, baseball cap, and the nonprescription reading glasses—half-diopter magnification—he bought at the CVS store on New Rochelle Road in Bronxville. Another cash purchase.

His New Balance leather walking shoes are well cushioned, comfortable, and thick-soled—perfect for what he'll be doing today and tonight.

At six thirty in the morning, traffic in the southbound direction of the Bronx River Parkway is heavy, but it's moving steadily at a moderate pace. It seems to Roddy that rush hour begins earlier and earlier each year. The world is getting crazier, he thinks. Streams of headlights and taillights make the parkway look surreal in the wintery darkness. Did he leave early enough to get to Arthur Avenue in time? It's very early—looks like the middle of the night—so it should be smooth sailing.

But traffic suddenly comes to a halt; then it's stop and go.

He slips into the left lane.

A half mile later everything stops again.

Ten minutes later he hasn't moved a single car length.

He grips the steering wheel tightly, worrying he won't get to the Bronx in time. If he's late, the plan will go belly-up.

Twenty minutes later, he's progressed maybe a quarter of a mile. It's mass inertia, as the lines of cars moving south move sluggishly, a few feet at a time. There's gotta be an accident farther down the highway. Tautness builds in his arms. Sweat prickles on his forehead. Exhaust fumes hang heavily in the morning darkness, backlit by headlights from cars traveling in the northbound direction.

Ahead, a string of taillights looks eerie in the cold night air.

He turns on the radio. It's 1010 WINS, all news, all the time, but he barely hears the announcer—there's something about the consumer price index and unemployment statistics. The financial news is followed by an ad for P.C. Richard & Son; it booms through the speaker, grating on his ears. The ad says something about Christmas shopping, which makes him think of Tracy.

Roddy snaps the dial, turning the radio off.

He waits behind a Hummer, stuck in a traffic clog for what seems like hours. Some drivers have turned off their engines. Christ on a bike, he's trapped in an endless line of idling cars and the torpor of stalled traffic.

A glance at his watch says it's been only twenty-five minutes, but time seems to be running away from him. His thoughts roil about his options should he miss the window of opportunity to get to the cheese store when it's empty and Charlie's wife isn't there.

Nothing comes to him.

A sense of trepidation floods him. His hands ache, so he lets go of the wheel and thinks about turning off the engine. That headache he's fabricated as an alibi threatens to become a reality.

Traffic finally begins moving slothfully. Cars cut in and out and drivers change lanes, trying to make up for lost time, intent on gaining a few feet here and there. Some drivers won't let others cut in front of them.

Horns honk.

Tempers fray.

More horns.

We live in an insane world.

More stop-and-go, bumper-to-bumper traffic, enough to make his temples throb.

Even though he's finally moving, it's very slow. Time passes too quickly. Roddy's left foot taps a tattoo on the floorboard. Maybe it would be best if he gets off at the next exit and forgets the whole thing.

But traffic picks up, moving listlessly at about five to ten miles an hour. If it keeps going at this pace, he'll be okay—he'll get there before the store gets busy.

Farther down the road, he sees it: yes, there was an accident. Two crumpled cars sit on the shoulder of the parkway. Police cars, tow trucks, and an ambulance are clustered nearby—lights flashing and blinking, people rubbernecking.

Traffic congestion and accidents: variables you can never know in advance.

Another mile and traffic thins; he picks up speed.

Finally, he comes to exit 7W, leaves the highway, and drives onto East Fordham Road, heading west. He crosses Crotona Avenue, then Belmont Avenue.

He glances into the rearview mirror and notices a black sedan behind him, a Ford Taurus, darkened windows. He can't make out the driver or occupants. Reminds him of the incident on Pondfield Road. In fact, one of the cars was a Taurus.

Are Cellini's thugs following him?

We know where you live. We know where you work. We know where your wife and kids live. We know where your wife works.

His heart pounds and his hands tighten on the steering wheel. After what happened the night of Merko's surgery, he can't take a chance.

He switches lanes; so does the Taurus.

He pulls out of the right lane and darts ahead.

Another glance in the rearview: the Taurus is behind him.

Seeing a BP service station, he thinks about pulling in and pumping some gas, even though his tank is more than three-quarters full. It's a good diversionary tactic to see if you're being tailed. The Taurus will either pull in after him or keep going and then park somewhere farther down the road and wait for him.

He's about to swerve into the station when it occurs to him: service stations have CCTV cameras. How many times has he watched *Most Shocking Videos* and seen a guy barge into a 7-Eleven outlet or a Chevron station with a gun or a baseball bat? How many times has he seen the recording of a fleeing bank robber pumping gas and then taking off? Not only is the suspect filmed, but the car and license plate are recorded, too.

No, pulling into a service station is a bad idea.

He slows down, peers again into the rearview mirror, and sees the Taurus behind him.

It's gotta be a tail.

He pulls over to the side of the road and parks with his flashers blinking.

In his peripheral vision, he sees the Taurus pass and keep going; it doesn't slow down.

Roddy waits for a few minutes and pulls back into traffic.

There's no Taurus parked anywhere along the road.

His imagination is working overtime.

As daylight breaks, the sky looks bruised by dark clouds.

Roddy turns from East Fordham Road onto Arthur Avenue.

Chapter 31

He drives along Arthur Avenue. It's a congested one-way street, and traffic crawls, so he gazes at the stores lining the avenue.

This early in the morning, very few pedestrians are on the street, but plenty of double-parked trucks clog the road while their drivers haul handcarts laden with deliveries down the cellar steps in front of the retail businesses.

Other than on Saturday, when he made his dry run, it's been several years since he's been to the Belmont section during the daytime. When he went to the cheese store on Vinzy's recommendation a year and a half ago, he barely explored the area.

Now, he sees that Cellini was right: despite a majority of Italian-sounding storefronts, many of the old-timers are gone, replaced by new ones with names like Ivana's Pizza and Beiska Groceries. Definitely not Italian. Farther down the avenue, he sees more of the change: a television store with the sign Kanale Shqiptare and another deli, this one called Kosova.

Are those Albanian-owned businesses? Looks that way.

After this mess with Cellini began, Roddy did some online research. He remembered the advice he'd been given in the army: learn everything you can about your enemy. And learn the terrain. He did a Google search and read about an Albanian crime wave that began some years back. Balkan mobsters rampaged throughout the Bronx and parts of southern Westchester. They took over gambling operations that had been controlled by the Italians. One group even had the balls to claim what had been John Gotti's table at Rao's in Harlem.

The Albanians were so ruthless, the Italians backed off from outright confrontation. It became a simmering stalemate.

He passes Vinzy Masconi's clinic, Carmel Medical Associates. He pictures Vinzy sitting at his desk, burying money and then funneling it to Cellini and wherever it goes from there.

See you tonight, Vinzy, after you're through cooking the books.

Perched on the corner of Arthur Avenue and 186th Street is Teitel Brothers, with its green awning spanning both Arthur Avenue and 186th Street. It's where Tracy and Angela often shop together. A while back Tracy mentioned she'd heard a rumor that the store is no longer in the hands of the Jewish family who'd owned it for years. It's now owned by Albanians.

There's no way he can park on Arthur Avenue. It's choked with cars and trucks. Besides, he doesn't want to be seen anywhere near this area. And there are probably lots of surveillance cameras situated on lampposts and storefronts along this commercial street.

He turns left at 186th Street, drives a short block, and makes another left onto Hughes Avenue.

Halfway down the block on Hughes, he sees a Honda CR-V pull out of a parking space. He maneuvers the Rogue into the empty space. A glance at his watch tells him he made the trip with time to spare and still has a few minutes to kill.

He's parked on a quiet side street in front of a store located in a five-story white brick building. The store's awning reads Cigars. The window advertises it as a cigar lounge. Another sign in the window reads Hecho a Mano. "Handmade," in Spanish.

Latinos have moved into the neighborhood.

And Russians.

And Albanians.

Change always comes to these ethnic enclaves.

It's the city's cycle of life, urban ecology.

At this hour in the morning the cigar store's closed; there won't be many smokers hanging around a stogie lounge.

Roddy kills another ten minutes, pushing thoughts out of his mind about what may happen tonight. He's thought about it and configured a hundred possible scenarios—no time to dwell on it now.

Donning the baseball cap and reading glasses, he gets out of the car.

The air is biting cold. Breath vapor plumes from his mouth and nostrils, getting whipped away by the wind. He raises his collar, thrusts his hands in the overcoat's pockets, and crosses the street. At this hour on a cold morning, Hughes Avenue is virtually deserted. A man stands on a stoop across the street, smoking a cigarette, talking on a cell phone. No one else is on the street.

The wind knifes into his face as Roddy walks toward 186th Street. He passes a three-story red brick apartment building, 2355 Hughes Avenue. As he noticed when he walked past the place on Saturday, the iron gate fronting the building is open. It leads to a breezeway along the side of the structure. Filled trash cans stand inside the gate, no doubt awaiting the arrival of a sanitation truck.

When he turns onto 186th Street, the first storefront he comes upon is Geppetto's. Roddy's heart rate accelerates at the sight of the red awning and that wooden Pinocchio sitting on a ledge inside the front window. Images of Cellini, DiNardo, and Vinzy flood his mind: that back room with thugs at the other tables, the threats, the veal chops, risotto, and wine; and Cellini's grotesque star sapphire ring. And that cigar, the end of it chewed, soggy, and wet with saliva.

His thoughts flash from that night to when he was stopped on Pondfield and then to the image of his son, bruised and broken, in that hospital bed. He shunts the image aside and keeps walking.

Roddy doesn't stop for a second; he's now abreast of Vesa, the Albanian travel agency. An image of Cellini comes to him.

Ten years ago it would've been an Italian agency. Get my drift?

A poster in the window depicts a pastoral scene of forests and mountains. Above the picture on the poster is the word Albania.

The poster triggers the memory of Edmund Merko when they spoke after the mobster's surgery. He seemed like a warm and gracious man.

But don't be fooled. He's a gangster.

The knee surgery is scheduled for Wednesday, the thirtieth, two days from now. Roddy feels a chill run down his spine.

He turns onto Arthur Avenue. Carlo's Latticini is three stores from the corner.

Roddy walks slowly, keeps his overcoat collar raised, and lowers the baseball cap. He saw no surveillance cameras on the street when he was here on Saturday, but there've got to be a few on a commercial avenue like this. There's no sense taking chances.

Cameras are usually inconspicuous, so just assume they're here.

He tucks his head down and holds on to his hat, as though protecting it from the wind.

He stops in front of the store.

It's a big chance, but I gotta get a gun.

He opens the door to the cheese shop.

Please don't let Mrs. Cheese be here. Please make sure she's at church.

A bell located over the door lets out a soft tinkling as he enters the store.

He looks to his right.

He's in luck. No one's behind the counter. The store seems deserted. The wife must be at church.

Now I gotta convince Charlie to sell me a gun. This could be tough.

No sign of a surveillance camera in the store, and why would there be one in a cheese store? But you never know.

He keeps the baseball cap on. The reading glasses are perched low on his nose.

Charlie trundles out of the kitchen, approaching him.

A white apron covers his rotund belly. He wears a white T-shirt from which thick, hairy arms protrude. He wears plastic gloves for making balls of mozzarella. Same bulbous-tipped nose, same closely cropped horseshoe fringe of hair around his otherwise bald scalp, same hangdog look Roddy recalls from when he last saw Charlie. Guy still reminds him of the actor who played Clemenza in *The Godfather.*

"Yes, sir. Can I help you?" Charlie says with a thick accent.

"Dr. Vinzy sent me."

Charlie squints and tilts his head. He obviously doesn't recognize Roddy from the earlier visit. *With glasses, a hat, and heavy stubble on my face, there's no way he'll remember me.*

"Dr. Vincenzo?" Charlie's bushy eyebrows rise in a quizzical look. He moves closer to Roddy and squints, as though examining him, trying to identify a stranger.

"Yes. He said I could buy some protection."

"Protection?" Charlie shakes his head. "Whaddaya talkin' 'bout? Protection? I got cheese, that's all."

Is he saying this because he doesn't know me? And because Vinzy didn't call him first?

"Dr. Vinzy said you could sell me something, not cheese."

Charlie shakes his head again, slowly. Doubt forms on his features; his lips tighten and his chin tilts downward as his eyes narrow again.

This isn't gonna work.

"You know, in the back room, from the safe. That's what Dr. Vinzy said."

"I know you?" Charlie says, ripping off his gloves, tossing them on the counter.

"No, but I know Dr. Vinzy. He said you would have something for me if I came in today."

"Funny. Dr. Vincenzo didn't say nothin' 'bout it. He always gives a call first."

Roddy shrugs. "I guess he forgot."

"He never forgot before."

"And Carmine said I could get something from you."

Charlie's forehead forms a deep V-shaped furrow. A hand goes to his mouth. "Mr. *Cellini* said this?"

"Yes, Carmine Cellini."

"I dunno 'bout that." Charlie's mouth twists, and an eyebrow rises. He looks befuddled.

Roddy can virtually see thoughts tumbling though the man's head.

I shouldn't have mentioned the boss. I'm too eager.

"I'm just telling you what Dr. Vinzy told me."

Charlie squints again. "I don't know nothin' 'bout it."

Roddy grimaces, feigns exasperation, and slaps his hands at his sides.

"And now Mr. Cellini say you should see me?" Charlie's voice virtually shouts skepticism. Mistrust.

"Yes. And I'll pay top dollar—cash—for something good. Fifteen hundred, maybe more for a good piece."

Charlie licks his lips and cants his head. After what seems a long pause during which he thinks, he shrugs. "Okay, mista. Here, you come with me and we'll see what we got."

He wants the money.

He follows Charlie through the same swinging doors as last time, beyond the tiled kitchen to a small rear office where a safe is located.

"Lemme see," Charlie says, squatting and fiddling with the dial on the safe. It's got a combination wheel; it's old-style, not digital. He turns the dial right and left, then right again, and pushes the safe handle down, but the door doesn't open. He mutters something in Italian, shakes his head, says, "I gotta start over," and turns the dial again.

Another full turn, a press of the handle, and the door creaks open.

Charlie stands, slowly slides the cloth-covered tray out from a shelf, and sets it on top of the safe. He pulls the cloth aside. His hand darts to the tray, grabbing a snub-nosed revolver, and he pivots toward Roddy.

A black hole looms in front of Roddy. The pistol points at his chest.

Roddy's blood hums in his ears. His hands go in the air, staying fixed at shoulder height.

Charlie cocks the hammer. His eyes narrow. "What's your name?"

"What're you doing?"

"I dunno you, and if you don't tell me who you are, you gonna get shot."

"I just came to buy protection."

"You gonna need protection, mista, 'cause I'm gonna shoot you dead if you don't tell me what you come here for. I gonna shoot you right now and tell the cops you come here to the backa the store to take the money from my safe."

Roddy peers at the pistol and sees the copper-jacketed bullets sitting in the cylinder. The thing is fully loaded, cocked, ready to fire.

Sergeant Dawson would say, "Always have a plan B, and act decisively." But I don't have a plan B.

And there's a loaded pistol a mere foot from Roddy's chest—pointed at center mass—and no matter what he does, Charlie can pull the trigger faster than Roddy can make a move.

Charlie waves the pistol left and right, keeps it level, pointed at Roddy's heart, and says, "Whadda you, some kinda wiseguy? You come in here to do somethin'? I gonna kill you."

Roddy knows as fast as he is—even though his reflexes are cat-quick—it'll take less time for Charlie to squeeze the trigger than for Roddy to cover the distance between them. And Charlie's zeroed in on him, staring right into his eyes. Roddy doesn't stand a chance.

Suddenly, a musical tone bursts from Charlie's right trouser pocket. He quickly switches the pistol to his left hand; his eyes shift down for a half second, and he reaches beneath the apron and begins extracting the cell phone.

An automatic ranger move.

Roddy's right arm streaks forward, bullet-fast. The knuckles of his clenched fist slam into Charlie's throat. The thyroid and cricoid cartilages crack. A sickening sound.

Charlie's trachea is crushed. His airway no longer works. A sputter of air blasts from his throat, followed by a choked sob. Charlie clutches his throat as his knees buckle; the phone and pistol clunk onto the floor.

He drops to his knees, grasping his throat. A guttural croaking comes from his closed airway and then a fluttering sound. His face reddens and turns purple. No air. His chest heaves. His eyes bulge and turn red. Eyeball capillaries burst.

He topples over, lies on his side, choking, gasping; his chest rises and falls, but there's no air, and his attempts to breathe sound like a ruptured bellows. He gurgles; froth bubbles from his mouth. Honking comes from his chest. His lips turn purple. He's oxygen-deprived, going cyanotic. His legs spasm and his body shakes.

Charlie's revolver lies on the floor next to Roddy's reading glasses. Roddy kicks the pistol away, picks up the glasses, and slips them into his inside coat pocket.

How calm he feels. There's no heavy breathing, no tremulousness. His heart rate is regular and slow, and his hands are steady.

An unexpected turn of events. Never could have predicted this. He doesn't even feel an adrenaline surge.

Looking down at Charlie, he shakes his head. He's just killed a man, but he knows he's done what he had to, and he knows what he must now do.

There are two kinds of soldiers: the quick and the dead.

That was Sergeant Dawson's mantra.

He turns to the tray sitting on top of the safe, seeing them all: five handguns in a row.

The first to catch his eye is a Ruger Mark IV, a rimfire semiautomatic pistol that fires .22 long rounds. The last time he saw one was years ago in the army, an earlier version. It's a deadly accurate target pistol with a six-inch barrel. He recalls learning the weapon is made to very close tolerances. As a .22-caliber piece, it's not a big-bang piece; nearly silent, it fires with a soft popping sound and won't draw attention. It's a target pistol. Built for accuracy. Perfect for his needs.

Foraging on a lower shelf, he grabs a box filled with Remington .22-caliber long bullets. He presses the push-button magazine release on the left side of the Ruger's frame, drops the magazine from the pistol's handle, and catches it in his left hand; it's empty. He loads it with ten rounds, careful to touch only the cartridge casings, not the lead bullet. He sets the loaded pistol on top of the safe, then puts the box with its remaining bullets into his left coat pocket.

A few last gasps come from Charlie.

A quick glance—the man lies on his back; his eyes bulge, and he stares at the ceiling. An empty look, lifeless.

Back to the tray.

A nine-millimeter Kimber Tactical Pro pistol lies next to where the Ruger had been. It's charcoal gray and has a self-illuminating tritium night sight—perfect for a firefight in a low-light environment. It'll give him a tactical advantage if things work the way he hopes.

If . . . if. Too many ifs in all this. But there's no choice.

The magazine holds seven rounds.

He grabs the Kimber along with a box of nine-millimeter ammo and slips it all into his right-side overcoat pocket. He touches nothing else, avoiding contact with the outside of the safe. No fingerprints. He leaves the safe door open.

He turns to Charlie. A weak gasp comes from the man's throat, but he's gone.

It's kill or be killed. That's what Sergeant Dawson would say. No regrets. Can't afford them. Not now.

Roddy gets behind Charlie, slips his hands beneath the man's armpits, and pulls him to the wall next to the safe. He props him up to a sitting position, his back against the wall. The man's chin rests on his chest.

Index and third finger on the man's carotid. No pulse.

His life's over. He died of asphyxiation.

What do I feel about this? Is this me, or some monster? I don't know. And right now I can't afford to care. Make the best of a lousy situation. There's no other choice.

Roddy stands in front of Charlie.

What to do?

He decides.

Holding the Ruger with its muzzle an inch away from the dead man's lips, he fires two shots into his mouth. The pistol barely makes a sound. Just a slight popping noise with each pull of the trigger. Very little recoil, only a gentle jump with each shot. The slugs shoot through Charlie's teeth, blast through his pharynx, and penetrate to his brainpan. Being small caliber, the soft lead of the bullets will flatten when hitting bone, either the vertebrae or the back of the skull.

Charlie is left with a gaping mouth wound.

Then two shots to the throat. A medium-sized hole forms in his neck. The slugs will either stay in his body, flattened against the cervical vertebrae, or pass through and lodge inside the wall behind him. No one will know his trachea was crushed by a throat punch.

Roddy raises Charlie's eyelids, looking into his dead eyes. Plenty of red splotches and squiggles in the sclera—petechial hemorrhages—

a sure sign of death by suffocation. The ME will know the man died of asphyxia, not bullet wounds. If the coroner notes very little blood was shed through the bullet holes, he'll know the bullets entered Charlie's body after his heart had stopped beating. And that'll lead to the conclusion the death wasn't caused by bullets.

Roddy wants it to look like a mob execution.

He places the heel of his left palm on the dead man's forehead and slaps the back of his head against the wall. Holding the pistol in his right hand, with his left pressing Charlie's head back, he fires a bullet through Charlie's right eye. He then blows out the dead man's left eye. It won't be obvious that asphyxiation was the cause of death.

He releases the head; it drops onto Charlie's chest.

The crime scene people and the ME will come up with an explanation. Even if it's the correct one, it won't matter.

Roddy collects the shell casings and pockets them.

He slips the pistol into the coat pocket, where it stays with the box of .22 long bullets.

He glances toward the kitchen and the front of the store. No one there.

Charlie's wife isn't back yet. No customers this early in the morning.

Can't go out the front door. Can't be seen near this place.

He turns, looking to the rear of the store.

Yes, just as he assumed, there's a door leading out to the back. It's the only way to get out unobserved.

Opening the door, he looks left and right.

The backs of the Arthur Avenue stores open onto a common area behind the buildings. The space traverses the length of the block, with each establishment's back area separated from the others by a wooden barrier or chain-link fence.

He's in luck. No one is in the back areas of the stores lining Arthur Avenue.

He pulls the baseball cap down and raises the overcoat collar.

He steps out behind the store. Two plastic trash cans stand beside a six-foot-high chain-link fence. The fence partitions the back of Charlie's store from the rear of the red brick building he passed earlier—2355 Hughes Avenue.

He hops onto the cover of a trash can and straddles the fence, thankful there's no barbed wire at its apex; the barrier is topped by a smooth metal pipe; he bounds over it.

Dropping down on the other side, he's at the rear of the building on Hughes Avenue. He dons the reading glasses and walks to the pathway alongside the building, passing a cluster of empty trash cans, a cracked box spring, a stained mattress, and a heap of discarded furniture. He makes his way down the passageway toward Hughes Avenue.

He passes through the open gate and turns left. Anyone seeing him will assume he's a resident of the building.

On Hughes Avenue, he walks toward his car. Keeping his head down, he holds on to his cap, again as if to prevent the wind from blowing it away. There's little chance a surveillance camera will have a clear view of his face.

When he walked the route on Saturday, he saw no surveillance cameras along this street. But still, it's best to take precautions. Worst-case scenario, a camera will pick him up entering his car and record the license plate. There's no choice; given the surprise development in the store, he must take the chance.

Reaching into his coat pocket, he presses the Open button on the key fob. The doors click open; he gets into the car, closes the door, starts the engine, and drives away.

Chapter 32

It's bitterly cold outside at ten o'clock in the morning on Monday, November twenty-eighth.

Edmond Merko sits at his dilapidated desk.

Here he is in his Alexander Avenue warehouse in the Bronx, a building situated on a dead-end street facing the Harlem River. Swiveling his chair, he gazes out the window at the Willis Avenue Bridge and the dark, dreary sky over the East River and Queens. He shifts his eyes to the freight yard below. Six trailer trucks—each forty-five feet long—are sitting there, backed into the loading docks. Men driving forklifts move pallets of wire-strapped boxes into the trailers. The growling sounds of diesel-fueled trucks and forklifts are supremely gratifying. Never have so many people wanted so many ladies' garments and, of course, other merchandise.

And the trailers, their shiny aluminum-coated bodies adorned with the logo for Merko Imports and Exports in bold red with black trim, the colors of the Albanian flag. People say his trucks stand out on the highways. Once weekly, they are hosed down in the freight yard, kept clean. No one would ever guess their secret cargo. After all, why would any smuggler want to call attention to his bright, shiny trucks?

He once arranged for a Merko truck to "stall out" on an overpass above the Long Island Expressway. It stayed for hours, as thousands of cars passed below, every driver seeing the Merko logo on its side. It was like a billboard for all below to see—free advertising.

Yes, America has been good to him. But after what happened in his belly, he must think about his future, and Masiela's as well. And does he need more money? Only a greedy fool wants more and more and then more.

There's a knock on the door.

"*Ejani në*, Baki," he says in Albanian. "Come in. No need to knock."

Baki enters the office.

"Baki, look out there," Edmond says, pointing to the window. "Isn't it wonderful to see so many trucks loading merchandise, my brother?"

Whenever he talks with Baki, Edmond reverts to Albanian.

"Sit, Baki. Sit. I want to talk with you."

Baki nods as he sits in the chair facing Edmond's desk.

"Baki, it is your ability to keep up with modern times to which we owe so much of our success."

"Edmond, you have been our family's leader—our *krye*—for many years. Without your connections, our clan would not be where we are."

Edmond laughs. "Yes, politicians and police love money as much as everyone else. So we owe our success to both of us."

Edmond leans back, clasps his hands behind his head, and regards Baki. The man has jet-black hair, a heavy stubble of dark beard, and rugged features. "You know, Baki, I think my oldest brother would have looked very much like you if he were still with us."

"He lived to be eighteen, if I recall."

"Yes, and my other brother was seventeen when he died. I was the baby at fifteen."

"You never think of going back for revenge?"

"I've thought about it." Edmond tilts his chair forward and sets his elbows on the desk. "But I think of an old proverb, 'By taking revenge, a man may get even with his enemy, but in passing over it, he is superior.'"

"Well said, Edmond. But if a man had killed my entire family, I could never have peace until I have had revenge."

"In that way, we are different, my brother. I have killed only two men in my life, and that was when I was young."

"I know. The hijackers from the Malota clan. That began your rise in the family. And, Edmond, as long as we're discussing violence, one of our informants tells me there's word on the street that you may be a target."

"A target for which clan?"

"It may be one of our clans, or it could be an Italian family. The Italians think we're stepping on their toes."

"Ah, Baki. Ambitious men leave much scorched earth behind them."

"Yes, you've made enemies, Edmond."

"What is it they say in the Western movies? Keep your ear to the ground."

"We will. Our informants will warn us."

"Ah, Baki, violence begets violence. I have grown to abhor it."

"Yes, but without the threat of violence, the jackals will eat us alive. If they come to harm our interests, you know very well, Edmond, what I will have our soldiers do."

"So long as I don't know about it, you have my sanction." Edmond Merko leans back in his chair and says, "Baki, you are now forty-two years old, correct?"

"Yes, soon to be forty-three."

"That's old enough."

"For what?"

"It's old enough to take over as supreme *krye* of the Merko clan."

Baki's eyes widen. His mouth opens.

"Baki. It's time for you to take up the reins. I'm going to be fifty-six soon, and after coming so close to death, I've been thinking of retiring. And now I must have my knees replaced. I realize how limited our time really is. I still think of what that surgeon said to me. He said, 'You know what to do to live a good, long life.'"

"But, Edmond, *you . . . retire?*"

"Yes, it's time, and I want to leave things in your capable hands."

"I don't know what to say, Edmond."

"All things must come to an end. Masiela and I will go back to Albania and live in the north country, where the air is clean and the forests are thick.

"And, Baki . . . you have been much more to me than an underboss. For me you are the brothers I lost as a boy, and you've been a loyal lieutenant. I cannot think of anyone else I would leave things to."

"But, Edmond," Baki says, standing, "without you we lose the police, the politicians, our contacts."

"Do not worry. A few meals with certain people will take care of that. I will tell them you are in charge, and it will be settled."

"I don't know what to say. I cannot think of the words . . ."

"Say nothing, Baki. Say that you will be happy to take over."

"More than happy. I am honored."

"I will keep half ownership of Tirana. You will own the other half. As for the apartment buildings, our lawyers will work out the details. Ownership will be transferred to you by legal means. And they will draw up the papers for transfer of control of Merko Imports and Exports."

"But, Edmond, what about your children?"

"Ah, my children." Edmond Merko leans back in his chair and smiles. "Masiela and I have always believed the young must succeed in their own ways. They don't know it, but when they each turn thirty, money held in trust will go to them. They will be well off for the rest of their lives, even if they don't become a doctor and a lawyer."

"Just like you, Edmond, to think ahead. I have always admired that about you."

Edmond smiles. "I am fortunate to have you working with me. In spite of the tragedy of my younger years, I think of myself as having been fortunate in my life. And I think we should celebrate our new arrangement by dining tonight at Tirana. Let's do this: you, Mirlinda, Masiela, and I—the four of us—will have a sumptuous dinner at the restaurant serving the finest Albanian food this side of the Balkans."

Chapter 33

After leaving the cheese store and getting back in his car, Roddy strips off his overcoat and tosses it along with the baseball cap and glasses into a Hefty trash bag. When he gets back to his apartment later this morning, the bag will go into the Dumpster behind his building before the garbage truck makes its pickup early this afternoon.

Entering Mount Vernon, he's aware his stomach is growling—sounds like a boiler factory. Shit, he's eaten almost nothing today—a lousy piece of dry toast and some instant coffee. He's ravenous. Reminds him of how he used to gorge himself after a boxing match when he was a kid.

He spots the Fleetwood Diner on Gramatan Avenue and pulls into the parking lot. Entering the place, he's seized by the aromas of bacon and coffee.

Sitting at the counter, he notices two truck drivers—guys in their forties, thickly built with big bellies—sitting a few stools away, to his right. One wears a red Peterbilt hat, jeans, and a red and black flannel shirt. The other wears brown Duluth work pants with a camo work shirt. Pseudo military. They talk loudly; their words pierce the hush of diner conversation among the locals. There're a few words about Trump, Clinton, then Syria—Aleppo—and something about a vote recount in Wisconsin and Pennsylvania.

Roddy tunes it out.

The waitress approaches with her Silex coffeepot and pours him a cup of coffee. He orders the Trencherman's Special—three eggs scrambled on top of French toast, bacon, sausage links, and a pile of hash browns with buttered toast—a coronary on a platter. The hell with that bullshit about cholesterol and saturated fat. So what if he gobbles down a mass of artery-clogging crap? Roddy doesn't know if he'll live beyond tonight, or maybe he'll end up in Attica or some other shithole for the rest of his miserable life, so what the fuck?

Waiting for his food, Roddy considers what he's done. He's killed a man with his bare hands—as he was taught to do as an army ranger. It was kill or be killed, or at the very least, suffer the consequences of Charlie telling Vinzy and Cellini he was trying to get hold of a piece.

After what happened with Tom, he can't imagine what might come next.

Fuck it. The guy was a criminal, a gun supplier for the mob. And of course he had bad intentions. Roddy feels lucky to be sitting in a diner at this moment.

The waitress appears with his food, sets it in front of him, and pours more coffee into his cup.

Roddy notices one of the truck drivers staring at Roddy's plate and elbowing the other guy. They snicker and whisper to each other. Roddy *feels* their stares—derisive, barely muted mockery; they're waiting for him to feel their contempt, expecting him to cringe. They think he's a suburban wuss, a goddamned pantywaist.

He feels a cold flutter in his stomach, looks up, stares at the wall behind the counter, and turns his head so his eyes find those of the trucker nearest him.

He stares, unblinking, knowing his eyes say, *What're you looking at?*

The guy stares back, holds Roddy's eyes for a few seconds, blinks, and keeps staring. Roddy's scalp tightens. His body coils.

It's a Brooklyn-style stare down, unrelenting, unforgiving, the prelude to fists flying and blood on the floor.

Roddy holds his stare and leans forward: badass body language. The guy looks away.

Moments later, the truck drivers get their checks and leave.

If they're waiting for him in the parking lot, he'll take out two more guys with his bare hands.

Roddy wonders if the dragons of his past will ever leave him, or if he'll be enslaved by them all his life.

Fuck it. He turns to his food

After devouring every morsel, he pays up and leaves the diner. The truckers are nowhere to be seen.

Roddy knows exactly what he'll do.

Still in Mount Vernon, he drives to an Army & Navy store he'd looked up on Google; he knows it has everything he'll need.

Virtually empty on a weekday morning, the shop is musty-smelling with a hint of camphor in the air. It overflows with camping gear, boots, service patches, old bayonets, ammo cans, survival kits, backpacks, belts, and armed forces clothing of every kind. He rummages through racks of surplus military apparel—some made of leather, others of nylon, cotton, wool, or canvas. Trying on three thickly lined and insulated winter coats, he settles on a vintage Korean War cold-weather parka with a heavy fur-lined hood.

Since it's military outerwear, the coat has huge side pockets and spacious inner ones, which can be used to his advantage. The parka is enormous: 3XL—so big, it swims on him, especially across the chest and shoulders. It's perfect for what he needs to do.

He then picks out a nearly formfitting lightweight ski jacket made of Thinsulate material. It's light tan in color and can be worn beneath the oversized parka without constricting his movements. A pair of gloves made of similar material is his next choice. Then a dark blue wool navy watch cap. He also picks up a pair of dark blue jeans.

The proprietor's a wizened-looking guy with a cigarette dangling from his lips. He nods silently as Roddy hands over cash for everything.

There'll be no credit-card paper trail.

From Mount Vernon, he drives north, eventually getting to Pondfield Road in Bronxville. He returns to the Regency, and after tossing the plastic bag in the Dumpster, goes to his apartment, where he unloads the remaining cartridges from the Ruger target pistol. Wearing powderless nitrile surgical gloves, he wipes down the rounds and then reloads the pistol with ten rounds from the box he'd taken from Charlie's safe.

Still wearing gloves, he loads the magazine of the Kimber. He then slips ten live rounds of .22-caliber bullets and ten live nine-millimeter bullets into the outside pockets of the parka. He puts both pistols in the two coat pockets, along with the extra live rounds. Returning to the basement garage, he removes the pistols and locks them both in the car's glove compartment. He leaves the live rounds inside the coat pockets.

He then removes the labels from the clothing he bought at the Army & Navy store. Using a scissors, he cuts each label into small pieces, puts them into a small plastic kitchen bag, and scatters the pieces in two separate Dumpsters behind the Regency.

Back at the apartment, he shaves his seven-day growth of stubble—uses a new disposable razor with extra thick lather and shaves down, then up against the grain. His face feels as smooth as a baby's ass.

He then turns on the TV to kill some time. He does his best to avoid thinking about Charlie, the cops, or what will happen with Vinzy this evening.

Though the TV is playing, he doesn't register a moment of whatever program is on. Charlie's wife must have returned to the store by now and found her husband. He tries to imagine her emotional state but then blots it out of his thoughts. This is no time for remorse or sentimentality. No doubt the cops are swarming all over the place looking for clues about what happened and why.

Roddy has time to spare. He thinks about the path he's chosen in his life and the obstacles he's now facing.

And ponders the likelihood his plan will fail or backfire and he'll wind up in prison.

Or dead.

If he dies, he'll leave Tracy and the kids behind, and they'll suffer. But at least the material things will be taken care of. There are enough conservative investments in his portfolio—high quality equities and plenty of tax-free municipal bonds—and there's his 401K through the hospital, along with his own IRA. The money will see Tracy and the kids through many years of their lives. Thanks to Dan's financial expertise, the kids' college accounts are well funded. Danny—the godfather to his kids—will take care of everything else to ensure the family's financial well-being. That's a given.

If he dies and everything comes to light, Tracy will know she was right about her husband: he was involved in some very shady dealings and couldn't be trusted. He never really left his past behind.

Like father, like son, she'll think.

With his death, Sandy will be devastated. Learning the facts surrounding his death will leave her with permanent wounds. But then, life leaves everyone with scars. An unscarred person is someone who hasn't lived.

As for Tom, who knows how he'll do in the long run? But he'll get through it. He's smart and resourceful. That's what people always said about Roddy when he was the kid's age, and he ended up doing well.

Or did he?

Another unanswered question: *Did I do well in my life? Has my life been little more than a series of bad choices—a parade of regrettable moments that overrode the good ones? The lousy choices I keep thinking about.*

But back to the moment. Yes, there's a damned good chance Roddy will die very soon.

Actually, it's probable.

Probability—a strange, even chilling concept—meaning there's a 51 percent or greater chance of something happening.

So it's probable he'll fail, meaning it's likely that tonight he'll end up dead.

But thinking about these last few weeks, any chance for his plan to succeed—even if it's only 10 percent—is a hell of a lot better than the odds he's been facing until now. And up to this moment, his life's been circling the drain.

But it's time to shelve all doubt and worries.

If you let yourself ponder failure, you've already lost.

After spending time in the apartment, he decides to construct a semialibi presence in Bronxville. He stops in at J.C. Fogarty's, a local watering hole on Kraft Avenue, down the block from the train station. Right in the heart of the village.

Yes, he knows he'll claim he had a headache if anyone questions him about not having gone to the Regency's rental office to break his lease. But he'll just say he decided to go for a walk and maybe down a beer to relieve the pain.

The only other patron in the place is a rheumy-looking guy sitting at the bar bent reverently over a glass of booze on the rocks. Roddy orders a mug of lager on tap and strikes up a conversation with the barkeep, a garrulous guy named Walt whose reddish-colored walrus mustache is the biggest Roddy's ever seen. He asks Walt lots of questions. The guy's an open book about his life. The only time he stops talking is when the scotch drinker signals him for another round of Dewar's.

Roddy barely hears a word Walt says, but feigns listening. If he attempted to recount three words of Walt's conversation, he'd fail miserably.

He nurses the beer for nearly an hour—drinks less than a third of the mug so he won't get buzzed— and pays up while the scotch drinker sits in a state of placid stupefaction. Roddy makes certain to leave a ten-dollar tip so if push comes to shove Walt will remember him.

Back at the apartment, he kills another two hours.

Finally, it's time.

He dons the Thinsulate ski jacket. He slips the 3XL parka over the ski jacket and then folds and stuffs the jeans—a different color from the black pants he's wearing—into the parka's spacious inner pocket. He slips the watch cap into an inside pocket along with a pair of nitrile surgical gloves.

A quick look in a mirror tells him he looks huge wearing the ski jacket beneath the parka, along with the clothing tucked inside the outerwear. Bundled up like this, he's so bulky-looking, he could pass for an NFL linebacker, but in frigid windy weather at the end of November, he won't stand out. He wears the same shoes he'd worn this morning.

He returns to the car, opens the glove compartment, takes out both weapons, and puts the Ruger target pistol in the parka's right side pocket, the Kimber inside the left outer pocket. The loaded Ruger in the right pocket sits on top of a bunch of live .22-caliber rounds. The fully loaded Kimber rests on the spare nine-millimeter bullets.

He sets out for his destination.

Driving within the speed limit, glancing occasionally in the rearview mirror, he does his best to avoid being pulled over by a cop. He also checks he's not being tailed.

It's seven p.m. Or nineteen hundred hours in military time, closing in on the time for the next step of his plan.

Once Roddy got used to the military life, the twenty-four-hour day enumerated by the numbers became second nature. After discharge, it took months to reaccustom himself to civilian time and the twelve-hour clock. Sometimes he still finds himself converting military time to the twelve-hour civilian clock. Some habits never go away.

He's very early for the meeting with Vinzy.

He thinks back on what happened at the cheese store this morning.

How strange to lack remorse—to feel nothing—after what he did to Charlie Cheese.

Am I trying to feel guilty? Am I blaming myself for not caring? If I feel guilt, does that make me a better person?

Maybe it's better to feel nothing. Why should he feel anything for the man?

He had every intention of putting a bullet in my chest.

Justification for the Mad Dog? Maybe, but there's no other choice. Do what must be done.

Roddy parks the car on Hoffman Street, a quiet residential enclave only one short block from where he'll meet Vinzy.

He'll sit in the car and wait before seeing Vinzy.

A gust of wind blows so violently, the car is buffeted.

The street is dark and virtually deserted. A lamppost projects a cone of light near the corner. Not a pedestrian in sight.

A sign says there's metered parking from eight a.m. until seven p.m. on weekdays. Since it's now seven thirty—civilian time—he doesn't have to shove a batch of quarters into a parking meter.

Roddy knows the parking meter's an important variable—one that must be taken into account. Every detail counts, no matter how seemingly inconsequential. He's made it a point not to rush with the execution of this plan. He did his best to calculate all the possibilities, though you can never account for everything.

Variables. Unforeseen possibilities.

The unknown.

Whether it relates to surgery or what he's doing now—if it relates to anything in life—the variables are ever-present and always have an effect. Especially something so seemingly trivial as a parking meter.

Roddy recalls a movie, *Summer of Sam*, about the serial killer Son of Sam. During the summer of 1976, over the course of several weeks, he shot people sitting in their cars, mainly young women with long dark hair. Some were killed; others were seriously wounded.

The city was in a panic. Throughout the boroughs, women had their dark hair cut short and dyed blond. A search of parking tickets in the area where one murder took place revealed a ticket had been issued to an illegally parked car.

Following up on the lead, the cops learned the ticketed car had been driven by a young man who was eventually identified as David Berkowitz, aka the Son of Sam. Because of that random fact—a minor thing such as a parking ticket—the serial killer was captured.

A simple variable determined the outcome.

So it's a good thing there's no need to plug coins into a parking meter. There's a smaller chance of a random event leading back to Roddy.

As for visibility, Hoffman Street is residential, so very few security cameras are positioned on buildings or lampposts.

He's brought a black wool scarf to hide his face in addition to wearing the parka hood up. He won't look suspicious with the scarf wrapped around the lower half of his face since the car's thermometer says the temperature has dropped to nineteen bone-chilling degrees. And there's a brisk wind. Not only will it keep people off the streets, but it'll make walking with a scarf over his face and a hood over his head appear sensible.

So far, luck is with him.

Chapter 34

Still sitting in the car, Roddy wonders what he'll say to Vinzy. How will he confront that snake?

What will happen when he's face-to-face with this so-called friend? What will Vinzy say or do when he's surprised by what Roddy's decided to do? It's another unknown.

There's no way he'll get Vinzy to try convincing Cellini to call off the hit on Merko. Nothing will change Cellini's thinking. As many unknowns as there are in this situation, that's not one of them.

With Vinzy, he'll let his instincts take over. Like he did in the boxing ring. Maybe it's not such a bad thing to go with your impulses. But still, you gotta stay in control. You can't be a wild animal. Remember Doc Schechter's words.

Waiting in the car on a dark, quiet street, he tries to distract himself. He turns on the radio. Again 1010 WINS. It's a medley of disparate voices: an ad for a storage company followed by another for a car dealership, more news—but it's meaningless palaver, background chatter as his thoughts tumble through the last few weeks of his life.

A turning point comes tonight.

He hopes.

At 7:55, he gets out of the car. It's very early—an hour and five minutes before the scheduled meeting with Vinzy at Rocco's.

But this is part of the plan. Ranger training taught him many things. One of the foremost was a simple truth: the element of surprise is very powerful.

The air is frigid. A gust of wind whips down the street and slashes into his face, making his eyes water. He wraps the scarf around his neck and over his face, allowing a small space for his eyes. He pulls the parka hood up.

The only part of his face visible is through the narrow slit for his eyes.

With his head bent downward, he walks along Hoffman Street, turning onto 188th Street. At the intersection of 188th and Arthur Avenue, he turns right and walks toward 2407 Arthur Avenue.

Vinzy's office.

Not Rocco's.

Vinzy's place is directly across the street from a Chase Bank. No doubt the bank will have surveillance cameras pointing toward the street. He's gotta be careful.

As he'd anticipated, on a bitterly cold Monday night, despite being a commercial thoroughfare, Arthur Avenue is virtually deserted. Gusting winds and temperatures in the teens keep people indoors.

At the door to Carmel Medical Associates, Roddy rings the bell. He's wearing his Thinsulate gloves and makes sure to keep his back toward the Chase Bank across the street. With the parka hood up, he's unidentifiable.

He peers through the Plexiglas door panel and sees a dim light coming from the hallway leading to the clinic's rear. The lobby is barely lit by rheostat-controlled recessed lighting. All the other lights are off. The place is obviously closed.

A moment later Vinzy emerges from a dimly lit corridor and enters the clinic's lobby. He's wearing a sports jacket, jeans, a dark blue suit, shirt open at the collar, no tie. He looks perplexed, moves cautiously to the door, and peers through the Plexiglas.

Roddy lowers the scarf and lets Vinzy see his face. He removes the gloves and stuffs them in the parka's inside breast pocket.

"It's me, Vinzy. Roddy."

Vinzy shakes his head, blinks a few times, and looks befuddled. His eyebrows go up; he shrugs his shoulders.

Vinzy unlocks the door.

"Roddy? What're you doin' here? You're early . . . and we're supposed to meet in Pelham."

"We'll talk here, and then we can go to Geppetto's."

Without waiting for a response, Roddy brushes past Vinzy and moves into the reception area, keeping the hood up and his back toward the bank across the street.

"I didn't think you'd wanna go back to Geppetto's," Vinzy says in a pitchy voice.

He locks the outer door.

"No problem. Let's talk."

Roddy stands in the dimly lit lobby, his back still toward the door. He wraps his arms around himself, pretending he's cold.

Vinzy says, "I don't understand." His voice sounds shaky. "What's up? Why not—"

"Forget it," Roddy cuts him off. "Let's talk in your office. It's important."

"But . . ."

"We gotta talk, Vinzy. Don't waste time."

Roddy walks into the corridor heading toward Vinzy's office. Vinzy follows.

"I don't understand," Vinzy says.

Sergeant Dawson was right. Surprise is a powerful tool—in the military and elsewhere. Stealth and the unexpected are your friends. Especially if you're an army ranger or if you're one man dealing with the mob. Vinzy's flustered and doesn't know what to say or do.

Once they're away from the reception area—deep enough in the clinic's interior to avoid the bank's cameras—Roddy pushes the parka hood back and lowers the scarf.

No CCTV in the corridor. It's a surprise, considering that Albanian maniac who burst into the clinic and demanded his wife's medical records.

Vinzy shuffles in front of Roddy and extends his hand toward a door at the end of the corridor.

"What's goin' on, Roddy?"

"I'll tell you inside."

Vinzy's office is sparsely furnished in dark woods, no personal touches. No family photos or decorations to make the place seem welcoming. Strictly utilitarian.

A quick glance at the walls and ceiling: no camera in sight.

Roddy sits in a chair facing the desk. An open ledger book and a laptop sit off to the side.

Vinzy perches himself in a high-backed leather chair behind his desk and closes the laptop.

"Jesus, what's up? Why the change in plans? Shit, Roddy, you look pale as hell. How're you doin'?"

"Not well."

"You look anemic. Have you lost weight?"

"A little."

"Look, I know this is one helluva stress, but you'll get through it. You're a strong guy. Just stay the course. It'll all turn around. But why here . . . and not in Pelham where you—"

"Forget about it."

Vinzy shrugs. His lips twitch, and he leans back in his chair. "Okay, Roddy, so whaddaya wanna talk about?"

"You mentioned things turning around; any chance you can talk Carmine out of this?"

Vinzy shakes his head and closes his eyes. His hands float up in the air, palms outward.

"I wish I could, Roddy, but there's not a chance." His voice quivers. He's nervous, never expecting Roddy to show up like this. He senses something's wrong.

"No chance Carmine'll change his mind?"

"Not a chance." He shoots Roddy a weak smile; it reeks of contrived regret.

"Tell me something, Vinzy. Why'd you ever mention me to Carmine?"

Vinzy presses his lips together; one side of his mouth rises as he closes his eyes and cants his head. "I don't know . . . It happened. But what're you—"

"It *happened*?"

Heat flares in Roddy's cheeks. His blood feels like it's on fire. A buzzing sensation begins in his chest, feeling like an electric wire. It travels down his belly into his legs.

His thoughts carom to Tracy at the hospital.

What if he dies? Tracy sobbing at the bedside.

Tom in that hospital bed—bruised and broken.

"So it just *happened*, Vinzy," Roddy growls. "Just like that?" Roddy leans forward and dips his head.

"Yeah . . . I guess. I mean . . ." Vinzy's lower lip trembles. A sheen of sweat forms on his forehead. He senses something's very wrong.

"You just throw people away, don't you, Vinzy? Three wives, me . . . we're all dispensable, aren't we? We're just trash in your life."

"Listen, Roddy, shit happens. But what's that got to do—"

"Really? Shit happens? Tell me something else, Vinzy. Why'd they run down my boy? My son? I said I'd do it, so why?"

Vinzy drops the baffled look. He clasps his hands on the desktop and leans forward. His face hardens. His amiability fades in a millisecond. He means business now. No more bullshit.

"You really wanna know, Roddy?" His tone is harsh, unforgiving.

"Yeah, I wanna know." Roddy crosses his arms in front of his chest.

"It's *your* fault, Roddy." Vinzy's eyes gleam. "You got no one to blame but *you*. You might as well've been drivin' that car yourself.

You fucked up when you operated on Merko. We know you were alone with him in his room and his IV was still in. That was your chance and you did nothin'. Did you think we wouldn't find *out*? We told you we have contacts at the hospital. The hit-and-run was ordered to convince you we mean business. Bottom line: you had it comin'."

Something flares inside Roddy.

Vinzy's eyes narrow. "Hey, man, how many layers of clothes you got on? You gotta be hot as hell in that coat."

"I'll tell you what's got me hot and bothered . . . what happened to my son. And the threats to my wife and daughter."

"You had it comin'. Your wife and daughter, I don't know shit about that."

Roddy rips the Ruger out of his pocket. With his elbow sitting on the desktop, he points it at Vinzy's head. Dead center of his forehead.

Vinzy's face curdles into a fear-filled mask that turns chalk white as blood drains downward. His hands fly up in the air and he pushes away, rolling his chair back from the desk. Sweat droplets prickle on his forehead. His eyes widen. "Hey, *c'mon*, man. That's not called for."

Roddy seethes but stays controlled. His hand is steady. A strange taste forms on his tongue, metallic, bitter. Like he imagines poison would taste.

Roddy keeps the pistol pointed at Vinzy. Locked into a spot on his forehead.

"*C'mon*, Roddy . . . what the fuck you doin'?"

"I'm pointing a loaded pistol at your head. That's what."

"Look, Roddy, I'm a friend."

"A *friend*? Don't bullshit me, you snake."

The pistol holds steady.

Vinzy's eyes fix on the weapon as he slowly rolls his chair closer to the desk.

"Listen to me, Roddy. I swear on all that's holy, the hit-and-run was Carmine's idea. And Tony DiNardo's. I had nothin' to do with it."

"But I had it coming, right?"

Vinzy swallows hard. His eyes flit from the pistol to Roddy, then back to the pistol.

"And you got me involved in all this in the first place, right?"

"C'mon, Roddy, be reasonable . . ." Vinzy's eyes look like huge marbles. Sweat speckles his upper lip. Flecks of saliva form at the edges of his lips. His hands move to the edge of the desk and then slip lower, to his lap. His eyes laser on Roddy's.

"Put your hands on the desk, Vinzy. *Now*."

Vinzy's hands flop back onto the desk. His cheeks shine with sweat.

"I know you keep a piece in there. If your hands go down again, Vinzy, I'll blow your fucking head off."

"I wasn't gonna do a thing, Roddy. Believe me." Vinzy's voice warbles. He swallows so hard, he gulps. Roddy smells the man's fear.

"You swear?"

"Look, Roddy, maybe I can talk to Carmine and convince him not to—"

"Not a chance. Isn't that what you said, Vinzy? 'Not a chance.'"

"Yeah, but maybe—"

"The time for talking is over. I'm all talked out."

"Whaddaya gonna do, Roddy. Shoot me?" Vinzy's eyelids flutter. Ribbons of sweat drizzle from his hairline, coalescing into streams leaking down his face. His lower lip quivers, and his chin trembles. "Jesus, you gonna *shoot* me?"

"Could be, Vinzy. Like you said, shit happens."

"Where'd you get the piece?"

"From Charlie Cheese."

Vinzy's eyes widen. His hands tremble on the desktop. "*Charlie Cheese?*" he warbles. "He was killed this mornin'. They shot the shit outta him. The cops're all over the store."

Roddy nods and moves the pistol closer to Vinzy's forehead, pointed at the kill spot.

"Jesus Christ. *You? You* killed him?"

Roddy nods, staring unblinkingly at Vinzy. He fights the urge to let a bitter smile form on his lips.

"Why? Why'd you do it?"

"Because like you said, Vinzy, I'm the same guy I was back in Brooklyn . . . and in the army. Nothing's changed. Remember saying that?"

"Hey, Roddy, I didn't mean it that way."

"What way didn't you mean it?"

No response. Just Vinzy shaking his head. His mouth hangs open. His eyes dart away; they seem to drift to a spot behind Roddy and off to the right. Vinzy's right hand drifts slightly lower.

"Talk to me, Vinzy. Tell me how you set me up because I'd be afraid *shit* would happen to my family. Talk to me."

In a strangled voice, Vinzy trills, "So this is because of your kid?"

"You can say that."

"So it's revenge?"

"It's more than that. Much more."

Vinzy's right hand lowers another half inch. "*What*? Why the *fuck're* you doin' this?"

"To protect the people I love, and frankly, Vinzy, my bullshit artist of a so-called friend, there's no other way."

"Yes, there is, Roddy. I swear there is. *Listen* to me, for the love of God. Jesus Christ, just hold on a minute," he pules, his palms now facing outward, like he's trying to push Roddy back, gain distance. "I got loads of dough." Vinzy nods frantically. More spittle forms at the corners of his mouth. "I can make it worth your while. Ease back on the dial, my man. Just cool it. Lemme take care of you. C'mon, be reasonable. All I gotta do is go to the bank and—"

"Don't insult me, Vinzy."

"Okay, okay." Vinzy's fingers tremble. But that hand sinks lower. "Just *wait* a second, Roddy. For God's sake, hear me out." Streams of sweat dribble down his pallid face. "*Listen* to me, man. You got no fuckin' idea who I know. I got lotsa connections. I know people who can make things happen. If I go to Carmine and—"

Vinzy's right hand shoots to his left lapel. His movement is quick as his hand slips beneath the jacket, grasping for a shoulder-holstered pistol. As quick as the motion is, he might as well be moving through syrup, as Roddy acts reflexively, in an instant.

He pulls the trigger.

The back of Vinzy's head slams against the leather chair as the slug cracks through his forehead. A small hole blossoms on Vinzy's forehead, above his left eyebrow. The bullet plows through his brain.

No exit wound, just mashed lead resting in his cranium.

Roddy stands and watches Vinzy's body slide down the leather chair; it slips to the floor behind the desk and lies in a limp heap. A thin stream of blood pulses from the .22-caliber hole in Vinzy's forehead; within moments it turns into a trickle dripping languidly onto the carpet.

The chair rolls back on plastic wheels. Vinzy's face is a mask of death. His open eyes stare at nothing, the light gone, life vacated.

He went for his pistol. Just what I knew Vinzy would do.

Roddy slides the Ruger back in the pocket of the parka. The shell casing lies on the floor; he decides to leave it. The hell with it. He'd wiped it clean back at the apartment, and it won't matter if the cops find it.

Vinzy's body will be discovered when the clinic opens in the morning. The forensic people will find gunshot residue on Vinzy's face—they'll know the shot was up close, personal.

The way it should be done when the mob kills a guy for a transgression.

Against whom?

Against Roddy? No.

Against the mob? Yes.

Just like Charlie Cheese was killed by the higher-ups.

Or maybe he was assassinated by the Albanians.

For what?

Who knows? And who cares?

Roddy surveys the room. He hasn't touched a thing other than the pistol. He's left no prints, no DNA, no biological evidence. And he's certain the bank surveillance camera across the street won't have footage identifying him.

He stands beside the desk and peers at the ledger. Vinzy was cooking the books, preparing for the meeting with Danny.

On the other side of the desk, a week-at-a-glance calendar is open.

Without touching it, Roddy checks for appointments on the twenty-eighth, today and tonight.

There are several entries, including one saying, "Rocco's, Pelham. 9 p.m."

Roddy's name isn't there.

And there's no reservation at Rocco's in Roddy's name. Never was—either in his name or Danny's—even the times he met there with Danny.

If he lives through tonight, and if he's ever questioned, which is unlikely, he'll simply say he and Vinzy had talked about meeting at Rocco's—there was no need to make a reservation on a Monday night—but Roddy was disappointed that his old medical school friend never showed up.

For a moment he wonders if he feels a thing about having shot Vinzy Masconi.

Are his nerve endings firing in a frenzy? No.

Is his heart thumping a sickening beat in his chest? No.

Is he racked by a swell of guilt? No.

Remorse? No.

Regret? Sure.

Regret for Vinzy? Not a shred of it.

Regret for everything that's happened? Yes.

Does he feel anything else?

Guilt? No.

Satisfaction? No. Not really.

It's too late to feel anything else.

Now he's going on the offensive, making things happen.

He won't be a marionette.

Maybe he'll be the one pulling the strings.

He'll do what must be done.

If the variables are with him.

If he's lucky. Very lucky.

After that? It's anyone's guess.

He pulls up the parka hood, wraps the scarf around his face, slips on the gloves, takes a last look at Vinzy's corpse, shakes his head, then turns and walks back to the corridor. He keeps his head down should a surveillance camera be anywhere on the premises.

A door in the reception area is located beneath a sign reading Fire Exit. He pushes the bar handle and it opens. A short corridor makes a right turn leading to a fire door facing Arthur Avenue. It opens only from the inside. He leans against the push bar, opens the door, and leaves.

He emerges onto Arthur Avenue. The bank is directly across the street.

A frigid wind shears its way along the street. With the parka hood up, most of his face covered, and looking down at his feet, he walks toward 187th Street.

Two down.

There's unfinished business. The riskiest part is still ahead of him.

He'll probably get there at about nine o'clock.

It may take time, but hopefully, with a bit of luck, it'll be settled.

Chapter 35

Roddy knows each street he'll travel to his destination. And he won't go by car.

Over the Thanksgiving weekend, he'd scoped it all out on Google Maps. Including street views. After familiarizing himself with the itinerary, he'd made a dry run so he'd know the precise route. On Saturday, after leaving the bank, he'd taken Metro North's Harlem Line local train from Bronxville, getting off at the Fordham station in the Bronx. It was a sixteen-minute trip, only a few train stops from Bronxville, heading south. Leaving the station, he'd walked each street he's taking to his destinations tonight. It's all been scouted out.

He begins the walk.

From Vinzy's office, he walks to Fordham Road and then turns left, heading west toward Webster Avenue. An occasional passerby scurries by on the other side of the street, but nobody's walking the same route he's taking. And anyone on the streets tonight is hurrying to get indoors and out of the cold. It's a good thing—less chance of an unanticipated complication. The weather's a variable in his favor.

Keeping his head tilted down, looking away from storefronts or buildings—minimizing the risk of being recorded by surveillance cameras—he turns right and walks north on Webster. He keeps his right leg slightly stiff and walks with a barely discernible limp—a gait very different from his normal one.

Stealth, surprise, and deception are indispensable tools of asymmetric warfare. And that's what he's fighting, a war. For his family and his soul.

After Vinzy's body is discovered in the morning, the cops will, no doubt, go to the bank across the street and examine its surveillance videos. The recordings are probably digital and can be easily retrieved. After going over the bank recordings—in slow motion and in real time, all digitally noted in minutes and seconds—the cops will do their best to track all CCTV feeds available from stores and residential buildings along the route he's traveling. As piecemeal as the recordings may be, they'll likely be able to follow him to his destination.

The videos will show a shadowy figure leaving Carmel Medical Associates. The unknown man will be wearing a bulky parka with its hood up and a scarf covering his face. The parka with the ski jacket beneath make him look as though he weighs thirty or forty pounds more than he does—maybe 240 or 250.

And, at night, any video capturing him will be grainy at best.

Walking slowly but steadily, he reaches Bedford Park Boulevard, turns left, and walks west. He moves at a measured pace, no need to rush. He stays on the street-level walkway, avoiding the underpass near the Grand Concourse.

He crosses the Grand Concourse at Bedford Park Boulevard and walks another two blocks, arriving at Jerome Avenue. Turning left on Jerome, he passes Edmond Merko's restaurant, Tirana, then turns left at the corner of 199th Street and Jerome.

When he did the dry run on Saturday, he timed the walk from Vinzy's clinic to Tirana—twenty-six minutes at a casual pace. Tonight, walking with an altered gate, it takes a bit more than half an hour.

It's now nearly nine o'clock on Monday night, two days before Edmond Merko's scheduled surgery and one day before Vinzy and Cellini were scheduled to meet with Danny—a visit that will never happen.

Roddy stands on 199th Street and leans against the wall of the building where Tirana is located at the intersection with Jerome Avenue.

He's about seventy-five feet from the restaurant's awning-covered entrance on Jerome, standing at the edge of the building on 199th, a quiet, tree-lined residential street. There's not a soul in sight on this dark side street. It's ghostly quiet but for the occasional whoosh of a car passing by on Jerome Avenue.

The only illumination at the intersection is an arching street-light hanging over Jerome Avenue. Across the avenue, a vast parking lot can be seen, beyond which is an elevated train trestle.

Tirana is a two-story building extending at least one hundred feet onto 199th Street. The restaurant's awning reaches the sidewalk curb and leads to its front door on Jerome Avenue. The entranceway is lit by fluorescent tubes tucked beneath the awning.

Peering around the building's edge, Roddy watches a stretch limo pull up to and park in front of the place. A uniformed chauffer gets out and opens the driver's side rear door. Four occupants get out of the limo. Bundled up, holding their hats, they move quickly to the entrance and enter Tirana.

At least ten people are congregated outside, clustered beneath the restaurant's awning, men and women. Everyone greets one another. Hugs and kisses all around.

Looks like it's a big night for the Albanians. They must be celebrating something.

From this angle at the building's edge, firing at the entrance area using a two-handed shooting stance, he'll be forced to expose himself from his position around the edge of the building.

It won't matter. He'll have the element of surprise, and to sow further confusion, he'll be firing from a darkened area into a well-lit one. Sudden shooting coming from an unseen source always leads to panic.

He takes out both pistols and sets them on the ground.

Take it one step at a time.

He removes his gloves and stuffs them in the parka's inside pockets.

Another car pulls up in front of the restaurant; three people get out and enter Tirana. The driver pulls away from the curb and departs.

Despite the frigid air, there's still a crowd congregated at the entrance. They huddle and talk as breath vapor escapes from their mouths and noses.

Yes, there must be some occasion for so many people to be out on a wind-driven Monday night with temperatures below freezing.

The only person left in the parked limo is the driver. He sits behind the wheel smoking. Every now and then the lit end of the cigarette glows orange. The engine is running; exhaust fumes hang heavily in the frigid night air. No doubt the driver has the heater going full blast. The headlights are turned off. The fact that he's waiting probably means the people he dropped off are important mobsters and their wives or girlfriends.

A Lincoln Town Car pulls up, drops off a couple, then pulls away.

Roddy makes sure the scarf covers his face from beneath his eyes down. The parka hood stays up.

He picks up the .22 and readies it. Then he racks the Kimber.

It's been years since ranger training. He hasn't run an infiltration course or practiced shooting for years. Decades have passed with countless nonmilitary activities—college, medical school, internship, residency, marriage, a surgical practice, and so much more—and he'll be rusty when it comes to firing a weapon.

Both pistols are racked and ready. He'll leave the shell casings lying where they fall.

The first two or three shots are crucial; they'll cause panic.

He raises the Ruger, steps out around the edge of the building, and assumes a shooting stance. He takes aim, but as he's ready to fire, it happens: his heart flutters and his pulse bounds in his ears. His bare hands feel frigid and begin trembling as adrenaline floods him. He can't fire accurately in this state of tension.

He's gonna screw it up.

Suddenly, his thoughts stream back in time, to Fort Benning. Sergeant Dawson's southern drawl during small-arms training comes back to him.

Take measured breaths—let as much oxygen as possible get to your lungs. Then, a long exhale. Relax your muscles. When you aim, keep both eyes open because it's a pistol, not a rifle. These are the steps to a kill shot.

And remember this, young troop: almost any pistol is more consistent than a human being. In the hands of the right shooter, this weapon can shoot the mole off a man's ass.

After one more deep breath, his hands are steady, and he knows he can do it. No more thumping of blood in his ears. He holds still, relaxes his muscles, lets out a long exhalation, and fires the first shot.

A dull, low-level popping sound, obliterated by the wind.

The left front tire of the limo deflates.

A perfect hit.

The vehicle sags.

Another shot through the limo's front window, to the driver's right.

A starburst pattern on the windshield—a small hole in the middle.

The driver ducks down.

Another shot, then another in the same area, but closer to where the driver had been.

The chauffer begins blasting away at the horn.

The crowd in front of the restaurant goes into a frenzy.

The limo horn blares.

Four more shots into the limo's body. One after another, a series of *thunk*s. Shell casings fly up and to the right, drop to the sidewalk, and clink softly onto the concrete.

Holes appear in the car. He's fired eight shots from the Ruger. Except for two rounds, Roddy's emptied the pistol into the vehicle.

The crowd mills about.

Some people duck into the restaurant.

Confusion.

Panic.

Shouting in English and Albanian.

They can't tell where the shots are coming from.

Down goes the Ruger. Up comes the Kimber. It's heavy but perfectly balanced, and with a tritium night sight, it's clear shooting.

Only one man remains on the sidewalk. He cranes his neck, looks both ways on Jerome Avenue, and doesn't move. He can't tell where the shots are coming from. The wind carried the sounds; they dissipate into the night. The guy's either very brave or very stupid. Or he's frozen in a state of panic. No matter.

Roddy takes careful aim, exhales, and squeezes the trigger—gently, slowly—not making the weapon move or jiggle, keeping it on target.

A burst of concrete powder blows up inches from the guy's foot. He jumps, frightened out of his mind.

A perfect shot, close enough to appear the shooter has lethal intentions.

The Kimber's first shell casing ejects, hits the wall, and plunks heavily onto the sidewalk. A beautiful sound. It lies there along with the casings ejected from the Ruger.

The man looks toward Roddy, rigid, unmoving. A deer in the headlights.

The club door opens; an arm pulls at the guy.

Keep shooting. Take your time. Make every shot count.

Two more shots. They hit the inside of the club's door before it closes.

Another shot ricochets off the sidewalk, raising a shower of sparks and a puff of pulverized concrete.

He turns the pistol toward the limo and empties the Kimber. *Thunk, thunk.* Slugs sink into the metal. Smoke pours from beneath the hood. The engine block's been devastated.

The driver is still hunkered down on the seat or the floor.

No one's in front of the club.

It must be pandemonium inside.

The wind gusts along Jerome Avenue.

Now the next step. Hurry.

Roddy slips on the gloves and empties the parka pockets. Of everything.

It all falls to the sidewalk—live .22-caliber and nine-millimeter rounds tumble to the ground in a series of dull *thud*s as intact bullets hit the concrete. The sidewalk is littered with shell casings and live rounds. He rummages through his pockets, making sure everything has fallen out. They're empty. It's all on the sidewalk.

He peeks around the building edge.

No one has ventured from the club.

To be expected.

When people hear shots, their first impulse is to duck for cover. It's human nature. Self-preservation. You wait it out until you think the danger's passed.

No one will leave the club for a while.

Roddy picks up both pistols and thrusts them into the parka's pockets.

One more glance down. Everything's on the sidewalk. Except for the pistols, his side pockets are empty.

Roddy turns and dashes across 199th Street, then strides briskly toward the Grand Concourse.

Looking behind him, he sees no one's coming.

He sprints down the street and doesn't look back. Not much time to get away.

When the Albanians finally step out of the restaurant, they'll move cautiously. They won't want to run into an ambush. He'll have a decent window of time before they venture out.

He crosses the Grand Concourse, walks one block north to Bedford Park Boulevard, turns right, and walks toward Webster Avenue, keeping his head down and his face away from stores and buildings. There's little chance of a frontal view of his mostly covered face, so he won't be recognized in facial recognition software—not that he's on any criminal database.

But you never know.

Now a good distance from Tirana, he slows and moves with the same altered gait he used on his way to Tirana.

He hears sirens in the distance. Fighting the urge to look toward the sound, he keeps his head down and continues walking.

The sirens' wailing comes closer.

Moments later two police cruisers race past him on Bedford Park Boulevard—their sirens shrieking, light bars flashing in chromatic madness.

More police cars streak by, heading west toward Jerome Avenue and Tirana.

Someone's called the cops. Probably a resident in a building on 199th Street.

He's only three blocks from Webster Avenue, walking along the south side of Bedford Park Boulevard. He comes abreast of a block-long expanse of a school campus, set above the street atop a steep hill. If he recalls, it's the Academy of Mount St. Ursula. He'd figured this side of the street, devoid of apartment buildings with their security cameras, would give him a better shot at evading detection.

Across the street is a row of six-story structures, prewar construction, some with an Art Deco style—typical older residential buildings in the Bronx.

Except for the wind whooshing through bare tree branches, all is quiet.

Suddenly the wind dies. An eerie silence envelops him.

He keeps walking, then senses something.

It's nearby, not far behind him.

He whirls around. Sees no one.

He stands there and listens. His pulse bounds in his ears, but he hears nothing else.

The wind picks up. A sudden gust blows against his back.

He waits and hears only the wind.

He turns and begins walking again.

The wind subsides.

He hears something. Is it his imagination?

He's primed. His skin tingles.

He could be in the Carolina forests or swamps, back in ranger school. Every nerve in his body is on high alert, firing voltaic impulses. His heightened senses take it all in: traffic whooshing by on Webster Avenue, a streetlight humming half a block away, tree branches creaking in the night air. His vision sharpens; the surroundings look sharply etched.

His body goes taut; a chill crawls through him.

He waits.

Sees and hears nothing unusual.

Yet he's primed, completely charged, amped.

For what?

Nothing's there.

He turns, about to resume his trek.

A faint sound from behind him.

Roddy pivots.

Emerging from between two parked cars is a tall, slim black guy wearing an army fatigue jacket and a knit wool cap. Both hands are thrust deep in his pockets.

This is gonna be trouble.

The guy's coming his way, and his intentions are easy to read: aggressive strut, chin thrust forward, shoulders back.

Roddy's about to be mugged.

Just what he needs, a street thug. Probably carries a blade. Maybe a handgun.

Wasting this guy will deep-six his plan.

The man is coming closer.

"Yo, brother," the guy calls. His voice is a giveaway: bad intentions.

"Don't *brother* me. Keep away." Roddy's voice sounds muffled by the scarf over his mouth and the hood over his head.

Two rounds left in the Ruger. Be prepared to use them.

Roddy's muscles tense.

Another quick assessment—the man's physical stature, attitude, beady eyes, mustache, maybe twenty years old, in the prime of life.

The streetlight down the block is behind Roddy. He's backlit and silhouetted; the mugger can't see him clearly, can't tell he's not some candy-assed punk.

"Why, man? Watcha gonna do?"

Thinks I'm easy pickings on a deserted street at night.

Roddy rips the glove off his right hand and holds it in his left. He slips his hand into his pocket.

"Yo, motherfucker. *Watcha* gonna do?"

He's closing in.

In an even voice, Roddy says, "I'm gonna kill you is what I'm gonna do."

The guy's six feet away.

The Ruger comes out, pointed at the man's chest.

A round is chambered.

Roddy holds the weapon steady, finger on the trigger, ready to fire.

The guy stops. His mouth opens; his hands come out of the pockets—empty, no weapon.

He whirls around, dashes between two parked cars, and races across the street.

"Crazy motherfucker," Roddy hears him mutter into the wind.

Roddy's heart decelerates.

Slipping the pistol back into his pocket, he watches the guy disappear down Marion Avenue into the darkness.

Roddy scans the street—right and left— and makes one more check to ensure no one is approaching. He looks both ways once again, sees no shapes, no moving shadows, nothing suspicious.

He moves on.

Beyond the isolated campus, he walks past shuttered retail stores. There are gonna be security cameras along this stretch. No doubt about it. With his head down, he passes a Chinese takeout joint, a liquor store, a hardware store, and a pizza parlor called Rocco's.

Ironic, same name as where Vinzy thought he'd be dining tonight.

His destination is just beyond Rocco's, at the intersection of Webster and Bedford Park Boulevard.

By now the Albanians are sure to have found the debris Roddy left on the sidewalk, unless the police spied it first. He can only hope the cops have been focused on the spent cartridges and bullets. The success of this night depends on Merko's crew seeing everything before the cops get there.

And if they did, there's no telling what comes next.

A few more steps and he comes to the place he scouted out over the weekend: Jolly Tinker, a pub.

Edon Bronzi, a thirty-year-old Albanian man, is Baki's cousin and second-in-command under Baki.

As a solid soldier, he long ago made his bones when he killed a rival clan's underboss. The enemy clan was trying to muscle in on the Merko clan's drug business. It was a quick kill when he caught the guy outside his apartment building late at night.

One shot to the back of the head. Problem solved.

Edon knows Baki admires his bravery and commitment to the clan. And he won't let the underboss down tonight.

It's a few minutes since gunmen shot up the boss's limo and fired at the crowd. He moves slowly. With his pistol drawn, Edon edges along the wall and approaches the darkened corner of the building at 199th Street, where the shooter, or shooters, were lying in wait. They're long gone by now, but you never know.

He inches his way along the wall, glad he's wearing rubber-soled shoes so it's unlikely they can hear him. He wonders if the assassination attempt on Krye Merko was orchestrated by the Ristani or Marku clan. Either one is a possibility, but he thinks the Ristani clan is more likely behind it. Relations with them have been icy. It's a good thing the boss was already in the club when they opened fire. Even if they weren't going for the boss, they disrespected the clan, and God help them if they're identified.

A noise behind him. He looks back.

It's his comrade Besim. He also has his semiautomatic drawn.

They near the corner of the building slowly. Carefully.

A few other men follow behind them. Each has a handgun drawn, ready to fire.

Edon stops near the building's edge. He waits, then spins around the corner, pistol racked and ready.

No one there.

Whoever they were, they're lousy shots with poor timing. Typical of the Ristani clan's soldiers. But they sure shot up the big boss's limo.

"They're gone," Edon says.

Besim comes up to him. "How many?"

Looking at the sidewalk, Edon says, "It looks like there were two. Different caliber shell casings. Go back to the club and get a flashlight."

Besim is gone and returns soon.

Edon squats down, holding the flashlight above the sidewalk. "Yes, there are twenty-two-caliber casings and nine-millimeter casings. And look at all this unused ammo. They must have panicked and ran, headed down One Ninety-Ninth. Cowardly bastards."

Sirens sound in the distance. They come closer. "Someone called the cops," Edon says.

"What's that?" asks Besim, pointing at the sidewalk.

Edom shoves the bullets and casings aside, picks something up, and holds it beneath the flashlight.

"Oh, man," he grunts. "Look at this. We gotta show it to Baki. Leave the bullets and casings. Let's get back inside before the cops get here."

Chapter 36

Before entering Jolly Tinker, Roddy thinks about what happened at Tirana.

He was very careful—didn't aim at or hit anyone outside the restaurant. And the episode with the mugger, though unexpected, didn't amount to a thing.

He's on schedule.

So far, so good.

Jolly Tinker's been around for nearly fifty years. It's the kind of Irish pub that used to pepper the working-class neighborhoods in all the boroughs. It's a watering hole and meeting place for people who work with their hands. Very few white-collar guys or professionals in this place. In addition to cops from the nearby 52nd Precinct and firemen from a local hook-and-ladder company, the Tinker attracts its share of college students from Fordham University, only a few blocks away. Except for the college kids, it reminds Roddy of John's Bar on Sheepshead Bay Road, the pub where he and Danny spent many a night bellied up to the bar, getting loaded even though, at seventeen, they were underage. Fake IDs did the trick.

With the parka hood still over his head and the scarf covering most of his face, Roddy enters the pub. Once inside, he lowers the hood and rips off the scarf, stuffing it into one of the parka's pockets.

The place is mobbed. It's a sensory assault, full-blown cacophony. It's wall-to-wall people—a horde of men and women, young and old, mixed ethnic types—drinking, laughing, and shouting at the tops of their lungs.

Just as he'd anticipated, despite the frigid weather, the bar is jam-packed because of *Monday Night Football*. The crowd roars with each play as the Packers and Eagles battle it out, and it's playing on a flat-screen TV perched above the bar. It'll be easy for Roddy to blend in, go unnoticed, and complete the plan.

The TV's the only modern trapping in the place. The pub has stone walls, weathered wood ceiling beams, and an antique bar, and nearly every inch of wall space is smothered by a glut of old framed photographs. An Irish flag hangs from the ceiling alongside an American flag.

The room is overheated, reeking of malt and beer and whiskey and the sweat scent of excited people amid the roar of alcohol-infused hilarity.

People are crammed together so tightly, there's no space between the bar and opposite wall. There must be 150 happy souls— maybe more—partying on a Monday night. And the place won't close until four a.m.

No one notices or cares as Roddy weaves his way through the mass of packed bodies. His adrenaline-sharpened senses pick up on everything—snatches of conversation, sights and sounds he'd never ordinarily register.

When he checked the place out on Saturday, there was no evidence of CCTV, though the pub has a motion-detector alarm, which is turned on at closing time at four in the morning.

He elbows his way through the mob, getting to the men's room door.

Once inside, he glances about: old tile walls, three toilet stalls on the right, three urinals on the left, and two sinks just beyond them. The smell of deodorizer cakes wafts from the urinals. As when he cased the place on Saturday, a large metal trash bin stands beyond the pair of sinks. It has a flap door for disposing of paper towels, but the top can be lifted off for emptying. A paper towel dispenser sits on the wall above the bin. You turn the handle and the paper rolls out in detachable squares.

He slips into the stall farthest from the entrance, closes and locks the door, and sheds the parka. From the coat's inside breast pocket, he removes a watch cap and jeans. He grabs two nitrile surgical gloves from an inside pocket and slips them on. Both pistols stay in the parka's outer pockets.

With the parka off, he now wears the tan ski jacket and the black pants he wore into Fogarty's earlier that afternoon. He rips the shoes off his feet, loosens and steps out of the pants, grabs the loose-fitting blue jeans, slips them on, steps back into the shoes, ties the laces, then dons the watch cap.

He's still inside the stall when, suddenly, the men's room door blasts against the tile wall. The bang is so loud, Roddy's ears ring. The crowd's roar caroms off the walls before the door closes. Two half-smashed guys stumble in, stand at the urinals, and empty their beer-filled bladders. They're college kids, seniors with booze-thickened voices, blabbing about graduate school—Fordham, Wharton, or NYU—all while they piss.

Roddy waits, planning his next moves. The guys seem to take forever to piss away the booze but finally shake, tuck, zip, and make a perfunctory show of washing their hands. They pull down on the paper towel dispenser—the thing clangs with each hard pull—dry their hands, and toss the towels into the bin. The bin's flap door squeaks. They talk and laugh raucously, open the men's room door to the crowd's roar, and they're gone.

Silence but for the crowd noise bleeding through the door.

Gotta move quickly before someone else comes in.

Still wearing the nitrile gloves, Roddy opens the stall door, moves to the towel dispenser, rips off two pieces of paper towel, and again locks himself inside the stall. He extracts both pistols from the coat pockets and wipes them down with the towels. Just in case. Don't take any chances. Because of his army service, his fingerprints are on file with the US government.

He rubs every surface of the pistols twice. When they're wiped clean, he slips them back in the parka's pockets. He opens the stall door, lifts the top of the trash bin, and sets it on the floor. Still wearing surgical gloves, he stuffs the parka into the trash receptacle. He moves quickly, thinking he hears voices at the door; if someone comes in now, it'll be obvious he's hiding something.

He pushes down harder.

The coat barely fits, but he presses down.

The voices outside the door seem louder, then fade and blend with the pub's ambient roar.

Luckily, only used paper towels sit at the bottom of the bin. Using his weight, he pushes the parka downward; it compresses the towels beneath and slides in, leaving only a few inches of space at the top of the bin. He rips off the nitrile gloves and pockets them in the ski jacket. He retrieves the black pants and stuffs them inside the trash bin along with the coat.

He pushes down again—with all his weight—and manages to press the clothing a few inches lower. The trash bin now holds the outerwear he wore entering the pub, along with both pocketed pistols, all jammed into the receptacle.

He rolls a bunch of towels from the dispenser, rips them apart, wets a few under the nearest sink faucet, tosses them over the clothing, and piles dry towels over them. After fifteen or twenty paper towels cover everything, it's clear: a casual glance into the bin shows only a heap of dry and wet paper towels. Nothing more.

Someone disposing of a towel will never suspect what lies beneath.

He replaces the top, making sure it's securely in place.

It's done. Everything's stashed away.

He rips off another paper towel and wets it. To make sure he's left no prints, he wipes down the towel dispenser's handle, the top of the trash bin, and the stall door handle; then he tosses the soggy towel through the swinging door into the bin.

Voices sound outside the men's room. They're close. The door opens to the crowd's clamor: the thunder of high spirits.

An older man enters the men's room.

The guy nods at Roddy; he nods back.

The man combs his hair in front of the mirror.

Roddy stands at a sink and peers into the mirror.

Tan jacket, different pants—jeans a lighter color than the black pants he wore on his trek to the pub—a navy watch cap, no scarf, no hood. He looks thirty or forty pounds lighter than when he wore the parka over the ski jacket. A different look—a new ball game—especially for any surveillance cameras that might have captured him on his trek to the Tinker.

Back in the pub.

The crowd seems to heave from side to side—shouting, cheering, or booing at the TV. It's the third quarter. The score is close— the Packers are ahead by four points—and the noise is deafening.

Roddy melts into the mob—an anonymous figure huddled in a roiling mass of beer-swilling patrons.

He's surrounded by snippets of talk, not really conversation— verbal smoke and mirrors—people's half-lit banter and convivial bullshit.

It's a crush of people—flirting, grinning, shouting, sipping whiskey, guzzling beer, and texting. He smells pheromones blended with the sour odor of malt and barley and the peaty smell of whiskey. The smell reminds him of wood stain, but it's mostly reminiscent of John's Bar back in the day.

One young couple—college kids, maybe twenty-one years old— are locked in an openmouthed kiss, tongues sloshing in and out, a kiss that goes on and on. The guy's eyes are closed; hers are wide open and she's peering at her cell phone held aloft behind the guy's left ear.

It's the fourth quarter, Green Bay scores, and it looks like the game's out of reach for the Eagles. The gaiety dissipates. People's attention shifts from the television to one another.

Roddy scans the people around him.

For some reason, an internal sensor sends a signal—maybe it's a tripwire—and a spasm of alarm tightens his chest.

A flash of familiarity, someone he's seen before.

To his left.

He looks carefully, but sees no one he recognizes.

The crowd mills about.

A space forms in the mass.

A closer look, two people away, part of the crowd, very close.

It's him.

The thug from the Pondfield Road stop. Same slicked-back hair, same hard face, same black leather car coat.

Roddy's to his left, just behind him.

The guy's eyes are glued to the TV screen. A sour look on his face; he's lost money on the game.

Is it a tail?

How could it be?

He couldn't have known Roddy would be here tonight.

Roddy threads his way through the crowd, moving toward the entrance.

With the game on ice, the crowd thins.

Roddy edges closer to the door.

People spill out of the Tinker in packs; it's a mass exodus. He joins a group leaving the pub. Four college-age guys, half-lit, laughing, slurring words, bundled up against the cold.

Outside, they horse around. One guy grabs another's hat, and they romp on the sidewalk, laughing and shouting, clouds of vapor pouring from their mouths. They walk in a loosely formed group, a few stumbling from the evening's overindulgence. He moves with them, normally now—no limp—should security cameras pick them up.

Trying to appear part of the group, he ambles a foot or two behind them. The guys argue about football; their hoarse voices dissipate in the wind. Just ahead, two groups of guys walk in the same direction, most likely heading back to Fordham.

To any surveillance camera, he's not the same guy who entered the pub. And he's one of many people leaving the place in droves.

Traffic on Webster is light; an occasional car passes by.

He spots a boro taxi—it's one of the apple-green-colored cabs licensed to pick up passengers in the outer boroughs but not in Manhattan. What luck. He won't have to walk back to Hoffman Street and risk another confrontation with a mugger or be seen by a passerby.

Roddy slips away from the group and raises his arm deliberately, not urgently, hails the taxi, watches the driver pull over, reaches out, grabs the right rear door handle, opens it, and fights the urge to look back to see if anyone notices him. He hops into the cab—casually, no hurry, doesn't look like he's running away—and once inside the cab he smells vanilla from a deodorizer dangling from the rearview mirror. He barely hears himself say, "Hoffman and One Hundred Eighty-Seventh Street."

"You got it, buddy."

Arriving at the intersection a block from his car, Roddy says, "Pull over here." The meter readout says $6; he fishes in a pocket, grabs a ten-spot, hands it to the driver, says, "Thanks," and gets out of the cab.

Hands thrust into his pockets, with the watch cap covering his head, striding normally, he walks a short block to the car. He unlocks the door, slides in, and sits behind the wheel. Now, he feels drained, suddenly realizing how wiped out he is. This morning seems like years ago, not the same day, and he closes his eyes, waiting for his rampaging heart to slow down.

He sits there and keeps his eyes closed, knowing he must wait for things to happen.

If they will. He can't know, but he has to hope.

One more thing, and maybe, with some luck, it'll be over.

Now he fights the fatigue, starts the car, pulls out of the spot, and heads back to Bronxville.

He won't go to the apartment.

He'll go to the place where all roads lead—at least for him.

He'll go home.

To the house on Clubway.

Home.

Where he belongs.

Back to Tracy and the kids.

Chapter 37

Detective First Grade Joe Quartararo has been a member of the NYPD for eighteen years.

Following a three-year stint in the army—Fort Jackson, then Fort Bragg, where the rednecks hated Italians from New York—he was accepted into the Police Academy and became a cop. After walking a beat, he passed the competitive exams, joined the detective division, and became a detective third grade. Since then it's been an upward climb to his current rank. Assigned to the Bronx, he's been investigating homicides since he became a detective.

The pay's a helluva lot better than it used to be. Decent benefits, too. Between his salary and the money his wife, Lisa, earns as an IT technician, they live well. The only problem with the division is the shortage of detectives for the huge population of the Bronx, nearly 1.4 million souls, according to the latest reports. Homicide detectives are spread thin throughout the borough, and the caseload can get insane. It makes for plenty of cold cases.

He's seen the Belmont area change from a strictly Italian neighborhood to one having a mix of ethnicities. The nearby Morris Park section is loaded with Albanians who've begun spreading into the Belmont section. Some Russians and Hispanics have moved in, too. The Darwinian cycle of gentrification won't happen in this area anytime soon.

No doubt, more immigrants are coming—from the Middle East and Africa. Refugees from ethnic conflicts, Jihad, persecution, and all the shit storms befalling the planet.

But mixed ethnic neighborhoods can create conflicts, especially when you have organized crime activity. The Balkan mob has grown enormously, and the Italians have much less control than before. Ethnic warfare never dies. It's amazing: people can't stand living side by side with others who don't share their values or beliefs. That's just nature.

He's been partnered with Mike Connor for the last three years. Mike's a great guy, a dyed-in-the-wool Irish cop, though Joe can't stand his taste in music—Enya's New Age Celtic shit, or U2, or Van Morrison with his bluesy gospel sound. Joe prefers Fleetwood Mac and Santana, but it doesn't make a particle of difference in their relationship. Along with Phil Kaufman, another homicide guy who'd been transferred from Manhattan's One-Nine, they joke about the three Is—Ireland, Israel, and Italy. They razz one another about their ethnicities, but it's good-natured banter.

Joe thinks about yesterday's homicide at Carlo's Latticini. He and Mike arrived at the scene soon after it happened. The dead man's wife discovered him in the back office after she'd returned to the store with coffee and pastries. Hysterical, she had no idea why it went down.

"What do you think of these wounds?" Joe asked the crime scene tech working up the case.

"Pretty sadistic," replied the crime tech.

"The wounds tells a story," Connor said.

"So, tell me the story," Joe said, formulating his own tale of retribution.

"The vic's throat is blown out, and so are his mouth and eyes," Connor said. "This poor bastard saw something he shouldn't have and talked when he should've kept his mouth shut. So here he is, no mouth, throat, or eyes."

"Agreed. This homicide talks out loud," Quartararo said. "It's a mob thing. You think it's the Italians?"

"Who else would kill a fat Italian who makes cheese for a living? There's no evidence the store was robbed. Another thing, if the killer used a twenty-two semiautomatic, he was a pro. No shell casings. He picked 'em up."

"Twenty-twos are a signature of the mob," said Quartararo. "A twenty-two semi is their favorite weapon for a hit. The bullet's destroyed when it impacts anything solid. So whatever we retrieve won't help trace the weapon."

"It's probably untraceable anyway," Connor said. "It was either stolen or bought on the black market."

"What about that piece on the floor?" asked Joe.

"A snub-nosed revolver; an old-time kinda piece. We'll see if there're any prints on it."

"And that cell phone?"

"Looks like he was making a call. We'll have to look into his contacts."

"Look at those guns in the safe," Joe said, pointing at the handguns. "This guy was into some mob-related crap. I guarantee those pistols aren't registered anywhere."

"Okay, so it's a mob hit. But who and why?" asked Mike.

"No idea."

It's just about twenty-four hours later, and Quartararo and Connor are back on Arthur Avenue. This time they're down the block and across the street from where the cheese store homicide went down.

They're standing in the office of Dr. Vincent Masconi's clinic. The Crime Scene Unit just told them it provisionally looks like the doc's been dead for about twelve hours. His body was discovered less than an hour ago by the clinic's receptionist, who reported for work a little after eight thirty. Her wails and a nurse's sobbing can be heard coming from the reception area.

Quartararo knows it's gonna be a long, long day.

"Looks like the same kinda pistol used in yesterday's hit at the cheese store," says Connor.

"And they left the shell casing on the floor," Quartararo says, bending down to get a closer look at the object. "Could be the perp was leaving a message. If I had to guess, I'd say this was a contract killing. We have a small-caliber bullet to the head—no exit wound . . . looks like another twenty-two, the same as yesterday."

"We'll see if forensics find any GSR on the vic's face," adds Connor.

Quartararo moves behind the desk. Masconi's body lies beneath it. "The poor guy musta been doing paperwork when this thing went down," he says, eyeing the open ledger on the desk. "And there's no sign of forced entry. So he either left the door unlocked, which is unlikely in this neighborhood, or he opened it for someone he knew."

"Hey, Joe, isn't this the same clinic where some guy came in demanding his wife's medical records and then went home and shot her?"

"Yup," says Quartararo. "I caught that case just before we became partners. I'll never forget that one."

"Look at this. The doc was packing," says Connor as he bends over and draws back Masconi's sports jacket.

Quartararo squats down and sees a Smith & Wesson .38, partly out of its holster. "You think he was going for it when he got clipped?" he asks.

"Maybe. Or it coulda slipped out when he hit the floor," says Connor, now standing.

"We'll see if he was licensed to carry," says Quartararo. "I can understand a doc wanting a little extra insurance in this neighborhood. But I wonder if this guy mighta been 'connected,' if you get my drift. There was something about him that didn't sit right with me when I was investigating that wacko husband."

Quartararo stands and looks around the room. "No closed-circuit TV in this place," he says. "Too bad. It could tell us a lot."

"CCTV solves plenty of cases."

Joe peers at his partner—Mike's face looks red.

Connor says, "Joe, let's get over to the bank and look at their camera feeds. That'll tell us a lot more than staring at a dead body. We'll take his office records and laptop and check out his apartment. But let's hit the bank to see what kind of video we get."

"Good idea."

"Yeah, let's get there real quick," Mike adds, his tone urgent. "I gotta take a wicked shit, and that bank's got clean bathrooms. Let's hustle over so I can make a deposit."

Chapter 38

Carmine Cellini and his men enter Geppetto's. There's safety in numbers.

The place is nearly empty on a Tuesday night. Actually, it's virtually empty every night of the week.

It's getting close to Christmas—only twenty-seven days away—and Cellini wonders why people aren't in a more celebratory mood. Dine out, live a little. Enjoy life. What the fuck. How many good years does anyone have on this earth? When he was younger, Christmas was a bigger deal than it is nowadays. Or is it just that as a kid, everything's a big deal? Or maybe it wasn't as commercial as it is now. Who knows?

Nothing's the way it used to be. It's all changing. And not for the better.

It's seven p.m. on Tuesday, November twenty-ninth—prime dinner time—and what does he have tonight? A lousy ten patrons in the restaurant, and that's all he'll get. Maybe ten or twelve covers for the night. The people who eat at his place are elderly. They eat early. Down in Boca, or Pompano, they'd show up for the early-bird special. They'd bring coupons, looking for every discount they can get.

Yeah, Geppetto's would be a real loser if he were running it strictly as a restaurant, but it serves his purposes just fine: a hell of a lot of business gets done in the back room, and he takes pride in continuing the tradition of serving authentic Italian food prepared by Italian hands, not like the shit being shoveled onto plates in those Albanian places.

Geppetto's is gonna be empty by eight. These old-timers gotta get home, take their stool softeners, and get to bed by eight thirty or nine o'clock at the latest. They're so old they fart dust. A fate that awaits us all, if we live long enough.

Why is he so down on old people? Maybe he's jealous because they've managed to live so long—something neither his mother nor his father ever got to do. They died in a house fire when he was five years old, while he and his kid sister, Angelica, were staying at his uncle Mike and aunt Vera's place in the Poconos for the weekend. Like a good aunt and uncle, Mike and Vera raised them, two blocks away on Lorillard Place.

Growing up, he knew Uncle Mike was in the rackets, so he fell into the life. He has no complaints. He made his bones long ago and has plenty of dough to show for it. The life's been good to him. But lots of friends from the old days are either dead or in prison. At least he's still alive and kicking.

But what the fuck's going on with these shootings? Cellini wonders, as he, Tony DiNardo, and seven of his best soldiers stand in the aisle leading to the rear room.

First Charlie and now Vinzy—gone. Not only did he lose two good earners, but Charlie and Vinzy were good friends. He and Charlie went way back, and he was like a big brother to Vinzy when the kid was coming up. On top of it all, he can't dope out who in hell would be starting a war now.

That old-timer Sal Branca and his wife are sitting at their favorite table in the front room. The Brancas have been coming to Geppetto's for years, twice a week, like it's stamped on their souls. Tuesdays and Thursdays. And they always take the same table. Habits are tough to break, especially when you're in your eighties.

Sal Branca has noticed Cellini's entrance. Sal rips the napkin from his neck, tosses it on the table, and totters over. Getting closer, he extends his hand. A sign of respect.

"Mr. Cellini, my wife, Carmella, and I extend our condolences to you on the loss of Charlie and Dr. Masconi. Such terrible things to happen. We are so sorry for your loss . . . and for the loss to Arthur Avenue."

"Thank you, Salvatore. I appreciate the sentiment."

They embrace and slap each other on their backs.

Two other old men approach, each wanting to pay respects. Cellini acknowledges them as his soldiers stand nearby.

Then Cellini, DiNardo, and the other men enter the back room and close the pocket door.

His best soldiers are now gathered together: Tony DiNardo, Vince Parisi, Johnny Fataruso, the Domino brothers, Frankie Santoro, Pete Falcone, and Ralphie Rizzo. All good guys, all made men. But there's no sign of Albie Sansone.

The other men sit at two tables close to the door as Cellini and DiNardo head for the rear corner table, where they always sit. Cellini signals for the Domino brothers to join him and Tony at that table—the one they call Carmine's desk.

The four men sit down.

"Where's Albie?" asks Carmine.

"He's out with the flu," answers Richie Domino, the older of the two brothers.

"Fuckin' guy's always out for one reason or another," says Carmine.

"Hey, boss, it's flu season," replies Richie. "Give the guy a break."

Franco approaches.

"Let's eat, and then we'll talk about this fucked-up situation," Carmine says. "Something's brewing, and we gotta get a handle on it."

As usual, he orders for everyone. Franco writes on his pad, nodding as Carmine rattles off the order. "I'm keeping it simple tonight, only rigatoni with marinara sauce and a small salad. And keep the Barolo coming," Carmine says, lighting up a cigar, a Cohiba Corona, his favorite—rich, earthy, and aromatic.

He points to the other table and says, "Bring my boys over there the same thing. We all eat the same tonight. And vino for everybody."

Gotta keep everyone happy and treat 'em all the same.

Carmine leans closer to Richie Domino and says in a half whisper, "Any word yet on Vinzy or Charlie Cheese?"

"Nah, Carmine. The cops ain't sayin' nothin'. I hear they're thinkin' they were mob hits."

"Who'd wanna clip Vinzy or Charlie?"

"No idea, boss."

"I've been thinking it could be the Albanians, but we've had no trouble with them. And the other families . . . doesn't make sense."

Richie shrugs. "Beats the shit outta me. I can talk to our guys at the Four-Six and Four-Eight, see if they find somethin' out."

"Yeah, you do that. Meanwhile, with Vinzy gone, I couldn't meet with that mick accountant, Burns, today. And we've lost our business with the clinic. Son of a bitch. Vinzy was a good earner. A good guy, too. I'm gonna miss him."

"Speakin' of Vinzy reminds me of somethin' . . . Isn't Merko goin' into the hospital soon?" Richie asks.

"Yeah, tomorrow, the thirtieth," Carmine says. "That's all set. And keep your mouths shut, you hear me?"

The Domino brothers nod. "Sure, Carmine."

"I don't want any leaks. Don't mention a thing to the other guys, got it?"

They nod again.

"Carmine," DiNardo interjects, "you think I should get aholda Dolan just to make sure he's still on board?"

"Nah. Not necessary. After what happened to his kid, he knows he'd better come through."

"Yeah," says DiNardo, smiling. "Dolan's a real family man. He'll do anything to protect his family." He snorts and lights up a cigarette.

"Yeah, and then we got plans for him, that no-good wiseass."

It's seven forty-five in the evening. Albie Sansone lies on his bed thinking about Donieta, his girlfriend of four months. What a beautiful woman. Intelligent, too. If he didn't know better, he'd think she was Italian, not Albanian. Just goes to show how you see people in a different light once you get to know them. He met her at the Fordham Diner, where she works part-time as a waitress while she takes classes at Fordham. She's gonna be an elementary school teacher. When they met, it was like something magical happened—an instant connection, one that's gonna last. He feels it in his bones.

Now they're an item—no, more than that, they're serious.

But what'll his mother think if he brings Donieta home? An Albanian girl. Not Italian. Could be trouble. Mom's old-fashioned, doesn't care for the Albanians. Calls 'em copycats. Fake Italians. Lowlifes. The old-timers have bias so deeply ingrained, it never fades. He's gotta think more about it, then decide what to do. Until he does, they can't start living together.

And he dreads the thought of meeting her parents. Would they ever accept her marrying an Italian? Sometimes he thinks it'd be better if they just eloped, like something out of a B movie.

And what about his situation with the Cellini crew? That'll be big trouble the second they learn he's seeing her—*if* they find out.

He can always pick up where he left off—finish school and become a court stenographer. He's kept up his skills, practicing at home, transcribing radio talk shows. A good job would be waiting for him at Bronx Supreme through Uncle Paulie's connections. Become a state employee and have security, good benefits, too.

So here he is, lying around in his apartment, pretending to have the flu. A few more days of this and he'll be bored to death. There's nothin' but reality shows on TV—*Keeping Up with the Kardashians, The Real Housewives of New Jersey, Survivor, Naked and Afraid*—real shit.

He glances at the bedside clock. It's seven thirty.

It's time.

He picks up the burner phone and dials the number.

On the second ring, a voice says, "Yeah?"

"They're there," he says.

There's a *click*. The line is dead.

Salvatore Branca and his wife, Carmella, have been eating dinner twice a week at Geppetto's for years—always at their favorite table. Franco, the waiter, doesn't let anyone else sit there. He reserves the table for them every Tuesday and Thursday night. Sal loves the calamari and linguini doused in fra diavolo sauce. And the veal parmigiana is excellent. "She's always the same," Franco once remarked.

And Franco's right. You can count on a dish being prepared properly *every* time, always the same—no variations. Mr. Cellini runs a fine restaurant. And the menu never changes. There are no fancy high-priced specials—not like these new restaurants, where you got young snots in the kitchen and waiters who don't give a damn, and where there's always some *pazzo* dish that no real Italian would ever eat. At Geppetto's, it's the real thing, the way your mama and nonna made it back in the old country, and it's always excellent.

He looks around the room. It's not a fancy place, just a good old-fashioned trattoria like they got back in Napoli. Simple white tablecloths, a quiet room, no music, good food. Too bad the place does such lousy business. It'll probably go the way of all traditional things—die out and be replaced by one of these new places with no tablecloths, loud music, uncomfortable chairs so you don't linger, and high-priced dishes, not authentic Southern Italian.

In a way he's glad he's on his way out. At eighty-two, how many years can he have left? And Carmella, at eighty, has bad emphysema.

Salvatore wonders why Mr. Cellini has all those men with him tonight. It looks like a big meeting. It must be about that murder at the laticini and at Dr. Masconi's office.

Salvatore feels a draft of frigid air, looks up, and sees four men wearing long coats and hats. They enter, close the door, and move through the restaurant along the side aisle. Tough-looking men, mobsters—more of Mr. Cellini's men. Yes, something's going on. The men head toward the door leading to the back room.

Yes, something big is going on, a war is brewing. It's getting to be like the old days.

Carmine Cellini finishes eating his pasta. He loves the taste of parmigiana cheese grated onto the rich, thick marinara sauce, and adores the taste of extra virgin olive oil mixed with tomatoes, onion, garlic, and whatever else goes into the sauce to give it a slight bite. His chef, Gino, knows how to make it the right way— with a touch of good Chianti. And rigatoni with its ridges holds the sauce beautifully; it's his favorite shaped pasta. Cooked *al dente*, it has a density other pasta shapes lack, and it does something in his mouth no other pasta can do. He sips his wine, then picks up his cigar and puffs.

He hears the pocket door slide open and bang into its slot. He glances up. Can't be Franco; he always enters the back room through the door from the kitchen.

No. It's not Franco, for sure.

Shit. The guy's bursting into the room.

It happens very fast. There's another man, then two more. Four men, and it's so quick, it's a blur. Confusing. What the fuck? There's a shotgun, and another gun pops out of a guy's coat, a machine pistol. Is it an Uzi? No!

A flash. Another one. Bright. A blast, sudden, deafening. Something slams into his chest, a hard blow, and his insides collapse, and he's falling back, and the room swirls, and it feels like a sledgehammer has hit him, and he's in the air, thrown against the wall, and another *thump*, and then something explodes in his head, and his world is gone.

Kostandin Dushku, a veteran soldier of the Merko clan, holds the Micro Uzi submachine gun and sprays the room. Back and forth the weapon sweeps, left, right, then again, set on automatic mode and firing nine-millimeter Parabellum rounds—seventeen hundred per minute. With a magazine capacity of thirty-two rounds, he can empty the weapon in seconds. The Uzi jumps in his hands as he fires, yet he controls it as he rakes the room.

Men go down—flesh flays, blood spurts, bodies fly. His magazine empties; he presses the release button, and it drops to the floor. He slaps another magazine into the weapon and continues firing.

He concentrates on the rear corner table where four men sit. He recognizes Carmine Cellini, blasts away, sprays the table, and gets the others, burst after burst, one- or two-second spurts of firepower so he doesn't spit the rounds out in one place. Control, control, that's what it takes. The other tables are decimated by Kostandin's comrades. Edon Bronzi and his comrade Besim are beside him.

Edon's twelve-gauge shotgun booms, spewing pellets and heat, while Besim fires a nine-millimeter Glock. The fourth man, Armond, discharges a pump-action sawed-off shotgun shot after shot. The weapon roars as he racks and clacks and fires away.

Muzzle flashes streak amid the thunder of gunfire. The air shimmers with heat, and Kostandin's eardrums feel the percussive blasts. Shell casings bounce on the floor amid smoke and splintered wood, glass shards, and clouds of plaster dust. The Italians go down, dead and dying. Two men spasm before falling to the floor, their bodies blown apart. Chunks of flesh are scattered everywhere.

Holes in the walls, tables overturned, bodies strewn in grotesque postures. One man's head is shattered, now barely a human face. Guts hang from his belly, a glistening pile of blasted innards.

Kostandin slaps a third magazine into the Uzi and keeps firing. The bodies buck as bullets impact them, shredding flesh, splintering bone. Blood spatters, spurts, and pools everywhere. Gun smoke fills the air. The room reeks of it.

When the third magazine is nearly empty, Kostandin raises his hand.

The firing stops.

Kostandin's ears ring. He swallows hard. Bubbles burst in his ears. He surveys the room through smoke and the acrid smell of gunpowder.

Death and devastation. Nine bodies. Not a sign of life.

"They're finished," Edon says. He bends down and picks up the empty Uzi mags.

Kostandin reaches into his coat pocket and extracts the little item Baki gave him—the one Besim and Edon found on the sidewalk, along with all those bullets and shell casings, outside Tirana last night.

He inspects it, turns it over, and smiles. "It's all over for you, *Don* Cellini. All over."

Cellini's body is slouched against the rear wall behind the overturned table. Tablecloth, food, silverware, and glistening shards of shattered glassware are all over the place. Everything's spattered with blood and flesh.

What's left of Cellini is filled with bullet holes—a few to his face, lots in his chest and belly. One eye is blown out—now a gaping hole where the eye had been.

Oddly, a lit cigar protrudes from what's left of Cellini's clenched teeth. Smoke curls from the cigar's end, rising in a wisp into the air.

Kostandin sets the object on top of Cellini's head. "Yes, it's all over for you. Geppetto's is no more, and your business is over."

Kostandin turns and waves to the other three.

The gunmen head back to the front of the restaurant.

Salvatore Branca huddles beneath the table. He drapes his arm over Carmella.

When he first saw those men enter the restaurant, he thought they were Mr. Cellini's associates. He trailed them with his eyes and saw them open their coats, reach inside, and pull out guns.

He knew what was about to happen.

He dropped his fork. "Get down, Carmella," he rasped. "Get down."

Despite their age, they both managed to slide beneath the table.

Then he heard the shots coming from the back room. Horrifying. He kept his hands over his head and his eyes closed.

Now, with his heart racing, he wonders if he should slip a nitroglycerin tablet under his tongue. His angina might act up. But if he moves, he might call attention to himself or Carmella. Her breathing is so heavy, Salvatore fears she'll have an asthmatic attack.

He keeps his eyes closed, pats Carmella's shoulder, and covers his head with his free hand.

In the silence that follows the back-room blasts, he whispers to Carmella, "Don't move and keep your eyes closed."

He hears footsteps as the men head toward the front door.

One man stops and fires a burst of bullets from his weapon. Salvatore spasms at the rattling of the gun, then hears plaster chunks falling from the ceiling.

Oh, father in heaven, spare my sweet Carmella and me.

"Albania forever," shouts the man.

The restaurant door opens, and a blast of icy air sweeps through the room.

The door slams shut.

The Albanians are gone.

Salvatore, Carmella, and the other patrons stay frozen in place. Carmella is shaking and crying. Wailing can be heard from beneath the other tables. Salvatore holds Carmella tightly, kissing her forehead.

Doesn't matter how old you are; you're never ready to die.

He hears car doors slam, then an engine guns, followed by peeling rubber, then silence.

Salvatore won't look in the back room. "Stay down, my love. Stay down," he whispers to Carmella. "Let's lie here for a little while and thank God we're still alive."

Chapter 39

It's eight fifteen on Tuesday night, the twenty-ninth. Joe Quartararo and Mike Connor sit facing Lieutenant Patrick Brady in his office. The call about the Geppetto's massacre came in moments ago, just as the two detectives were packing it in for the night.

"I had a feeling this was gonna be a long day," says Joe, knowing he and Mike will soon be headed back to Arthur Avenue. When they caught the cheese store homicide, he wondered if it was an isolated event, but Masconi's murder added more fuel to the fire. Now this bloodbath at Geppetto's?

Shit. He never anticipated an all-out war was about to erupt.

"Before you head over to Geppetto's," Brady begins, "what've you got on the Masconi hit? I read your reports from yesterday on the cheese store. Anything new to add there?"

"The only thing new is it looks like the weapon used there was a twenty-two pistol, the same type that killed the doctor," answers Joe. "As for Masconi, Lieutenant, we don't have much sorted out there yet, either. We need more time.

"There're prints all over the office, and the place was dusted pretty good; we don't expect to find anything useful there. Hell, we might pick up a few that're on file; after all, I'm sure the clinic had its share of unsavory characters visiting. If we do get some hits, we'll track 'em down."

"The doc let the perp in," says Connor. "The video from the bank across the street confirms that. The ME set the death between eight and nine last night, which jibes with what's on the video."

"It's grainy and shot from about seventy-five feet away," Joe adds, "and on it we see a big guy—must weigh in at about two fifty—ringing the clinic's bell a few minutes before eight. He's wearing a huge coat with a hood covering his face. He keeps his back to the camera, and his head's down. Cagey bastard knew he was under surveillance. Anyway, the doc opens the door and lets him in."

"Twenty minutes later," Joe continues, "the guy comes out of the clinic through the fire exit door. He keeps his head down and walks away. He has a slight limp. We couldn't make out his face because not only was he under a hood, but a scarf covered his face."

"The doc let the guy in?" Brady asks. "Means he knew him."

"Right. We're looking to see how 'connected' the doc was."

"The Bronx mob?"

"Looks that way. And the bullet hole in the doc's forehead looks like a typical execution."

"What else you have?"

"It's only been one day, but we hit some retail outlets and apartment buildings and managed to partially track this guy on CCTV. That limp of his . . . we'll have the forensic people look at it to see if they can make out the guy's problem. It might help identify him.

"We got him going from one video feed to another, and he eventually got to that Albanian restaurant, Tirana. We lost him there because no surveillance cameras are at that intersection."

"No cameras?"

"Nah. Those Albanians must've undone the CCTV. Doesn't matter because we get more video of him after he leaves the area."

"What happens then?"

"We don't know for sure that it's him, but the Five-Two is look-ing into a shooting that happened right outside the restaurant at the same time our suspect was in the area. People from the apartment house on the corner of One Ninety-Ninth reported shots fired, and when the cruisers responded, they found the sidewalk littered with spent shell casings and live rounds—but of course the Albanians wouldn't say a thing, even though one of their limos looked like Swiss cheese. A couple of bullet holes were in the front door of the place, too."

"What happens next?"

"The feeds are pretty sparse, but we tracked him going into that pub Jolly Tinker. Guy had that same limp and was wearing the same coat and hood."

Quartararo pauses, sighs, and shakes his head.

"What?" asks Brady.

"I hate to tell you this, Lieutenant, but that's the last we see of the guy."

"What do you mean?"

"We watched the video feed three times," says Connor. "No one wearing a black, hooded coat ever left the club. People were coming and going all night long. *Monday Night Football* was on— and when the game was over, they left in droves."

"So the guy must've changed clothes in the pub," Brady says.

"That's what we figured," Joe replies. "So this afternoon we went over to the Tinker to go through the trash, and maybe get to talk with someone who was there Monday night. We struck out on both counts: the garbage was picked up early this morning—we have a call into Sabado's Carting to follow up with them.

"And the guys working behind the bar last night aren't due back until tomorrow night. We called both of them, but the calls went to voice mail. We planned on dropping by tomorrow, but with all this other shit going down, we'll keep calling until they answer. We've got their addresses, too, so we'll interview them tonight, one way or another, after we're finished at Geppetto's. And in the morning,

I guess we'll be sorting through piles of garbage at some dump. It'll be like looking for a needle in a haystack."

"You mean to tell me the Tinker doesn't have any security cameras?" asks Brady, shaking his head.

"None," replies Joe, stifling a yawn and thinking about how many more hours it'll be before he gets to hit the sack.

"Okay, guys, thanks," Brady says, getting up from behind his desk. "Get over to Geppetto's. The crime scene people are working the place up. Kaufman and Correlli are already there. They'll bring you up to speed."

Entering Geppetto's, Quartararo is certain he and Connor will find the remnants of a vicious gangland massacre. The first reports sounded grim, but what the hell, he's seen plenty of corpses in his time. Captain Brady said the crime scene was reported as being "gruesome. A real slaughter."

But Joe's seen everything—from the dead junkie who OD'd in a piss-stinking back alley, to the gutted crack whore slumped dead on a garbage-strewn staircase, to the twelve-year-old girl who'd been raped on a rooftop and then thrown to her death.

And plenty more.

He's lived and worked through it all—the shootings, stabbings, and drive-bys; the turf wars, whether the warriors are black, Puerto Rican, Dominican, Albanian, or Russian gangbangers; home invasions and random homicides; domestic violence turned to murder; and every conceivable means by which people succumb to their violent impulses.

The back room of Geppetto's is taped off. The crime scene people are swarming around in full regalia. They wear booties and surgical masks, stepping carefully over the bodies strewn about the place. Camera flashes throw bursts of light through the place.

Kaufman and his partner sit casually at a table in the front room. "Welcome to hell," says Kaufman. "CSU's nearly finished. We'll be able to go in there soon. Better hold your noses."

A few minutes later they enter the back room.

Slipping beneath the police tape, Quartararo realizes he's never seen anything like this in his eighteen years on the job. It's something right outta hell. A slaughterhouse. Looks like a Hieronymus Bosch painting. Or better yet, a war zone.

Total destruction.

The coppery smell of blood and the stench of feces assault him. Ruptured guts are strewn throughout the room. The reek of it all hits the back of his throat and sits on his tongue like a foul vapor mixed with the odor of gunpowder and plaster dust.

Quartararo stifles a gag, fighting the reflex, but incipient nausea rolls up from his belly. Joe knows the pong of this room will stick with him for a long time. When he's least expecting it, the stench will fill his nostrils and invade his sinuses even when he's not anywhere near Geppetto's—it's only ten seconds and the scent memory's already imprinted on his brain. Nearly choking, he rips a handkerchief from his pocket and covers his nose.

Connor coughs, sputters, then retches and stumbles from the room. He returns moments later with a cloth napkin covering his nose.

The scene is unbelievable. Never in all his days has he seen such wholesale annihilation.

Two of the dead still have open eyes—inert, lifeless, like doll's eyes. No matter how many times he's seen dead men with that stare to nowhere, it always gets to him. And the other corpses lie in twisted disarray, torn apart by a tsunami of lead.

Bullet holes are everywhere. Spent shell casings litter the floor. Yup, the place looks like a war zone.

And the blood. It's amazing how much blood the human body contains. It's everywhere, all over. Slick puddles of it, some congealed—it looks like shiny pools of currant jelly. The stickiness says the shootings went down a short time ago; the blood hasn't crusted over yet, not even at the edges of the pools.

The tables are blasted to pieces, splintered, overturned, riddled with holes. Chairs are upside down. Dishes, silverware, glasses, uneaten food, and blood-soaked linens are everywhere. Blood spatter covers every surface, and bits of bone and brain are on the floor and walls.

My God, it looks like something ISIS would do in Iraq or Syria.

Quartararo steps over six or seven bodies and looks down at one he knows all too well: Carmine Cellini.

Cellini's corpse reminds Joe of a dropped marionette.

The mobster is propped up against the wall, behind what's left of the table where he must've been sitting when he was blasted to hell. Bullet holes are everywhere—maybe twenty or thirty of them on the wall behind the body. Plenty of holes in Cellini, too.

And a cigar is sticking out of his mouth, protruding between clenched teeth. Strangely, the stogie's still smoking. Like what happened to Carmine Galante in Brooklyn a whole bunch of years ago.

One of the guys from the Crime Scene Unit snaps pictures of Cellini. For sure, there'll be plenty of photos in the morning edition of the *Post*.

And what's sitting on Cellini's head is very strange.

Right there, on top of his carefully coiffed, dyed black hair, is a little matchbox. No doubt it was put there by the Albanians.

It's a message, for sure.

It's from Cellini's restaurant, this very place that he owns and where his mangled corpse sits propped against a wall—Geppetto's.

A little matchbox.

It's the kind you don't see much of anymore because restaurants don't allow smoking.

It's a small thing, holds maybe ten matchsticks.

Joe bends down and looks at it closely: the box cover has this picture of Geppetto carving his boy Pinocchio out of a chunk of wood, right out of the Pinocchio story. It's the restaurant's logo.

Geppetto and Pinocchio.

That matchbox was probably lying on the floor of this room.

Probably sat there in the middle of all that blood and gore and cartridge casings.

Maybe as a joke one of the gunmen picked it up and put it on Cellini's head.

Or, maybe it's a message, like "Albania forever." Isn't that what the old-timer Salvatore Branca said one of the gunmen shouted before leaving the restaurant?

How else could that silly little matchbox have gotten there?

It's eleven thirty p.m., a little more than three hours since they spoke with Lieutenant Brady in his office.

On the way back to headquarters, Quartararo thinks he's seen enough blood and guts to last a lifetime.

In a couple of years he'll have put in his twenty and will have a decent enough pension. Maybe he'll take his brother-in-law up on the offer to buy him out of his restaurant in Chappaqua, a charming little bistro on King Street, right in the center of town. He's always liked cooking, especially French food, and enjoys being with people. Meet and greet. It's a fun thing to do.

So maybe he'll become a restaurateur.

But back to the job at hand—trying to figure the who and why of a bunch of homicides.

He looks over at Connor behind the wheel. "Those barkeeps had nothing to offer," Quartararo says. "How *could* they? There must've been a few hundred people watching *Monday Night Football* at the Tinker."

"Yeah, that place is a gold mine," says Connor.

"Think we'll find anything at the dump?"

"Nah. What're we gonna find?" Connor asks, shaking his head. "I can't imagine going through a dump site and coming up with a damned thing. Even if we find the guy's coat, so what? I'll bet he ripped out the label and it'll lead us nowhere. But we'll give it a shot. I'll tell you, though, this is some big-time shit."

"Yup, and it's all mob-related," Quartararo says. "These homicides: the cheese store guy, Dr. Masconi, both shot with a twenty-two-caliber pistol. Mob hits for sure. Shots fired at Tirana. My guess from the shell casings and live bullets is there were two shooters, probably a couple of hit men. Edmond Merko's limo's all shot up. They must've been trying to clip the big guy."

"For sure."

"You know there *had* to be payback."

"It looks like a war's starting," Connor says. "And that witness, Mr. Branca—same name as the guy who threw the home run pitch to Bobby Thompson in the fifty-one pennant playoff—the old guy said one of the gunmen shouted 'Albania forever.'"

"This shit happens when these ethnic types live too close to each other."

Connor nods. "Yeah, Joe . . . to quote Rodney King, 'Can't we all just get along?'"

He makes a left turn, and they pull up in front of the precinct. "You know what, Joe? I'll probably have a bad dream about what we saw tonight. It was a fucking nightmare."

"Yeah, I'm not gonna forget it." Joe says. "I'm bushed. I'm headed home to catch a few hours of shut-eye. I know Lisa's waiting up for me. And tomorrow we have to sift through all that garbage."

He gazes at the precinct building, shaking his head. "I'll tell you something, Mike. I made up my mind tonight: I'm gonna retire in two years, as soon as I've put in my twenty."

January 2017

Chapter 40

Tirana is far more elegant than the building's exterior led Roddy to believe. The impression from the street is of a two-story place that once housed a group of retail stores. Maybe the original structure was home to a Dunkin' Donuts and Baskin-Robbins, or possibly a Subway shop next to a video game arcade. Something tacky and contemporary.

But once you enter the place, you get a different impression. The entranceway floor is covered with rich-looking red carpeting. A black double-faced eagle is emblazoned in the middle of the crimson-red carpet—the symbol of Albania.

Beyond the entranceway, the room opens to a lovely expanse. Black leather banquettes line the walls, giving the place a sleek, clubby feel. The chairs are soft and comfortable. It's modern, but not overly so. It's not state-of-the-art streamlined stark. And it's not overdone in an old-world style, either. Dark woods abound. Heavy table linens, small bouquets of flowers, and small candle-lit lamps sit atop each table. A cadre of waiters carrying trays of food create a homey, comfortable feeling. The lighting is subdued, but not too dim, and there's nothing glitzy or overly done about the decor.

There's no canned music coming from hidden speakers, no boisterous drinking crowd bellied up to the bar as there was with McLaughlin's. There's simply a small service bar. It's not a singles joint or a drinking crowd. The room allows for intimate conversation and has a subdued European elegance.

A small, slightly elevated stage says there's occasional entertainment with room for three or four musicians. A black baby grand piano sits off to the side.

Tirana's food is sumptuous, the portions generous. To Roddy, the preparations seem exotic but have a welcome tang of familiarity—chicken with walnuts and baked leeks for him, lamb with yogurt for Tracy. Danny and Angela love their dishes—seafood with complicated names Roddy doesn't even try to remember.

The waiter, a gracious older man who's proud of his profession, said Albanian cuisine is basically Mediterranean in style, influenced by Greek, Italian, and Turkish cooking.

And while the food is excellent, the prices aren't celestial.

Not that cost matters tonight: they're guests of Edmond Merko.

Sitting at a banquette with Tracy, Dan, and Angela, Roddy feels a swell of tranquility wash over him—something he hasn't experienced in a long time. Two glasses of Albanian wine have done the trick. It's good stuff; he may buy some and give it a real tryout.

Tracy leans against him, and he slides his arm over her shoulder.

For a change, Dan looks comfortable in his skin—doesn't have that nail-bitten, goose-bumped look he gets when he feels the world's coming down on his head. In fact, for the last few weeks, Danny's seemed more at peace with things—even with himself—than he's been in a long time. It's a good thing.

"I hope you guys'll forgive me," Dan says, leaning toward Roddy and Tracy, "but I gotta say I'm glad you're back together. When you were apart, it felt like nothing was the same."

Angela nods. "I agree."

"You're not out of line," Tracy says. "Nothing *was* the same, and we're really good now."

She pats Roddy's hand and rubs it gently.

He places his hand over hers.

Dan and Angela seem to be waiting for Roddy to speak.

Roddy thinks about what he could say but decides to let the moment pass in silence.

He could say he'd been too taken up by work and office politics, or even say he'd been suffering from some sort of male menopause, but that wouldn't be the truth.

Even though Danny's unaware of the recent horrors, he'd know it's a lie.

And Roddy made a solemn pledge to Tracy.

No more secrets or lies. From the time I made that promise, I'll share everything with her.

And he'll abide by his pledge to never keep anything from her again.

Now, in this moment, he feels her love for him. It's durable and deep and has survived the spasms of the last year and a half, when his life devolved into such a disordered mess.

At this moment, the dinner and company are superb, and it's beginning to feel like old times with Danny and Angela, before they were derailed by Kenny Egan's blandishments and blarney.

Roddy feels lightness in his chest—as though the world is a better place.

He finally says, "We have to cherish the people we love, and"— he feels his throat close as his eyes grow wet— "I love you guys, all of you."

And there's not a particle of mistruth in his words; they're as genuine as anything he's ever uttered.

Danny's eyes glitter. He nods, then smiles. His face reddens in that blotchy Irish blush of his. "Oh, Cisco," he says, recalling a bit from TV reruns of *The Cisco Kid* they watched as kids at Danny's house.

"Oh, Pancho," Roddy says with a chortle.

They all laugh.

Tracy leans her head on his shoulder.

"I know what you mean," Danny says. "I really do."

"So you won't be a wreck any time a client doesn't show up?" Angela asks with a smile in her voice.

"Nah, it's all small stuff. Like Roddy says."

Edmond Merko appears at the table. He's using a cane, and he walks with a slight limp after his knee surgery. Though he's a massive man, Roddy can tell he's lost some weight.

"How are my special guests doing?" he asks in that basso Balkan voice.

"The food is wonderful," Tracy says. "And this wine is heavenly."

Merko laughs. "Ah, Albanian wine is very underrated," he says with a grin.

He slides into the banquette, sitting next to Roddy. The man is Kodiak bear big, exudes a boatload of bonhomie, throws a huge arm over Roddy's shoulder, and says, "This is a wonderful doctor. I wanted to thank him for saving my life."

Roddy smiles and shakes his head.

"No, *no*," Merko protests. "I would have paid a heavy price for my indulgences over the years, but I say to you all, divine intervention brought this man to me."

Merko pauses, regarding Tracy, Danny, and Angela. "And you know what?" he asks. "He is a modest man—*too* modest. He saved me from death, and I wanted to thank him, but I had to call and *beg* him to be my guest here. He thought I was making an empty gesture by inviting him, but I'm not that way. And here you are, on a beautiful evening in the new year. It is an honor to have you at Tirana, and I hope you are all having a good time."

"We are, Edmond," Roddy says. "It's a beautiful place, and I'm glad you invited us."

Merko pats Roddy's back with a lunch-box-sized hand and says, "Good, good. Enjoy the evening. And please, stay for the entertainment. A lovely young woman will be singing, along with

a violin, a clarinet, and a piano player. She sings Albanian lulla-
bies and love songs, and she has the voice of an angel."

"We look forward to hearing her," Roddy says.

"I must tell you one other thing," Merko adds in that husky
voice. "After my stay in the hospital, I decided what is worthwhile
in this life. In the spring my Masiela and I will be going back to
Albania for good. My partner, a young man named Baki, will be
running things. And I hope you will visit Tirana again."

"We will, Edmond," says Roddy. "We will."

Merko lets out a hearty laugh as he gets up, waves goodbye,
and limps away.

They sit comfortably, finishing their wine, enjoying one
another's company.

Then an after-dinner drink.

Sitting at a banquette in Edmond Merko's restaurant with
Tracy and Danny and Angela, Roddy ponders the unlikely chain
of events—happenstance or not—that took his life along such a
dark terrain. It all streaks through his mind as decades contract
in seconds: his poor, damaged mother, his dead father whom he
never met, the depravity of his early years, his boyhood days with
Danny, the tender kindness of Peggy Burns, the botched burglary
from which Kenny Egan escaped, and everything afterwards—a
progression of good things—until the return of Kenny Egan, the
arrival of Grange and the threats, the extortion, then murder, and
Roddy knows his life became a tangle of lies; and finally came
Cellini, DiNardo, Masconi, and Merko, and now, here he is with
Tracy and Danny and Angela, at peace with his world, sitting in
Edmond Merko's restaurant.

Yes, there are moments that alter the arc of our lives, Roddy
thinks.

As Roddy looks back on his life, it seems linear, as though
everything was planned from the beginning—until this very
moment in time.

Maybe in retrospect life always seems a seamless affair, a unified procession of connected events telling a story.

But has it truly been an unbroken road—a clear chronicle—that brought him to this moment in his life?

Or was it simply a matter of chance with random events occurring in an indifferent universe, and only in looking back does it all seem to tell a seamless tale?

Is it fate versus free will?

Roddy cannot know.

There are so many beguiling mysteries of the mind.

But Roddy knows there *was* a single random thing—a fluke in his forty-seven-year stream of time—and it came from nowhere, jogging his mind, and when it did, it managed to bring them all to Tirana tonight.

It was such a trivial thing, one barely worth noting in the overarching scheme of things: on Thanksgiving Day, a votive candle died and a utility lighter ignited something.

That small flame evoked a memory of that little matchbox with the picture of Geppetto and his little son, Pinocchio, on its cover.

He never recalled pocketing it that first night at Geppetto's.

And that little matchbox morphed into a plan.

Awhile later, as the musicians are setting up, Roddy leans back in the banquette, his arm still over Tracy's shoulders, and she leans against him with her eyes closed.

He gazes across the restaurant, seeing other diners enjoying an evening out. He sees two men—rough-hewn guys, men who look like veterans of the mob life—sitting at a table across the room.

Things have happened and more things will come to pass.

The papers write about a likely war erupting between the Italian and Albanian mobs. Roddy noticed a police patrol car parked outside Tirana tonight.

And Tracy had mentioned a heavy police presence on Arthur Avenue when she and Angela went food shopping for specialty items just before Christmas.

He knows he's unleashed a potential tide of savagery and retribution, and it's likely men will die.

But he won't let himself wallow in guilt. Those men have made their choices, just as he's made his. They must live—and some will die—traveling the roads they've chosen.

He never meant for these things to happen. He could never have known what awaited him when he made the choice to become a partner in the restaurant. He only wanted to make Danny happy and share something—an opportunity—with his lifelong friend and blood brother. He could never have foreseen the evil, the threats, the horror of it all.

He's lived through it and his family is now safe.

There's nothing to fear.

What began with the return of Kenny Egan to his life and ended with the massacre at Geppetto's has lost its power over him.

He and his family are free.

But he'll never be free of one thing: he must live a riven life—one as a husband, father, and physician and the other, a life of secrets.

And the crimes he's committed will always be with him.

Will the ghost of what he did haunt him?

How can he know?

Life is filled with uncertainties, and he'll never know how the past may drag him back, no matter how much he's changed.

Is he at fault for not having realized how one bad decision could beget a stream of horrors?

Perhaps, but it would be self-blame for a string of unforeseeable events.

And when things got worse—whether with Grange or Cellini or Charlie Cheese or Vinzy—he made his choices.

He did evil things.

But it wasn't vengeance that drove him. It wasn't a wish to slake some retaliatory bloodlust.

It was to protect the people he loves.

Could he have done things differently?

Maybe so, but his decisions were made in the moment, in the face of deathly threats to the people he loves.

Would he do it again without benefit of hindsight?

Yes, he would.

Maybe it's merely an attempt to ease the pain of picking at the scabs of his guilt, but there was no choice.

And there's no choice now. He must live with his crimes—and those he forced on Danny—and must never let Tracy know of them.

That's his life now—with its deceptions and flaws.

No matter what he's done, despite the darkness of his past and what he did, he must seek the light. Roddy knows he must do all he can to love and care for his family, to understand, nurture, and encourage his children, to cherish Tracy, to do all he can for his patients, to be a good friend to Danny, to accept all he has done, and to live a life of grace and compassion.

He must savor the love and beauty in his life and the good fortune bestowed upon him.

And he must be thankful the horrors of the past are gone.

Life goes on, and we never know what awaits us.

A Note from the Author

So ends the Mad Dog trilogy. Roddy, Danny, and their families will go on with their lives.

I never knew if there would be a third Mad Dog novel. When Roddy and Danny were left at the end of *Mad Dog Justice* wondering if Snapper Pond would be dredged and the bodies of Grange and Kenny Egan revealed, along with Grange's star sapphire ring, the pistol, and the shell casings, I thought it was the conclusion of a two-book adventure.

Since Roddy and Danny aren't detectives or lawyers, their lives as a doctor and an accountant didn't provide opportunities for new cases. Their story had to have a finite timeline.

I was satisfied concluding their story after the second book, leaving open the question about any possible revelations and complications. Yes, it was ambiguous, but as Roddy surely knows, life is filled with many uncertainties.

After the second book was published, I received e-mails and missives on Twitter, Facebook, and Goodreads asking when Roddy and Danny would be back. It was clear some readers didn't want to give them up facing an uncertain future.

And in time I came to realize I too had misgivings about saying goodbye to them.

Roddy Dolan is the first fictional character I ever created, in the first novel I ever wrote. In a sense, he's my firstborn. It was difficult to let him go.

But something else drove me to write the third novel.

I enjoyed hearing readers speculate about Roddy and Danny and what they did under extreme duress. Were they moral or not? Were they victims of their pasts, or did they simply make poor choices?

And the discussions expanded beyond the novels. Many questions arose. What impact does fate have on our lives? Can we successfully reroute our lives—alter the road we chose and travel the one not taken? Readers at library talks, interviews, and author panels mulled over questions about the power of the past, about friendship, truth, secrecy, marriage, loyalty, and character.

And there were the *what-if* questions. Many people can single out a *what-if* situation that changed their lives. *What if I hadn't met _____ that night; would my life have been different?*

I hope readers have enjoyed the Mad Dog trilogy—or if you will, have derived pleasure from this *one* story told over the course of three interconnected narratives.

I never planned to write a trilogy.

I guess it's sort of like life: things happen, and as you look back, it always seems linear.

Mark Rubinstein
Connecticut, 2017

Acknowledgments

Writing a novel is arduous, sometimes frustrating, but above all, exhilarating. For me it's also an exploration of the unknown. While it's a solitary endeavor, most authors acknowledge the importance of other people's contributions to their work. Yes, you must trust your imagination and your readiness to look at your own demons, but you must also depend on the willingness of others to offer advice, criticism, and support. No writer creates alone. Least of all, me.

I owe a great deal to so many people it would be impossible to list them all.

Kristen Weber has helped me in many ways. Above all, she was the first to show me the way of the novel.

I am indebted to three great psychiatrists who were formative influences during my years of training in psychiatry: Drs. William A. Console, Richard C. Simons, and Warren Tanenbaum.

I owe a special debt to Harvey Morgan, a great friend for many years and a gunsmith without equal.

Throughout my writing life, friends and family have generously supported my efforts. They include Cindy Armor, Edie Bernstein, Steve Campbell, Ann Chernow, Dr. Michelle Cohen, Claire Copen, Rob Copen, Barry Eva, Elissa Grodin, Martin Isler, Natalie Isler, Helen Kaufman, Phil Kaufman, Craig Kennedy, Jeffrey Ketchman, Niki Ketchman, Jill Stanley Kotch, Fran Lewis,

Barry Nathanson, Susan Nathanson, Daniel Pildes, Nancy Quinn, Bob Rubenstein, Carole Rubenstein, Tina Schwartz, Bert Serwitz, Joyce Serwitz, Jill Sklar, Alan Steinberg, Mindi Steinberg, Elaine Tai-Lauria, Martin West, and Judith Marks White. Their kind and encouraging words have always meant a great deal to me.

Over the past few years I've interviewed many of the most successful authors on the planet as part of my contributions to the *Huffington Post*. I've learned from every one of them. A few of them are people to whom I owe special debts of gratitude. They include Joseph Badal, Louis Begley, Michael Connelly, Patricia Cornwell, Linda Fairstein, Lisa Gardner, Andrew Gross, Jonathan Kellerman, Raymond Khoury, Jon Land, Phillip Margolin, David Morrell, Sara Paretsky, Scott Pratt, James Rollins, John Sandford, Simon Toyne, and Don Winslow, all great writers and wonderful, giving people.

My gifted wife, Linda, is not only my soul mate, adviser, creative muse, and first editor (conceptual and otherwise), but she's a superb grammarian, my willing confidant, and the CEO of my life. She lifts me up when I'm down and moderates the absurd flights of fancy occasionally seizing me. With each book, I end up thanking her for putting up with my writerly routines and for simply putting up with me. She makes both my books and my life far better than they ever would be were she not with me. I could never thank you enough, babe.

And I thank with all my heart Sidney, Billy, Maggie, Hannah, Hank, Jenny, and Jake for enriching our lives in ways beyond description.